Trapped in the R.A.W.

Trapped in the R.A.W.

A Journal of My Experiences during the Great Invasion

by
Kaylee Bearovna

With an Afterword by Pearl Larken
and Appendices Compiled by the
"We Survive" Series Group

by Kate Boyes

Aqueduct Press
PO Box 95787
Seattle, WA 98145-2787
www.aqueductpress.com

Library of Congress Control Number: 2019936765

ISBN: 978-1-61976-159-9
First Edition, First Printing, July 2019
10 9 8 7 6 5 4 3 2 1

Cover Illustration: Portrait of a young woman with books or loose papers. *The Wasp* Vol. 5, 1880. Wasp Publishing Co.
https://archive.org/stream/waspvol51880unse

See page 301 for list of text illustrations.

Book and cover design by Kathryn Wilham

Acknowledgments

Many thanks to Pearl Larken and the other members of our book group—Darcy Hogan, Lucy T. Furuheim, J. Lawrence, Kris Conner, Nikki Atkins, Jerry Murray, Pat Fitzpatrick, and (especially) Norma Taylor: when I was in a dark place, you inspired me, fed me, and gave me a reason to go on.

Thanks, also, to Kath Wilham and Timmi Duchamp, whose publishing expertise and kindness turned a pile of ripped pages, scribbled notes, tape, and dreams into a book.

And from all of us to Ishi Kenai: Thank you for giving us the gift of hope.

Dedicated to those who love books,
libraries, and all things rare and wonderful,
including the indomitable spirit
that helps us survive.

Day Eight

Rip out pages from books? Never! I never harmed a book before I took this job in the special collections library, and I wouldn't risk losing my job by doing such a thing now. Even during seminars, when professors encourage us—actually, given what's happening outside, I should start using the past tense—encouraged us to make margin notes in our texts and then shamed students who did not, I came to class w/ dozens of tiny slips of paper sticking out from between the pages of my books because I couldn't write in them. I forced myself to make a margin note once—w/ a #3 pencil, and very lightly but I erased the mark & felt physically ill for hours.

I never harmed a book...before the invasion.

Everything changed eight days ago. I was alone in here, closing the library for the day, when I heard screaming outside. I climbed a sliding shelf ladder to look out a high window, & I saw....I....

I can't write about it now. I can't even think about it. Too soon? Why do people say that when they know it's not funny? Yes, it's too soon. Too disturbing. Too incomprehensible. Plus, the light is fading so I need to wrap things up for the day and go into hiding because the invaders are most active around dusk & dawn.

"If I should die before I wake...."

My grandmother taught me that bedtime song. I've hummed it often during the past week because there have been many times when I thought I might die. Or was sure I would. Best to fall asleep w/ a clean conscience, just in case.

So before I crawl under my bench in the far corner of the Science/Medicine section of the library and try to sleep—

while listening to annoying scratching sounds coming from someplace inside this building & horrifying howling coming from outside it—I say: I am sorry. Sorry I've been ripping out blank pages from rare books in this library for the past seven days. & very, very sorry I ripped out this printed page today.

Day Nine

I tried to calm down enough this morning to write about Day One, but my hands started shaking as soon as I thought about it. I gave up. Besides, I've decided to deal w/ the worst aspects of my situation on even days. Today is definitely an odd day.

The only thing I can say about Day One at this point is that as soon as I realized what was happening, I slid down the sliding shelf ladder (didn't even use the rungs), locked the two library doors, then shoved tables, chairs, & shelves against the doors to form barricades. Still don't know where I came up w/ the strength to do what, in retrospect, seems like a bona fide tiny-woman-lifts-car-w/-one-hand-to-rescue-infant kind of thing.

When I finished securing the doors & took a moment to catch my breath, a physiological reaction to the fear & adrenaline pumping through my body struck me. Yes, that. I ran to the bathroom, turned on the light, closed the door, & …no toilet paper.

My friend/choir buddy/co-worker Benji, the only person who had been working w/ me that day in the RAW (our nickname for this library), had called the campus custodial office earlier to tell them our bathroom needed to be stocked. No one came. After Benji left for the day, I tried calling them again on my cell phone while I was closing up the library. No signal (hasn't been a signal or Internet connection since then, so cell phone towers must still be down, & now my phone battery is dead). I continued closing up, heard screaming, climbed the ladder, looked out, & that was that.

Amazing how little paper there is in a special collections library. No due date slips because items in here can't be checked out. No card catalogues, which I've seen only in old movies & photographs, because all info is on computers. No tax booklets & forms because they're available on-line. We used to give patrons scrap paper if they needed to take notes (only w/ a pencil, of course; no pens allowed for patrons), but now we have a digital-only policy for note taking.

Our head librarian is—was?—a recycling fiend, so no paper towels in the staff kitchen, just cloth napkins & rags the kindly old library volunteers take—took—home to wash for us. There was—is?—a little box of tissues in the head librarian's office, one box for the entire staff. We were encouraged to bring a cloth handkerchief, & we were glared at if we forgot and had to slink into her office to take a tissue. But her office was locked on Day One, peons like me weren't given keys to it or the book conservation room, & I was still too afraid of her then—& in too much of a hurry—to break the lock.

Where are the creeps taking stealth videos when you need them? A clip of me running around the library w/ a bad case of the hurry-me-ups while trying to figure out what to use as a substitute for toilet paper would go viral for sure. A cloth napkin or rag? No, I would need to wash it, & I wanted to conserve water because it could be turned off at any moment. My hand? See previous response & eeeeew, just…eew. A sleeve from the head librarian's lab coat? Deeply satisfying, but only momentarily, & not practical. My hat? A sock? The smoking-gun letter Professor G sent me, the one I hid in the case w/ my sunglasses? No, no, & absolutely not.

Fun fact about how most books have been made over the past couple of hundred years: pages of text are printed on both sides of a large sheet of paper; the paper is folded several times to create a signature (a booklet thingy); after enough signatures are printed to include all the pages of text, the signatures are bound together into a book. Because of the folding process, the number of pages in a book created this way will be a multiple of eight. If the text doesn't come out to a multiple of eight, there will be blank pages, usually at the end of the book.

Yes, it's amazing how little paper is in a modern library—except between the covers of books. I wish I could say I hesitated for a long time before ripping out that 1st blank page. I didn't. Once I settled on the solution, I found a book w/ blank pages, ripped one out, & ran for the bathroom. Just like that.

Later, curled up under a bench in the Science & Medicine section—the bench farthest from the doors, the one that can't be seen from any windows—I thought about ripping out that page, & I cried for hours.

Silly to be upset about a small thing like that in the midst of massive death & destruction, right? But here's something I've noticed during my time in the RAW: Many of the really horrible things that happen leave me feeling zoned-out. I don't think that means there's anything wrong w/ me. I think of that reaction in terms of the pain scale from 0 to 10 that doctors use: if a scale existed for emotions, & if the most intense negative emotion it was possible for us to feel in the normal course of human events—aye, there's the rub—was a 10 (as I felt when my mother died), then what happens to our emotions when the basis of the scale changes? When the world ups the horror ante & the old 10 is now a 1? Or a .001? When we've felt as badly as we can feel & then things get worse? It makes sense that our emotions would be off, at least during a period of adjustment, under those circumstances. So it's the small things, the things I can react to based on the pre-invasion emotional pain scale, that upset me the most.

Also, destroying books means one more piece of the old world, the old me, is lost. Maybe forever. How many more pieces of me can I lose before there is no more "me," before the "I" that I was before the invasion disappears completely?

I fell asleep before dawn, then woke from a dream about earthquakes. I was shaking so hard that the book cart next to my sleeping bench was vibrating. I almost threw up, but I took deep breaths to calm down.

A few blank pages a day to take care of necessities, that's all I needed. I discovered early on that pages are scratchy, especially when applied to delicate areas, so I tried something we did in elementary school: Crumple pages into balls, open them, smooth them out, then repeat until the pages are soft & more absorbent.

& so it went until yesterday. I ripped out a blank page, hurried to the bathroom, & didn't realize until I was in there that I had torn out an additional page by mistake. A printed page. A page of text.

The pages of the book were so thin. Gold gilding on the fore-edge had stuck the pages together. I was in a hurry. Yadda, yadda, yadda. I could make a list of reasons. But I can't provide even one good excuse because there is none.

So that happened. Mea culpa. My bad. I was sorry about using blank pages; I was appalled about altering a book forever by removing a page of text. I spent hours yesterday looking through books to estimate the supply of blank pages available. I considered, for the 1st time, the possibility that there might not be anyone left except me to read these books. Ever. I decided I should

Oh, no!

Day Ten

Last night was a nightmare. Again.

The invaders have been trying to break down the front door since Day One. No luck, which explains why I'm still breathing. The doors resemble those of a castle: Oak slabs, iron straps, monstrous bolts. Built to withstand attacks by Huns, Visigoths, or other marauding hordes that might pass by this little town in the middle of nowhere & have a sudden overpowering need to visit a library. I always thought the doors looked pretentious; now I love the way they look & perform.

But when I was writing in this journal yesterday, the invaders hit the door w/ something really big & really heavy. Something like a battering ram.

BAM!

I started humming "Love Shack" to drown out the sound.

BAM!

I hummed a little louder, baby.

BAM!

Even though I was humming as loud as I could, it wasn't loud enough to drown out the sound of wood cracking.

BAM!

The last bash knocked down some chairs from the barricade. That, plus the sound of wood cracking, made me feel sick. I hid under my bench, rolled the cart in front of it so invaders couldn't see me when they broke in, & waited for the door to give & the invaders to swarm the RAW.

Then—Why? Why?!!!—they stopped. Maybe their arms were tired. Maybe they saw other people trying to escape & had to go kill them. Maybe it was supper time. I don't know.

I stayed hidden until long after the last bash. I needed to check the door for damage, but I didn't want to emerge until the invaders were gone. While I waited, I kept humming "Love Shack" as loudly as possible to drown out the sounds of feet running past the building, people howling as they died, something scratching frantically.

Two things made last night worse than previous nights. 1st, the amount & intensity of activity: In addition to the ramped-up assault on the door, I counted nine howling sessions. 2nd, & almost as disturbing, my sighting of an invader looking in a window.

The windows of this one-story building, which is almost as tall as the two-story buildings on either side of it, are long, narrow, & located near the top of the high walls. The architect—son of Dowager Gulick, who donated the money to build the library—said he designed the windows that way to protect the books from sunlight. The design didn't work, & the campus maintenance crew had to install Roman shades on the windows to fix the glitch.

From outside, the shape & location of the windows, plus the rough concrete walls (How is Brutalism still a thing?) & oak doors, make this place look like a small castle fortress w/o the charm. From inside, the lack of windows through which to view the campus & town (w/o climbing a shelf ladder) made it feel a bit like a prison even before the invasion. (To be fair, though, the windows do provide a nice view of the sky.)

Anyway, the invader must have accessed the roof using the maintenance ladder next to the wheelchair ramp by the back door, laid on his/her/its belly (or whatever), & hung his/her/its head & upper torso (or whatever) over the edge of the roof—& I mean way, way over the edge—to look in.

Because the enemy should have a short &, if possible, disgusting name (the better to express one's hostility toward them), I have decided to call the invaders "pacz." That's plural:

"pac" is singular. I have no idea what these things are. During long nights when I can't sleep, the question spins around in my head: What are they? What are they?!!! People? Aliens? Robots? Creatures (i.e., animals) of some sort? Or—in half-awake moments, when dreams & reality merge & turn into the stuff that makes heads explode—zombies? I had no idea on Day One; I have no idea now.

I decided to use the 1st letters of "people," "aliens," "creatures," and "zombies" to name the invaders, but I refuse to dignify them by capitalizing the name. I nixed the 1st letter of "robots" because the top two names I came up w/ that incorporated an "r" were "crapz" and "parcz." The former is too common &, given the color of the invaders' suits, not terribly creative. The latter brings to mind pleasant places: Great Barrier Reef, Grand Canyon, Galapagos, Disney World. Plus, the "r" softens the sound of the names too much. Saying "pac" feels like spitting. Saying "pacz" feels like spitting & then hissing (I like to say "paczzzz" to accentuate the hissing effect).

Anyway, I wouldn't have noticed the pac that (I refuse to use "who," too) looked in the window if not for the full moon. I expect that's why so much was going on, since pacz are most active in half-light. There was no real darkness last night, so there was no respite from the horrible things they do.

The scratching sound has become a huge problem. The sound started on Day Three, I think. It was barely audible at 1st. I thought it was the sleeve of my jacket (it's cold in here) brushing against things. But the sound was still there when I played what Matilda & I call the statue game—make no sound & don't move.

The scratching was so irritating last night, my need to check the front door for damage was so pressing, & the library was so easy to move around in because of the full moon, that I slid my protective book cart to one side & crawled out from under my bench to investigate.

Trapped in the R.A.W.

I checked for the source of the scratching in every part of the RAW that I could. 1ˢᵗ, the main section, which looks like any ordinary library, w/ many rows of book shelves that patrons can access by themselves, plus a section in the middle that used to have lots of long study tables before I used them for door barricades. Then the area around the front desk, where Benji & I worked. Then the three SoDoc rooms (SoDoc = special objects & documents), which have no doors & contain items only people who work here can access. After that, the staff kitchen area, also w/ no door. Finally, the bathroom, which, thank goodness, does have a door.

I found nothing that could be causing the scratching, so it must be coming from either the Head Librarian's office or the book conservation room. As I mentioned before, the doors of those rooms are locked, & I don't have the keys.

Trundling back to my sleeping nest after a fruitless search, I noticed something strange about one of the long, narrow shafts of moonlight on the stone tile floor. There was a roundish dark spot at one end.

I looked up, & there was the pac's head in the window, backlit by the moon. That mesh part of its head covering, the part I'm guessing is over its face, was almost touching the glass. Of course, it was viewing me upside down, since it was hanging over the edge of the roof.

No trouble playing the statue game at that moment. I couldn't move. I don't think I was breathing, either. The pac seemed to be playing the same game. There was a long period of absolute stillness. Did it see me? I had to find out. I took a step to the right: the pac's head turned in that direction. I waited for a minute, then took a step to the left: the pac's head turned that way.

Did it see me? Absolutely.

Any chance I had of sleeping was blown to bits right then & there. I backed up until I was behind a book shelf, then slunk to my bench & hid under it.

But today, as I covered the new hole in the front door w/ a table and then rebuilt the barricade, I couldn't hide from the questions. Did pacz peek in the windows every night? Did the pac realize I was the enemy? One pac knew I was in the RAW on Day Three because it chased me back here after my failed rescue attempt. I was hoping that pac had decided I was long gone: I was hoping the pounding on the front door was something pacz did to every campus building. But now....

Now that the invaders, the pacz, know for sure I'm in here, will they intensify their efforts to get inside?

Day Eleven

Storm clouds moved in yesterday just before sunset, lightning shot through the sky, thunder shook the RAW, & then heavy rain began to fall. It was the 1st real storm since the invasion began, the 1st of the big storms that hit this area every year in late autumn or early winter. Clouds covered the sun, then the moon. The world became dark in the most comforting way possible.

I watched every step in the progress of the storm; I read every chapter in its story. That's why I've kept the shades open on the windows. It's hard to be locked up in here. If I couldn't see the outside world, if I couldn't look up & see the sky, even if it is only a very thin slice of it, my life would be much harder.

Between lightning cracks & thunder rumbles, everything was quiet. I climbed the ladder often during the evening to peek outside, being even more cautious than I was before, in case the peeping pac was still around. No pacz. Anywhere. Usually I see a few any time of the day or night out in the Quad, on a soccer field, or slinking between buildings. It seems too good to be true, but I have a hunch pacz don't like rain.

Ha! Take that you evil so-&-so(s), you loathsome whatever-you-are(s)! And if you hate rain, trust me, you are really, really going to despise snow....

I love rain. W/ all my heart & all my senses. Even as a small child, I took long walks during storms. My mother never stopped me. She would rub my hair dry w/ a towel when I came back home & say, "That's my Kaylee, soggy but satisfied."

I had an almost overpowering urge to go outside last night, to have that rainy day feeling again. Open the door. Step into the world. Stand on the grass w/ my hands & face turned toward the sky. Feel something powerful again, something other than fear.

I was full of nervous energy, my body charged by the clash between an intense desire to be outside & an intense desire to stay safe inside. I couldn't read. I couldn't sit still. Exercise was the only way to get rid of my agitation.

Exercise became part of my daily routine after I recovered from the events of Day Three. Being slapped in the face that day w/ the realization that my life, & maybe the lives of others, would almost certainly depend at some point on my ability to run fast enough to escape death gave me a great incentive to keep as fit as possible.

I had created an empty space in the middle of the RAW when I used the tables & chairs to barricade the doors. But running in tight circles in that space made me irritable. It reminded me too much of the similarities between my situation & that of a caged hamster. Spinning, spinning, going nowhere.

I needed longer stretches of cleared space to give my heart & lungs a work-out. By stacking in one corner the small study desks that had been in the perimeter aisles, I was able to create a large loop to pace around. Ninety-two paces from the front door, around the perimeter of the main section of the library, & back to the front door again.

For over an hour I paced around the perimeter aisles of the RAW to the sound of the storm. My speed grew faster as the storm grew more intense, as I recalled more walks in the rain, as I thought about my mother & all the people who are gone now.

& then, suddenly, I was running. I was lapping the aisles in great loping strides, around & around, singing.

"I can hear the thunder
of that great strange world of wonder,
Like a voice out in the distance calling me."

At one point—heart pounding, breaths coming in quick gasps—I grabbed a table from the pile barricading the front door & threw it. Across. The. Room. The table crashed into 18th-Century Literature, dislodging several books from a shelf, & sending them skittering along the slick tile floor. Something about the way those books moved, like terrified animals scurrying away to escape my great fury, made me laugh. Doubled over. Gasping for breath. Until I cried.

When I calmed down, I wedged the table back into the barricade. Then I flopped down on the floor & crawled on my belly across the stone tiles until I was as close to the door as I could be w/o causing items in the barricade to cascade down on my head. Through the narrow crack between the bottom of the door & the threshold, a draft of air flowed toward me. Rain-laden. Fresh. Cool.

The smell of freedom.

Day Twelve

I slept the night before last—& I mean really slept—for the 1st time since the invasion began. The sound & smell of rain, & the lack of pacz, helped me drift off into nothingness & stay there for a lovely, long time. No pacz meant no howling or door-bashing, & that meant no awful nightmares or jolting awake in a cold sweat. When I woke yesterday in the dark, I thought it was the middle of the night, but it was 7:00 a.m.! I climbed the ladder, peeked out: No pacz.

Then, because it rained all day yesterday & the pacz were no-shows again, I took my time following a routine I came up w/ early in the invasion—wash face, eat, brush teeth (my tiny travel tube of toothpaste is long gone, so I use water), tidy up, crumple pages, read, work on special tasks, read, eat, brush teeth, & top off water containers. At some point, when my fingers warm up enough to work properly, I write a journal entry.

I've added exercise to my daily routine, but I've demoted one task from daily to only-when-I-absolutely-can't-avoid-it-any-longer status: Combing my hair.

That seems like such a simple thing to do every day. Or even several times a day. I've never had trouble keeping all my long brown hair going in the same direction before.

Of course, I've never worn a wool knit hat 24 hours a day before. Seriously, it is VERY cold in here just about every minute of just about every day, almost freezing at night, so I seldom remove my hat (or anything else). The wool rubbing against my head makes terrible tangles. "Rat nests," my mother called them. There's no "running a comb through" my hair now.

I try picking the tangles apart at times, but mostly I take off my hat, stare at the comb, sigh, & put my hat back on again.

My special task yesterday was washing—clothes & self. I didn't think I would need to wash very often in the RAW, especially after most of the soot from Day Three was cleaned up. I'm not doing much more than sitting around. But I wake from nightmares soaked w/ sweat. & there's a gaggy scent associated w/ fear, too (turns out it's not just horses who can smell fear). It's like I'm wearing the stinkiest perfume ever: Eau de invasion. Also, one does not wish to look & smell too badly when greeting one's liberators, probably troops from the Yakima military training center south of here, when they arrive to kick the invaders' butts & free the world. (Seriously, when are all you buff ROTC-type gals, guys, & glorious others going to get here?!)

Thank goodness for the lab coats hanging by the book conservation room door. And a very special thank you goes out to the universe for the lost-and-found (LAF) box.

I layer on lab coats to keep warm at night, but their other function is to keep me decent on wash days. I turn on the oven in the staff kitchen, open the oven door, then, while the area around the oven warms up, take off my clothes—in the bathroom, w/ the door locked, because old habits die hard. Fill the bathroom sink w/ water; add dirty clothes to soak (& try not to glance in the mirror because I'm looking a little haggard these day). Throw on lab coat, return to kitchen, stand close to oven, & use a rag & hand soap to take the post-invasion version of a sponge bath.

Sure, I could wash in the bathroom. Or I could stand naked in the kitchen to wash, because there's about zip chance anyone or anything would see me. But that bit of warmth from the oven feels good while I'm washing, & I am not quite ready to give up on proper behavior just yet.

Trapped in the R.A.W.

Now, the LAF part. Here's what was in our LAF box when the invasion began: A black umbrella used by an Emeritus professor who came here to do research almost every day; a glove, mitten, long scarf, & ugly pea green/lavender/neon orange hand-knit hat—I wear all of them to keep warm, even though they make me look ridiculous, because, hey, I've never been a glamazon; a crimson nylon gym bag w/ an XXL pair of crimson sweatpants, an XXL crimson tee-shirt, a huge pair of crimson socks (guess what our school color is), a jock strap, a tube of alpha-male deodorant, & a pack of condoms. The last three items will remain in the LAF (somebody might need them someday; I certainly don't), but the big tee-shirt makes a good dress, & I think the other items could come in handy at some point.

Then I wash my clothes (but not undies—to simplify my life, & for comfort's sake, I am going commando now, top & bottom), climb the ladder, & drape them over a clothesline I made from Roman shade cords. Takes forever for them to dry. I tried drying them in the oven once; I still have interesting grill marks on my plaid flannel shirt. Anyway, as it turns out, I have all the time in the world to wait for clothes to dry.

That's what I did yesterday. Then, like a cherry on top of my pac-free day, rain fell last night again, & I slept again. It helps that the irritating scratching sound has stopped, although I've started hearing footsteps on the roof (not sure what the pacz are doing up there, but it can't be good).

Old business: I just read through my entries & realized I cut short Day Nine. I was finishing it up when the pacz got serious about breaking down the front door. I dropped the pen & hid under my bench. That was the beginning of hell night, the night of the full moon, the worst night (oh, powers that be, please let that be true) of my life.

I'll finish that entry today, but, from now on, I'm not going to edit this journal. Spelling, punctuation, grammar, odd abbreviations, uneven spacing: I've obsessed over those things my whole life, & taking college courses only made it worse. I used to feel as if I had to get everything just right. But what if I didn't? Would the world come to an end? No need to worry about that problem any more.

The Virgo rising part of my chart explains this obsession, my mother said. She didn't get into astrology until after her cancer diagnosis, but she figured out the basics quickly. She said even though I'm an Aquarius, the Virgo rising thing makes me, to put it politely, detail oriented. Or just plain picky.

Whatever. But I vowed before putting ultra-fine-point black Sharpie marker to book page on Day Eight (words don't stand out from pages of text when written w/ a pencil) that I would cross out nothing in this journal, correct nothing, edit nothing. (Proof of this: I should scribble "redundant" after that list. I won't. Take that, Grammarzons!)

After I made that decision, I felt light, free. Who cares about split infinitives? Why worry about gerunds? Those don't matter to someone surrounded by the enemy.

Okay: Day Nine. I spent the day looking through books to determine how many blank pages are available for necessities. Enough for a few months, I think. I considered using blank pages for my journal, too, but scrapped that idea: I might be under siege for a long time &, as bad as I feel about using blank pages for bathroom trips, I would feel even worse if I ended up using printed pages for that purpose.

But how to decide which printed pages to use? One thing that struck me as I flipped through books were statements like "No preface is necessary for this book." Then the author/ editor added one anyway. Most are flowery ways of saying, "Here's my two cents"; or "See how clever I am?"; or "I'm not sure you're going to like this book but please do." A few add something; most are totally useless; some are so egregiously self-serving they are painful to read. I decided to use preface-type things for my journal.

Sure, I feel guilty about altering texts. I feel guilty every time I rip out a page, w/ or w/o text. But I think about what other people would do if they were in a situation that forced them, in their struggle to survive, to destroy what they had always tried to protect. What would they be willing to sacrifice? It makes me feel better to think that other people would be okay w/ doing what I'm doing if they were in my shoes.

Bottom line: What is happening outside my window is more important than what is written in some of these books. Dowager Gulick was way off base when she gestured around the library & said that all of these books are rare & wonderful. Not so. But it did give us the great nickname for this place: rare and wonderful—RAW.

Actually, I wrote the preceding mostly as a way to put off the main topic of the day. I've been stalling for hours now. For days, really. Because….

New business: Day One. When I dream, the events of that day are what I see. Over & over. I hear screaming, I climb the ladder, I look out the window, & I see people running across the Quad, shoving each other out of the way, falling, trampling the too-still bodies of other people. Dying.

The cause? Waves & waves of some type of beings, more or less the size & shape of humans, inundating the area from all directions. Ugly things, dressed in brown, that just won't stop. So many of them. So many. & they just keep coming.

One man stops, pulls out a gun, & shoots an invader point-blank. No effect. A Good Guy w/ a gun cannot stop these things.

I look out across the valley at Jefferson City, my sweet little town. The place is covered w/ hundreds of the things. All moving at once. The town has turned into a great pool of undulating sludge. Row after row of the strange, deadly invaders rolling into this university, this town, places that were, only a few minutes before, calm.

If the invaders were aiming for shock & awe, they Crushed It!

The invaders—what I now call pacz—wear baggy brown uniforms that cover them completely. Even their hands, feet, & faces. The uniform fabric shimmers when sunlight hits it (I noticed that Day Two). The suits have loosely woven mesh over the area that, I assume, includes the invaders' eyes, nose, & mouth. From my window, I can't see what's behind the mesh.

Whatever they are, they seem to have two arms, two legs, a head, & a torso. For all I know, they might actually be humans under all that brown fabric. At 1st glance I thought they were animals. The sun was about to set when I 1st looked out the window, & there was so much going on (all shocking), it was hard to tell. Maybe they are trained animals or animal-like creatures, but the brown is definitely not skin or fur.

They could be human invaders from a foreign country, I suppose. But after I lock & barricade the doors & have my bathroom episode, I begin to doubt that they are foreigners. There are so many of them, & they appeared so quickly: How could humans do that w/o being noticed? I didn't hear air or land transport vehicles, & I didn't see anything like that from my window. Very odd.

Then there's the way they kill. No guns or spears; no light sabers or lasers. They just touch people. That's all. Not a hard touch, either, not like a slap or a punch. As soon as people are touched, they howl in pain, fall to the ground, writhe for a minute or two (or longer) while blood & other exudates come out of their bodies from places I never could have imagined. Then they die.

The howl is hideous. Screaming is human, but that howl.... I would never have imagined the human voice capable of making such a sound. & "writhing" is an understatement.

Grotesque twitches, spasms, & contortions of the limbs & torso; jerks so quick & violent they seem to break the necks of the victims.

The howling, writhing, & bleeding of humans. The massive number & awful unstoppability of the pacz. Those are what overwhelmed me on Day One. Those are what haunt me now.

Day Thirteen

I'm glad this is an odd-numbered day because writing the entry yesterday wiped me out. Did I have nightmares last night because of it? Yes. During my few bits of sleep. But, while lying awake, I came up w/ the perfect journal topic for today: food.

I couldn't think about food during the early days of the invasion. The horror going on outside made me nauseous constantly, & the thought of food made the nausea worse. I didn't eat anything until the 4th or 5th day (I took a few bites of a cracker in the night, so I'm not sure which day it was), & I lost what I ate almost at once.

I sipped water. Not enough. I'm sure some of my problems during the 1st week (my temporary semi-comatose state, for example) were caused by dehydration. I was afraid the plumbing & electricity would quit, so I was doing some serious rationing.

Hunger hit me hard on Day Six. Although I was still nauseous, I forced myself to open the refrigerator in the staff kitchen. Big mistake. Nothing to lose in my stomach, but dry heaves kept me busy for an hour.

Then, slowly, I tried again.

In the refrigerator door: condiments & an assortment of foo-foo leftovers from the pre-Thanksgiving library donor & volunteer recognition reception—kosher pickles, capers, Jack Daniels mustard, wasabi mayo, sun-dried tomatoes w/ herbs in olive oil, huge green olives stuffed w/ bleu cheese, Kalamata olives, organic ketchup, rice vinegar, Thai sweet red chili sauce, peach chutney, a good-size block of asiago cheese, & an unmarked jar of something that looks & smells like KY jelly (don't ask me what they did w/ that at the party: peons like me are not invited to those swanky affairs). Lots of items to put on food. The trick—finding food to put them on.

On the refrigerator shelves: Four cloth lunch sacks & a glass container. Each held the remains of what was, most likely, the last meal the staff members would ever eat in this library. Maybe the last meal they ate anywhere. 1st sack—green salad, too far gone to eat. 2nd sack—a stinky glob of brownish-green goo. 3rd sack—green salad (inedible), orange (okay), & (Yes!) peanut butter & seedless raspberry jam sandwich on whole wheat bread. 4th sack—baby carrots, mozzarella sticks, & two Little Debbie cosmic brownies (Thank you, Cosmos!). Glass container—roasted cauliflower (edible).

In the drawers: a bag of raw cranberries.

In the freezer: a pile of frost.

So much for the refrigerator. On the staff kitchen counter: a bag of herb tea & a bear-shaped plastic container of honey. I had to get a special dispensation from the head librarian to bring that little bear into the building, thus polluting her world w/ plastic. I won her over by arguing that the container had been a gift from my mother (recently deceased), I didn't want to throw away a plastic object, & I would refill it when necessary w/ organic honey from the local farmer's market.

In the cupboard: a huge bag of corn chips, a box of single-serving packs of instant oatmeal (37 in all), a tin of hot cocoa mix, & a bag of mini marshmallows. Not sure where the corn chips came from, but the last three items are the treats we got when we attended, on our own time, staff breakfast planning sessions each

Here we go again....

Later—

The pacz started ramming the front door while I was writing earlier. I thought they'd given up on that particular way of annoying me, but no such luck. I hid under the bench in case the door gave way. It's silly to do that, I guess. I mean, they know I'm in here &, since they seem to be a persistent lot, they would most likely keep searching for me if they happened to get into the RAW. Still, what else can I do but hide & hope for the best? There's no place I can go where I'll be safer than I am here.

They managed to get in a few solid, stomach-churning whacks during this ramming session. Chairs fell off the barricade again, & a table (the one I'd shoved tight against the hole they made last time) fell over & took another table w/ it. More sounds of wood cracking; more shaking of the building.

Then—just like last time, & for no reason obvious to me—they stopped. I checked the hole in the door: It was big enough to poke a finger through before the attack; now it's big enough for three fingers. There are hairline cracks in the wood. One hinge is a little loose (it will be interesting to see what comes unhinged 1st, the door or me). Otherwise, the door seems strong enough (as am I), & the lock is holding on (ditto). I shoved a table against the hole, rebuilt the barricade, & sat down to finish writing my journal entry.

Side note: Why, you might ask, don't the invaders try to break down the back door? That is a question I've asked myself many times. I will never know for sure, but I have a theory. The front porch is wide & deep, w/ lots of space between the top of the steps & the door. Several invaders could stand in a row in that space, all holding something long & very heavy, & swing it back & forth to smash the door. But there is only a small landing outside the back door, just big enough for one or two people to stand on at a time, & then a long wheelchair (accessibility) ramp leading down to the parking lot. It would be difficult, even for a fairly large group of invaders, to bash something long & heavy against the back door because most of the pacz would need to hold the bashing object far over their heads as they stood on the ground several feet below the landing. Not an easy thing to do. Also, the front porch is covered, so invaders are protected from precipitation there, but they would be totally exposed by the back door.

Back to my favorite subject…. Near the end of my food search, I remembered my package from Powell's book store. I had a campus P.O. box (mail tended to disappear when it was sent to my place at the YWCA), & the package had arrived the day before the invasion. I stored it in my RAW cubby. I knew which books were inside—two for me, two for Matilda. They were Christmas presents. But I had gone out for tea once w/ a guy from the shipping department at Powell's, back when my mother was seeing a cancer specialist in Portland every month or two, & he always threw in a treat for me when I ordered books, usually candy from Quin's, a little shop near the book store. Should I open the box & add that food to my inventory? No, I think not. I'll wait until there's a day when I need a sweet surprise.

I expected food—more precisely, the lack of it—would be my biggest problem. But at the end of my inventory I was pretty sure I had enough to make it through Christmas if I was careful. Hey, Benji & I saw "The Martian" on the big screen: when I feel deprived, I think of Matt Daman (in exactly the same way Benji does), sip hot cocoa, & count my blessings.

Now that I have been in the RAW ~ two weeks & can see how well my rationing is going, I think I have enough food to make it a week or two into the new year. After that….

Supper tonight: Nachos (three corn chips w/ asiago cheese & a stuffed green olive on top, broiled), the last bite of roasted cauliflower (it kept fine in the freezer), & a cup of steaming peppermint tea.

Day Fourteen

Two weeks in, & my life before the invasion is beginning to feel as much like fiction as the contents of the novels stacked around my writing desk in Pre-16th-Century Literature. I had a life before the invasion. Sort of. But now, well, it's all about the RAW, about the RAW....

I have decided to read my journal entries out loud while pacing around the perimeter aisles for exercise. I realized the other day that I was asking myself questions out loud, answering them out loud, &, when I didn't like the answers, arguing w/ myself out loud. What I am about to say would shock anyone who knew me pre-invasion, but I miss the sound of the human voice. Hard to imagine a dedicated introvert like me craving that, but it's true.

Sure, I sing now & then, & that sound comforts me. Sometimes I sing on purpose, like when I was trying to block out the odd scratching sound before it stopped, & now when I'm trying not to think about what the pacz are doing stomping around up on the roof. & I sing when I exercise, of course. Sometimes I'm busy doing a task & suddenly realize I'm singing. But that's me saying someone else's words, which is not the same as speaking my mind, as saying "Here's what I think."

I'm not worried about ending up a mumbling misanthrope, someone who wanders around dirty & unkempt debating the state of the world w/ herself. 1st, I don't expect to live long enough to reach that state. 2nd, I'm not dirty, I'm scruffy in an ecologically sound sort of way, I'm not unkempt (except for my hair, which I consider a piece of evolving organic art), I'm elegantly disheveled. 3rd, there are many people who talk to themselves out loud. There was a lawyer in our neighborhood who practiced her court arguments while riding her bike around town. & it was easy to spot the kids on the debate team in high school because they were the ones talking the loudest as they walked (all by themselves) down the hall. While I'm not a fan of lawyers or the kids on the debate team, I'm sure they would be considered both respectable & sane.

Something about speaking & hearing their words helped them come up w/ ideas & sort out complex situations. I guess my mind might work that way, too. I'm definitely in a complex situation, & there are so many things I need to figure out. Like why did the pacz turn off the campus steam plant—the heat— at the beginning of the invasion, but leave the water & electrical systems on? Were they trying to make it so uncomfortably cold in campus buildings that we would evacuate? Don't they understand that turning off the heat but leaving on the water will lead to frozen pipes at some point? Or do they understand that & it's all part of some long-range diabolical plan? Or was it just a mistake? & why leave the electricity on? & why…?

"Read your work out loud." Professors urged us to do that before we handed in term papers. I resisted at 1st, but when I got over the embarrassment of hearing my own voice, I found it helpful.

Actually, I whispered my papers out loud most of the time because even when my mother was dying her hearing was excellent. Sometimes late at night, after she fell asleep, I would forget & use my normal voice while reading a paper, & the sound would wake her. She would call out: "Why are you mumbling, Kaylee? Speak up. I can't help you if you don't speak up." I would go to her room, make her as comfortable as possible, then hold her hand until she fell asleep again. We never mentioned this, but both of us knew she hadn't been capable of helping me w/ anything for a long time.

Trapped in the R.A.W.

After she died & I sold the house to pay for graduate school, I had to be quiet because I moved into a dorm room at the YWCA (the house sold in the middle of a semester, when all the JSU dorms were full, and then the manager of the Y gave me a part-time job in the office in exchange for my rent, so I stayed). Up to eleven other women living in the dorm at any given time, most recovering from addictions. Some talked to themselves or screamed in the night, which led to some nasty fights. I kept quiet because I didn't want to be on the receiving end of a punch.

When I read my journal out loud for the 1st time yesterday, I was whispering. I've been whispering most of my time in the RAW because that's what people do in libraries (I raised my voice on Day Three, but that was an involuntary reaction).

I see similarities between my decibel level & my movements. I started out sitting most of the time, & moving about slowly & quietly only when necessary, because that's what people do in libraries. Over time, I began to walk around more in the large space in the middle of the RAW. Then I began doing laps around the perimeter aisles for exercise. Now, sometimes, I dance.

No need to be quiet in the library anymore. I can talk if I want to, I can shout & sing, I can howl—not like people touched by pacz, but like wolves in the arctic—whenever the moon shines. Or even when it doesn't.

After my 1st wimpy reading yesterday, I cleared my throat & started over. I read my journal entry again & again, raising the decibel level each time until I was shouting. Shouting at the top of my lungs.

Day Fifteen

This morning....

It was raining this morning, &....

Look, I tried.

I can't write about it now. I've already used a week's worth of blank pages today to deal w/ my physical reactions to what happened.

I just can't.

Day Sixteen

Stupid, stupid, stupid. & slow. Way too slow. & clumsy. Clumsy oaf.

Can't do anything right. Can't do anything. Right?!?!

Adulterer.

Murderer.

Spent all day in the bathroom. Not because I'm sick, but for penance. & to keep myself from hobbling out of this library, this dreadful prison, right here & now. To get what's coming to me. "Here I am, pacz. Yoo-hoo, here I am."

Which I should do. I really should. I should do it right now.

But there is nothing I can do to atone for my short-comings. My bottomless ineptitude.

My sins.

Day Seventeen

I wanted journal entries to be upbeat on odd days, but, because of what happened two days ago, no way I can be upbeat now.

Most humans on this side of campus were killed, or ran off, the 1st day of the invasion. At least as far as I could tell. A few dozen more were killed near my building the 2nd day. Thirteen, I think, on the 3rd day. After that, the killing slowed down.

There were holdouts. Like me. I don't know where they were hiding, but it must have been in places less secure than mine because every day—mostly between dusk & dawn—I would hear at least one howling session when a human died. On that awful night of the full moon, I heard nine distinct howling sessions, several of them w/ multiple voices (at least those people didn't die alone). Since then, none.

There was a slight chance another human was still alive here on campus. Very slight, but a chance. Because on the evening of the big storm, when I peeked out the window to check for pacz, I thought I saw a human standing in the doorway of the Ag Science building across the Quad. Just a glimpse, then he or she was gone. It was dark & I was highly agitated that night, full of wild thoughts & feelings, so I chalked it up to poor visibility & an overactive imagination, too iffy even to mention.

Strange: I would have guessed seeing another human would make me happy. Just the opposite. All it took was one middle-of-the-night howling session for me to realize that my best survival mindset was to assume everyone in town, especially the person I love—loved—was dead already & not still facing the awful agony of death by pac.

Trapped in the R.A.W.

Rain started falling mid-morning two days ago. Not a big storm like before. Just enough, I hoped, to make the pacz disappear for a bit. I climbed the ladder to confirm that they had all slunk back into whatever dark & loathsome place they go to when they're not outside. Yes; no pacz. But....

A human!

Jeans, gray hoody, black boots. Not a speck of brown on him or her—I couldn't tell which because the hood was up & the person was crouching behind juniper bushes by the front of the Ag Sci building. Not moving a muscle. Looking in my direction.

I scanned the area again for pacz. None.

Then I did something w/o analyzing all aspects of the potential action & its myriad consequences, w/o spending hours or days trying to figure out whether or not I should do it, w/o obsessing over my decision, as I would usually do.

I waved.

No response. I waved again, this time w/ my hand closer to the window.

The human stood up a little, looked around, looked around again, then, slowly, raised a hand.

Contact! I felt giddy. I raised my hand & flashed the peace sign, the two-fingered V for victory. S/he looked around, then made the same sign—w/ both hands.

There was a long pause. I'm guessing he or she was thinking the same thing I was: What do we do now? (Of course, I was also calculating how much food I had left, how long it would last for two people instead of one, how much longer it would last if I—or we—cut our intake by a hundred calories per day, how many blank book pages were left for daily necessities, how long those pages would last for two people instead of one—almost as long as for me if it was a man; not long at all if it was another woman).

My calculations were cut short by a gesture from the other human: Both hands palm up, shoulders raised, head to one side. I translated this as "So…?"

I thought about waving the other human over, signaling for him or her to cross the Quad & join me here in the library. But, when & if that happened, it had to be done quickly, & I needed time to take down the barricade against the front door, which faces the Ag Sci building.

You see that? You see what I said there? I was thinking about what I was doing. I was being careful. I was trying to do things the right way.

I raised one hand, palm out, & extended my arm toward the window & then back several times. I was trying to signal "Stop" or "Wait." It worked: The other human gave me a thumbs-up & crouched lower behind the row of juniper bushes.

I slid down the ladder, ran to the barricade, & began tossing tables & chairs to one side & pushing shelves out of the way. Furniture was flying; books were flying. When the barricade was down, I left the door locked—because it would be dangerous to unlock the door until I had to—& climbed the ladder again.

At 1st I thought the human was gone. No sign of human or pac. But then there, farther to the left, I caught a glimpse of a pant leg. I held tight to the ladder, leaned over until I was almost touching the window, & waved for her or him to come over.

Why didn't I look up? Both of us looked around for pacz, of course. But why didn't I look up toward the sky? Why didn't I notice that the rain had become little more than a drizzle or a light mist?

By the time I realized that the rain had basically stopped, the other human was already running. Head down, fists pumping, feet flying. So were the same four pacz I see all the time now, the only pacz I see around this area: a tall one, a plump one, & two short ones who are always together. I don't know where the pacz came from; they weren't there, then they were. Far behind the human & coming fast, but, thank goodness, not fast enough to reach the human before he or she reached the library.

I slid down the ladder, hit the floor running, &....

Tripped.

Fell.

Stupid, stupid, stupid.

Clumsy.

Clumsy oaf.

& slow.

Can't do anything.

Right.

The human reached the porch just as I realized I couldn't stand because my ankle was sprained or broken. The human beat on the door while I crawled toward it across the floor. He—I could tell now from his voice—screamed "Let me in" over & over while I grabbed a table beside the door & pulled myself up. Our faces were on opposite sides of the hole in the door when he screamed "Let me in" for the last time, the warmth of his breath touching my cheek.

The pacz touched him just as I reached out to unbolt the door.

Howling.

He slumped onto the door stoop.

Howling.

The pacz left.

Howling.

I fell to the floor &, through the crack between the door & the threshold, watched the man writhe in pain. On his last spasm, his face turned toward me.

"I'm sorry," I whispered.

Silence.

Day Eighteen

Hobbling. Using the old umbrella from the LAF box as a crutch.

Ankle throbbing, the slightest touch an electric shock. Swollen so large I can't wear a sock or shoe on that foot; my foot is always cold, but the injured ankle is always hot. Is that normal for a sprained ankle? Or a broken one?

If the fact that I'm trapped in here—alone, half starved, & constantly cold—in the middle of an invasion didn't keep me awake all night, or, even worse, the fact that my stupid clumsiness just led to the death of another human, the pain in my ankle would. "On a scale from 0 to 10, how would you rate your pain, Miss Bearovna?" I don't know, Doc: which of those numbers means the pain feels like a spiked metal mace beating against an eardrum?

My ankle is my guilt: excruciating, blistering, so enormous my skin will surely split open around it.

Doesn't help to say it could have happened to anyone. Doesn't help to tell myself I did my best. Because, based on what I've seen out my window, no one is awarding trophies for participation anymore. No one is handing out ribbons marked "Good job!" Not at this point in human history. Now, you either take 1st place, or somebody dies.

A human—maybe one of the few left in the world—is dead. If I had been more competent or less clumsy, he would be alive. Only one way to describe my performance the other day: major fail.

Forget those last two words. They're flippant. Insensitive. Just a little bit of lingo layered over the tragedy to take out the sting. If I could cross them out, I would. They don't describe how I really feel about what happened. This is how I feel: I murdered that young man.

The pacz came back for his body. They leave during the dying, then come back later. I think they hate the writhing as much as I do. But at least they clean up after themselves a bit. The bodies, anyway. The blood & other fluids & solids that erupt, spurt, & ooze from bodies as they die: those stay behind.

There is a large blood stain on the stone doorstep at the front of the library now. Lest I forget....

After the pacz took the man's body, I realized I should do something to honor him. After all, he defied the pacz for over two weeks. I don't know what he had to do to stay alive for so long, but I know it was hard.

Who was he? Did he have a family? Friends? Anyone who might want to know what happened to him? If there are other humans alive out there, they might feel comforted by knowing whether or not their loved one is dead or alive. To have closure.

I couldn't see the man well enough to describe him. Young, that's for sure. Probably my age. & hazel eyes. That's about all I could see by peeking through the crack under the door. Not much to go on for identification.

After I was sure the pacz were gone, I crawled to a bookshelf, pulled down some books, ripped out the 1st blank page I found, crawled back to the door. Slid the page through the crack under the door until it reached the closest puddle of blood. Waited until the paper was half soaked. Slowly—didn't want the wet section to catch on anything & rip off—pulled the paper back into the library.

Left the soaked page near the door, then crawled all the way to the other end of the library to reach the kitchen. Pulled myself up, leaned against a counter. The pain was intense before I stood, almost unbearable when I was upright. Dumped marshmallows out of their plastic bag, slumped to the cold floor w/ the bag in my teeth, & crawled back through the library to the front door. Placed the blood-soaked paper in the plastic bag. Crawled to the writing desk. Put the blood sample in the drawer that holds my beloved Sharpie marker.

Someday—if there are still humans around & still some way to test DNA—this man might have a name. People might wonder why his blood sugar level was so high, but there is a chance that he will have a name.

Day Nineteen

I didn't put the barricade back against the front door until today. I told myself I couldn't do it because of my ankle, & it's true that being upright is painful & walking is almost unbearable. (Climbing the ladder is totally out of the question for now.) I couldn't imagine shoving heavy items around; lifting them seemed impossible.

As it turns out, redoing the barricade almost killed me, & not because of the effort or pain. I was so focused on dragging chairs & tables around, & on dealing w/ my ankle, I forgot about the hole in the door. Yeah, not good. After every few steps, I had to lean against something to rest: At one point, I leaned against the door &—Surprise!—a pac finger poked through, almost touching my ear. Like I said, not good. I inched away from the door &, after a few seconds, the finger was withdrawn. But I had the feeling a pac was peering through the door. I waited until I heard the sound of feet plunking down the front steps, then I replaced the table that covered the hole.

Later, while lying down to rest & to calm the throbbing in my ankle (I wanted to take a nap but couldn't fall asleep because of all the stomping on the roof) I had a long, serious talk w/ myself about the importance of being honest in this journal. So, here's me being honest. The real reason I didn't replace the barricade until today was....

Why? Why should I bother to put it back up? By making pacz work harder to enter the library, I was simply delaying the inevitable—my death. Why put that off? Why did I deserve to live when so many people died? I'm nobody. Flawed, broken.

I almost opened the door & hobbled outside so many times in the past four days. To end the waiting. To end the pain.

I find myself humming "Stayin' Alive" at the strangest times. That was one of Benji's favorite songs. We used to sing it together, very fast & upbeat. Not now. Now I sing it slowly, like a dirge. Because, in a way, that's how it makes me feel. The song, like the process of staying alive here in the RAW, seems like the prelude to a funeral.

I've never been a drama queen. I've always been the level-headed one, the one who could evaluate a situation, develop a solution, implement it, & remain calm during the process. Solid. Dependable. My mother called me her rock. She told people she could always count on me to get things done w/o a lot of fuss. & here I was, considering actions that would lead to my death.

In my defense, I would argue that contemplating those actions was not necessarily being dramatic. Not in this case. Given the grim future I'm facing, either in the RAW or outside it, such thoughts might be considered reasonable.

But I woke up this morning w/ a voice in my head so insistent & border-line obnoxious that it could only belong to one person: Benji. No matter how loudly I hummed songs by his beloved Bee Gees to block out the voice, no matter how tightly I pressed my hands over my ears & sang "la, la, la, la, la," he just kept shouting at me.

"It's not about you, Doofus! It's about the books!"

Day Twenty

One week until Christmas. Can't believe how happy that makes me. It's a totally ridiculous reaction, I know, but that's how I feel.

Still hobbling. Still using the old umbrella for a crutch. Still unable to climb the ladder. Still in pain.

I remember when my best friend in middle school sprained his ankle during our ballet class. I went w/ him to the walk-in (in his case, hop-in) clinic because his folks were both at work. I remember the doctor saying it was too bad the ankle was sprained instead of broken because he could actually do something for a broken ankle.

My friend had to give up ballet. I refused to go to class, too. I said it was because I didn't want to go w/o him, but, really, I hated that class. My mother thought taking ballet would help me develop balance, agility, & poise. Anyone who saw me attempt a pirouette knew those things were never going to happen.

Here's the point: It took many weeks for my friend's ankle to heal at his young age, so I'm sure it will take the ankle of this old lady of twenty-four—almost twenty-five—at least that long.

I'm doing exercises to keep my ankle muscles from freezing up. Mostly rotating my foot, then pointing my toes toward & away from my body. No books on physical therapy in the collection, but I remember a few exercises my friend did.

Realizing I'm here to protect the books has made a big difference in how I view my situation. I don't deserve to live any more than all those people who died outside my window. True. But somebody needs to keep these books safe. Maybe this is all just a cosmic comedy show but, for whatever reason, it turns out I'm that person.

Sure, I use book pages for daily necessities & for my journal. But those actions affect only a tiny fraction of the books in this collection, & they help me survive so I can protect thousands of other books.

My food supplies are ~ half gone. Pretty much on track w/ my earlier calculations. I didn't eat for a few days after what happened on Day Fifteen. That gives me a few more days of food. Actually, for every day I didn't eat I gained two days of food because I've cut my daily calorie intake in half. I might be down to meals consisting of nothing but globs of expensive mustard & smears of snooty ketchup by the end, but that's okay. Whatever it takes.

I'm planning a Christmas feast. When I can't sleep at night—because of the bitter cold, my deep sense of guilt, or the patter of invader feet on the roof—I consider tasty condiment combinations for the meal. During the day, I read cookbooks from all over the world, some dating back almost two thousand years.

I think the feast will include the last crumbs of asiago cheese & one pickle slice for the appetizer, four crushed corn chips w/ a lovely caper-mayo-chutney sauce for the main course, hot cocoa w/ six micro marshmallows (I cut minis into four pieces to make micros) for dessert. Can't wait.

I've made a big decision. Tomorrow, I break into the head librarian's office.

The time for proper behavior has passed. I've seen or heard only one other human in the last ten days, so I don't think anyone will fault me for securing supplies wherever I can. Plus, it will be emotionally satisfying after putting up w/ her for so long. Closure is very important.

I don't know what else she has in there, but she has tissues. Want. Now.

Yes, tissues are the things we lust for in this brave, new, invaded world.

But my primary objective is to retrieve the bonsai tree on her desk. After all, it wouldn't be much of a Christmas w/o a tree.

Day Twenty-One

Chocolate! OMG!!! Great gobs of the ridiculously expensive kind! Who would have thought the old sourpuss to have had so much bioflavonoid in her?

I was wise not to take up crime as a profession. Took me almost 3 hours to break into the head librarian's office. A video of my attempt would be the funniest thing on youtube that doesn't include kittens. I tried for most of that time to open the door w/o causing lasting damage to it, the wood around it, or the lock. Then it dawned on me: Who cares if the door paint is chipped, the jamb is splintered, or the lock is broken? The door police?

In the end, I went w/ brute force. I dragged a metal chair over to the door, leaned against the wall to take the weight off my ankle, & smashed that lock w/ everything I had. Biff! Bam! Bop! & then, when the lock gave way, Bahdah bing!

The bonsai tree was on an automatic watering system—the head librarian would never trust one of us to water it properly—so it was still in good shape. The tree really is beautiful. Head Lib (that's what Benji & I called her) paid a doctoral student from Japan big bucks to do the pruning & shaping. The staff held a birthday party for Head Lib each year, & I was warned ahead of time that attendance—present in hand—was mandatory, so I gave her three rare polished agates to decorate the tree's shallow pot. I bought the agates in Queensland, Australia, during the year I was a research assistant there (on one of the few days—I can count them on one hand—during that year when I had time to do anything except research). The agates were nowhere to be seen: the head librarian probably tossed them in the trash as soon as the party was over. Oh, well.

I left untouched most of what I found in the office. Seemed fitting to set aside the place as a shrine to Head Lib, supreme goddess of control freaks. All I took was the tree, the box of tissues (Ha!), & a fistful of ultra-fine-point black Sharpies from her stash.

Side note: allow me to explain why I use a Sharpie to write my journal when pens are forbidden in the RAW. The restriction applied not only to patrons: None of the staff— at the front desk (Benji & me) or in the book conservation room—could use pens, either, except the head librarian, of course. There was only one pen outside her office, the Sharpie used to address manila envelopes for interdepartmental mail. That pen was attached to a wall in the staff kitchen w/ a chain, & liberating it was the 1st thing I did when I realized my journal entries would not show up against a page of text if I wrote them w/ a pencil.

The bonsai tree (I call her Bonnie), the box of tissues, & the pens are the only items I took from Head Lib's desk. Because I happened, quite by accident (NOT), to discover a remarkably large stash of food elsewhere in the office.

& what wonderful food it is.

Mostly candy: a box of Guylian Belgium dark chocolate sea shells w/ hazelnut filling (one missing); a Scharffen Berger dark chocolate & candied orange peel bar (sealed); a Green & Black's organic dark chocolate bar (half eaten); a bag of Ghirardelli dark chocolate blueberry squares in foil wrappers (full); & a Ghirardelli dark chocolate sea salt brownie bar (sealed).

Some cookies: a tin of Fortnum & Mason Piccadilly Biscuits—Lemon Curd (sealed), & a tin of Fortnum & Mason Biscuits—Chocolossus (half full, but w/ lots of yummy looking crumbs in the bottom of the tin).

A few savories: a bag of Bath Oliver Fortt's biscuits (three-quarters full); a box of Grate Britain All-British Smoked Cheese biscuits (sealed); a tin of Williams-Sonoma assorted cheese straws (almost full), & an unopened package of gluten-free crackers, five years past their expiration date.

A much-needed cache of protein: two jars of macadamia nuts (no salt; sealed), & a very large jar of Blue Diamond roasted almonds (no salt; half full).

Finally, some liquid vitamin C: two unopened bottles of organic mango juice.

Now it's mine, all mine!!!

The weird part is Head Lib never allowed the rest of us to keep anything edible at our work stations. No gum, no cough drops, not even a breath mint. To be fair, none of her food was in her desk, so I guess she wasn't breaking the rule. Technically.

Her food was in an antique pie cabinet in the sitting area at one end of her office. The place where she held quiet tête-à-têtes w/ the most generous donors & influential university officials. Two overstuffed chairs w/ green silk upholstery; a dark green marble coffee table; a Jacquard throw draped over the back of one chair; & an iPod Touch, plus accoutrements (Yes! Oh, yes, yes, yes!). On the floor, a thick & very comfy hand-woven wool rug, probably from an outdoor market in some exotic place.

I sat in the office for a long time today. Nibbling chocolates & biscuits, sipping tea, listening to music for the 1st time in weeks. Most of Head Lib's music collection ranges from ho-hum to seriously snore worthy, but there are some fine pieces, too. A few that Benji & I sang when we were in the town-&-gown choir. & Smetana's "Má Vlast," one of my mother's faves (it was on the program when my father took her to the symphony for their 1st date).

I left the iPod in the office. I might become addicted to listening to it, which would be dangerous. To stay safe, I need to hear everything going on around me.

The whole experience was so lovely, so peaceful. So very pre-invasion. I fell into a delicious state of drowsiness, then drifted off into a long nap.

I need to re-think my Christmas feast.

Day Twenty-Two

The pac came back last night. The tall one. It was looking in a window right before all the destruction began. Had to be the tall one the other time, too, because the pair of short pacz—the ones I call The Twins, who I see most often around here & who have been messing around on my roof for days couldn't lean far enough over the edge of the roof to look in a window. & I don't think the other pac in their foursome, the one I call Pudgy, could haul itself up the maintenance ladder.

I suppose the other pacz could look in a window if they had sticky stuff on their brown suits. But then they would be crawling up & down the facades of buildings like The Fly (that's what I'd do, for sure, if I had the ability), & I haven't seen them do that.

It's getting colder & colder at night in here. W/o heat, the temperature inside the library must drop close to freezing. I sleep w/ all my clothes on, plus my hat, coat, glove, mitten, scarf, & all of the conservation staff's lab coats that fit over my clothes, & I'm still cold.

My foot—the one I can't wear a shoe or sock on yet because of the sprained ankle—felt almost frost-bit last night. I needed to warm it up, so I slid the book cart to one side, crawled out from under my bench, & hobbled to the end of the shelf row. Looked up at the window: no pac. Hobbled across the frigid stone floor to the kitchen, turned on the oven, & stood near it for half an hour to take the chill off (most of that time I stood on one foot, holding the naked one practically inside the oven). Went to the bathroom. Snuck into the head librarian's office & stole her throw & wool rug.

While hobbling back to bed w/ my pilfered goodies, I looked up, & there it was—the dark round blob of a pac head blocking out the pale moonlight.

I stopped. For a long time. The toes on my uncovered foot became painful & itchy. Chilblains? I think that's what my grandmother called it. Whatever it was, it hurt. The tall pac didn't move. I didn't move.

Then I heard those annoying footsteps on the roof again, so The Twins must have climbed up there at that point. The tall pac's head turned in response to the sound of the footsteps. Suddenly, there was a loud whoosh, then another, & then: Ka-boom! Pause. Ka-boom! Two explosions, each powerful enough to rattle windows, break something big, & blow clouds of white dust through the library.

The tall pac almost fell off the roof when the bombs exploded. Its head twisted, & one hand must have lost its grip on the roof edge because that arm began to flail wildly. Its torso & feet swooped by the window as they slid off the roof, then the tall pac swung back & forth in front of the window, dangling from the roof by one hand. Its other arm kept flailing, & I expected to see the pac fall at any moment. As much as I hate pacz, I didn't want to watch that happen, & I really didn't want to hear the thud of a body hitting the ground. After a few (long) seconds of dangling, the tall pac's loose hand must have grabbed the roof edge again because it pulled itself up & out of my view.

Everything happened so fast. I stood still & tried not to cough while the pac was dangling, even though the dust in the air was burning my eyes, nose, throat, & lungs. I wanted to put the throw over my face to keep the dust out, but that movement might attract attention, so I just stood there.

After the tall pac returned to the roof, I heard the sound of stomping feet up there, then several loud crashes, then running feet, & then all was quiet again.

Until I started coughing. I couldn't hold it in any longer. At that point, I didn't know where the dust had come from (& I still don't know what the pacz put in the explosive devices to make them so caustic). All I knew was that the dust was mega-vile. I felt like tiny pacz carrying flame-throwers were running around in & on my body scorching everything they saw.

I stood still until I was sure the pacz were gone, then I coughed & hobbled back to my sleeping spot. While adding the throw & rug to it, I coughed so violently I had to stop several times to catch my breath. Perhaps I should have surveyed the library to assess the damage, although, in my defense, it wasn't very bright last night & my eyes were watering so heavily that I wouldn't have seen much anyway. Plus, I could barely breathe. Plus, I didn't want to stir up more dust. Plus My. Foot. Was. Freezing!

So I crawled into my cozy nest & lay still so I wouldn't cough too much. Aside from a few coughing fits, I slept better than usual. Even after being bombed & watching a pac almost die. I've been living in the valley of the shadow of death for so long that this sort of thing seems normal.

Seriously, at this point in my captivity, just having warm toes is enough to make me feel content.

Day Twenty-Three

Didn't take long after I woke up yesterday to discover where the noxious dust came from: the huge holes in two of the bathroom walls. Most of the plaster & tile had been stripped off those walls by the explosions, which were powerful enough to embed dozens of large, jagged chunks of tile in the two walls that don't have blast holes.

I stood by the bathroom door & stared at the damage for a long time before the reality sank in. If the bombs had gone off a minute earlier, I would have been in there. If I hadn't been killed instantly by the blast force, or by projectiles slicing me into pieces, I would have spent the rest of the night, maybe the rest of my life, trying to extract tile chunks from my body w/o bleeding to death or dying from infected wounds.

I gasped at that thought, which made me cough, which made me unable to breathe, which made me panic. I needed to run, but I couldn't because that would stir up dust & hurt my ankle. I needed to calm down, but I couldn't because I kept imagining myself lying on the bathroom floor, covered w/ blood, dead.

The door on Head Lib's office was shut when the bombs went off, so there wasn't much dust in there. I hobbled in, closed the door, crawled under her desk, & curled into a ball. Coughing. Taking shallow breaths. Coughing. More shallow breaths. No relief.

I had considered death coldly, rationally the other day; now the thought of it threw me into turmoil. I had slept soundly after the bombing; now the effects of it ripped apart my sense of well-being. I used to be a rock; now I was a quivering blob.

I remembered the iPod. I listened to Beethoven's 5th: I think of it as a war song, & the fact that I am at war had smacked me full in the face. Da-da-da dum; da-da-da dum. At 1st those notes sounded like "I'm-going-to DIE, I'm-going-to DIE." As the symphony went on, though, they made me think of people in England going about their business during World War II while bombs were falling around them. Just doing what they had to do, even though they could die at any moment. After the 4th time through the symphony, my coughing slowed, my pulse was normal, & I could breathe again. I uncurled & returned to my new normal—dealing w/ destruction.

The wall behind the bathroom sink was hardest hit. The blast hole didn't pass through the outside wall of the library (no daylight, so happy-happy-joy-joy about that), but it reduced the inner wall to a few damaged studs, broken pipes, & frayed wires. It's a miracle the sink & lights still work. The other blasted wall, between the bathroom & the kitchen, wasn't quite as damaged, but light was passing through the hole in it.

Also—Shocking Secret Revealed!—the bathroom was littered w/ pieces of something my mother called "girly" magazines, & she didn't mean zines for girls. They're mostly piles of confetti now. I have no idea who stashed them in the wall. Maybe construction workers when they built the RAW. Maybe somebody in the book conservation room (Benji & I call it the con-lab). Maybe the head librarian. I'd bet a fiver (if I had one) that it wasn't Benji.

The vent pipes on both of the blasted walls have jagged holes in them, so here's my theory: The Twins made two explosive devices, added chemicals to make the blast debris more caustic, & dropped them down the vent pipes that are exposed on the roof.

I spent most of yesterday cleaning up debris in the bathroom, wet-wiping surfaces in the kitchen to keep the dust out of my food & water, & mopping dust off the library floor so I don't stir it up whenever I hobble through. I was coughing the whole time, even w/ a dishcloth tied around my face.

While I was cleaning up dust in the kitchen, I kept the oven on for a special treat. But I was careful to set the timer for thirty minutes. I discovered early in my captivity that the oven acts up if it's on longer than that: I smell wires burning, then the oven starts sending out little puffs of smoke. Which is too bad because my life would be so much easier if I could keep the oven on all the time & just hang out by it to stay toasty.

Of course, I need to stand very close to the oven to feel much warmth because there is no door on the kitchen, & this building is like a great big super-frigid sponge. I can almost hear it sucking up any bit of heat it finds. I dreamed a few nights ago that the RAW was a beast, big & weird, like those hairless cats that were all the rage a while back but the size of a saber-toothed tiger. It lurked around my sleeping nest, lapping up the warmth of every breath I exhaled. Another time I dreamed this place was playing the old Hansel-&-Gretel trick on me, offering pizza & lasagna if I would just crawl into the oven. If the temperature in here was a little lower, or if there was Canadian bacon on the pizza, I might consider it.

All in all, yesterday was miserable. I had been happy lately about spending less time cleaning because most of the soot from Day Three was finally gone. Now…. Yuck. Dusting this stuff off books, shelves, tables (& on & on) will take FOREVER.

The only good thing about the bathroom being bombed is that the mirror over the sink was almost totally obliterated. All that remained were scattered sparkly bits, which are now safely in the trash, & one shard the size of a tennis ball, which I'm saving because every survival kit I've ever seen includes a small mirror.

I've been avoiding the mirror for a long time anyway because of my tangled hair & my, ahem, elegantly disheveled appearance. Recently, though, I've been a little afraid to look in it. My face is starting to look like my mother's did after her chemo treatments. Pale skin, hollow cheeks, dark circles under my eyes.

I know my health has gone downhill because I just don't feel well much of the time. I've dropped more than a few pounds, too, & I didn't have that many extra to begin w/. I know this because of the pants test—my jeans are so loose at the waist & in the thighs that I'll need to find something to use as a belt soon. Let's face it: scales can be manipulated fairly easily, but the pants, oh the pants, they never lie.

So that was yesterday. & then today....

I woke up this morning &, just like that, the running water is gone. & I mean gone gone. Tried to flush the toilet, & nothing but a gurgle.

"You never miss the water till the well runs dry."

I kept singing that old song today. When I wasn't screaming in frustration.

The pipes must have frozen & burst. I bet there's water spurting out of a broken pipe somewhere on campus, probably making a nice big ice-skating rink. When I realized early on in the invasion that the water & electrical systems were still working but the campus steam plant—the heating system— was not, I figured the pipes would freeze eventually. But, like death, knowing it will happen & then actually having it happen are two different things.

I've saved water in every container possible, & I refill them every night, & sometimes after I take a sip. I won't have water to clean up the dust in the library or wash clothes, but I have enough drinking water for a week. Maybe longer if I'm very careful. After that, I don't know. I'd better start praying for rain. Or snow. Or a rescue....

I have a feeling the tall pac was not involved in the bombing. From what I saw, he was as surprised by what happened as I was. & it certainly looked like he came closer to dying than I did.

Wait…. He?

I just realized I've started to think of the tall pac as a male. How did that happen?

Maybe because it/he seems to be in charge of the others (although not on the night of the bombing) & is taller than the others, two qualities I associate w/ males. I know, I know—that is totally sexist of me. Absolutely. Indubitably. I'm embarrassed to think it, let alone write it. I admit my sexist sin freely & w/o reservation, & I promise to surrender my unplayed feminist card as soon as I find another human to take it.

I have no idea what sex that particular pac might be. I don't know if pacz even have distinct sexes. Or any sex at all. But for lack of compelling information to the contrary, & because there is no one around to argue w/ me about it (sigh), I will, for now, refer to the tall pac as a male.

I'm going to stop thinking about the lack of water until tomorrow. Stop singing about it. Stop screaming about it. I decided yesterday while cleaning up bomb debris that I would reward myself today by decorating the bonsai Christmas tree. & that's what I'm going to do.

Take that, Universe.

Day Twenty-Four

The Christmas tree—Bonnie—is beautiful. I cut tiny stars from the foil wrappers of two chocolate blueberry squares. Blue on one side, silver on the other. Unraveled a thread from the hem of my shirt & used that to hang them on the tree. The ornaments weigh nothing, so they won't hurt Bonnie's branches. When I breathe or cough on the stars, they spin, flash, & sparkle. They make me feel like dancing.

I set Bonnie on a (dusted) book shelf near my sleeping bench. Even though it's around the time of the new moon now, there is enough light for me to see her when I peek out from under my bench at night.

Good thing it's fairly dark out, because my period started. Yeah, I guess the Universe decided being bombed & running out of running water wasn't enough of a challenge for me. So now I need to make a few trips to the bathroom every night (crumpled paper is not as absorbent as one might hope). After the bombing, I'm spooked about using the facilities after dark. That's silly, I know: The Twins could just as easily drop a bomb during the day. But being blown up in the dark seems worse somehow.

Made a discovery today that will save many blank book pages. Couldn't have come at a better time because, believe me, I am blasting through paper at the moment. I found a box, the kind used to store magazines, on a shelf in Contemporary Literature w/—wait for it, wait for it—the complete works of Professor Gulick.

I had to laugh when I saw it. I remember when he told me his entire oeuvre was housed in Special Collections. Yeah, but it's one box, three inches wide, & most of the contents are course outlines. Not much to show for several decades of work. He must have been too busy doing, to put it politely, other things.

I wish I could show Benji Professor G's skimpy contribution to the world of "leet-rah-tour," as Benji always called it. He would appreciate the absurdity. He would do his famous Prof G imitation & make me laugh. He would....

I miss Benji so much. Sometimes I think about how different my time in the RAW would be if he hadn't left early on the afternoon the invasion began. If he had stayed ten more minutes we would be here together, keeping each other's spirits up, telling jokes, singing. I try not to think about that too often, though. It makes this place seem even colder, & it makes the silence in here too painful for my ears to bear.

When I feel sad about Benji, I transmute those negative feelings into my loathing for Prof G. I sing a few choruses of Pink Floyd's "Another Brick in the Wall." Beat my fists on my writing desk. Sometimes bang my head against it, too.

So much fun preparing those papers for a higher purpose. Crumple, open, flatten; crumple, open, flatten. Repeat. Repeat. On the last crumple of each sheet, I made sure the printing was on the inside of the ball because, you know, ink. Then I stuffed as many balls as possible into the box & stored it in the bathroom.

I tried a Gulick paper ball the last time I used the facilities, & it did the trick. Then I tossed the bloody thing into a paper grocery sack beside the toilet.

She shoots!

She scores!

& I thought, "Rare & wonderful, indeed."

Day Twenty-Five

Tomorrow night is Christmas Eve! After finding the exquisite food in Head Lib's office, I've had many lovely middle-of-the-night planning sessions for the feast. During those sessions, I am filled w/ joy.

More good news: My injured ankle is feeling a little better—still swollen & painful, but not nearly as bad as before. I can wear a sock on that foot now. No shoe, but baby steps.

Of course, I'm coughing like someone who's smoked 2 packs of cigarettes a day for decades. My ribs are sore from coughing, which makes certain critical movements excruciating. I checked the lower right-hand section of my ribs today; it has a huge bruise. Bruised from the inside out by coughing.

On this 3rd day post-running water, the bathroom is beginning to smell like an outhouse. At some point, I must collect water (or melt snow) to flush the toilet manually. But since that means going outside, I'll put up w/ the smell for now. It's not too bad on my reading/writing/sleeping side of the RAW when the bathroom door is closed.

I'm exhausted, probably due to several factors: lack of fruits & vegetables, lack of protein, low caloric intake in general, ankle injury, burning eyes, period, breathing issues, constant cold. Oh, & a little number I like to call The Great Invasion.

I spend so much energy trying not to think about things: what might have happened to Matilda & Benji, what might happen to me & these books, the lack of food & water, my ankle/cold foot/coughing, the footsteps on the roof (The Twins are back; I'm thinking of renaming them The Brats), the strange odor coming from the book conservation room, the bashing on the front door.

My body is wedged tight against a conglomerate of real & potential disasters, a boulder of trouble on a steep slope above me, & I'm trying hard to pretend it's not there. But my feet keep slipping, & my arms are tired, & it gets to me. It's not a Sisyphus situation: there's no way I could push that boulder up a hill. I just need to keep it from rolling over me.

It's an odd-numbered day, so this entry is supposed to be upbeat. But thoughts of Christmas have allowed me to save up enough positive psychic energy to write about Day Two. I jotted down notes during the 1st 7 days (on those occasions when I was capable of such higher-level functions as thinking & writing) w/ my tiny golf-score pencil on the back of the letter hidden in the case for my sunglasses. I'll re-create events of that day, as I did for Day One, based on those notes. It won't be totally authentic because my memories of it are influenced by what I know now, but I'll do my best.

Day Two. I don't know how I survived the 1st night. Screaming & howling outside. Inside, a tight fist clenching my stomach, squeezing it harder as the night went on, making me gag over & over. Groaning from the front door when something bashed against it. The thumping of feet running past the library. More howling.

I found the safest place, my sleeping nest, & I hid there, turning my face toward the wall so I wouldn't see those things when they came for me. I wanted to put my hands over my ears, too, but I was sure Benji would come back & I needed to hear his knock on the door when he did.

No sleep. In the morning, I looked out from under the bench & saw nothing unusual. Crept down the shelf row, looked around the open space: except for barricades against the doors, the library looked like it always did. Ripped out another blank page & went to the bathroom, locking the door behind me.

How silly to lock the door. If the invaders break through the heavy outside doors, it will be a piece of cake for them to break down the bathroom door, & then being caught w/ my pants down will be the least of my problems. Still, I locked the door.

Then I climbed the shelf ladder & peeked out. The invaders were still there, but not in waves like the day before. They were roaming around in bands of 4 to 8. As I watched, 3 women sprinted out of the Natural Resources building & ran toward the river that flows along the edge of campus directly behind this library. The invaders were right behind them. The pacz hadn't caught up w/ the women by the time they sprinted out of view, but I heard their voices howling a few seconds later.

More gagging. Deep breaths so I wouldn't throw up.

I evaluated my situation. Cell phone signal—no. Heat—no. Electricity—yes. Water—yes. Essential plumbing—yes. Food—don't even think about it.

Water was the most critical factor, so I searched the staff kitchen for containers. Glass pitcher, vases, cups, glasses, tea kettle, serving bowls, punch bowl, fish bowl, sauce pan. I filled them, covered them w/ tea towels. Sipped a little. Must ration water.

Six more howling sessions.

Next, making my sleeping/hiding area more secure. The bench ends & wall behind it protected three sides, but the front was open. I used a rolling book cart, the kind w/ angled shelves on both sides, to block the front. I filled it w/ the heaviest books I could find—*The Complete Works of Shakespeare*, volumes of an old encyclopedia—so the invaders would need to work a little to get to me.

Five howling sessions.

What next? A protected writing/reading space. Wasn't sure I would get to use it, but I needed to keep busy. I used the antique writing desk near Pre-16th-Century Literature: no one is supposed to touch it, let alone use it. But now, why not? It's sturdy, the wood glows when the light hits it, & it has intricate marquetry on both sides & on the section intended to hold an inkwell. I pushed it into a corner, stacked books around it on the other 2 sides. I didn't use books from Pre-16th-Century Literature, of course: too fragile; too valuable. But over 12 feet of shelf space is devoted to a collection of contemporary romance novels, & we're not talking *Jane Eyre*. I used them, stacking the books ~ 5 feet high around the desk, leaving a narrow gap between the stack & one wall so I could squeeze into the small sanctuary.

Halfway through the project, there was a howling session that went on for ~ 40 minutes. I tried to keep working, but I couldn't. There was a world-wreck going on outside, & I couldn't look away. Someone, I told myself, needed to be a witness. I climbed the shelf ladder to watch.

Three bodies already writhing on the ground.

Four older professors from the Art department huddled together as they hurried across the open space. When the pacz reached them, the 3 men made a barrier around the woman. A last &, as I'm sure they realized, useless attempt to be protectors. Then all were touched by the pacz & fell.

Next came 2 women I knew well because they worked in the cafeteria & gave me leftovers for the picnics I had w/ Benji & Matilda. They didn't run. One of them was injured, & the other was helping her limp across the Quad. A tall pac strode up & reached out to touch them. The women looked at the pac, no fear on their faces, no hate, no anger, just weariness & resignation. The pac hesitated—odd behavior based on what I'd seen so far—then touched the women & left.

One at a time, over the next 20 minutes or so, 5 people tried to cross the Quad. Some ran, some walked, all died.

Then quiet. No humans; no pacz. I climbed down the ladder, vomited, & went back to the task of building walls around my desk.

There were 8 more howling sessions during the day, but I didn't climb the shelf ladder to watch. I had witnessed enough. I finished building the book wall, squeezed into the sanctuary, sat at my desk until just before dusk, & thought about the 36 people who had died today in the little bit of the world I could see through my window.

When the sun began to set, I climbed the ladder one last time & looked out. Pale sunlight was reflected in dozens of west-facing windows on campus, & in hundreds of windows in town & on the small farms scattered across the valley. If 36 other humans had died within sight of each of those glowing windows—&, based on what I had observed, such a thing seemed possible—thousands of people had died in this area today. I thought of windows in the many small towns in this part of the state: Wenatchee, Cle Elum, Cashmere, Starbuck, Othello, Moses Lake. I thought of Seattle & Portland, Spokane & Boise, Bellingham & Salt Lake City. All of the windows in all of those places. Each multiplied by 36.

Day Twenty-Six

Christmas Eve. Finally. Huzzah!

I've read all day today. Yes, I know what you're thinking (because the "you" I'm talking to is probably just me): I read for hours almost every day. But I do that for what my mother called "edification." Which doesn't mean I don't enjoy it. I do. But today I decided to read just for fun, because it's a holiday, & I can.

I had planned to read only works related to Christmas. I've read most of them many times; Christmas is my favorite holiday. But I made one exception—*The Foolish Dictionary*, a side-splitter best taken in small doses. I nibbled at that today, too.

Here's what else I read: O'Henry's "The Gift of the Magi" (my mother & I took turns reading it to each other every Christmas); Dickens' "A Christmas Carol" (ditto); Dostoyevsky's "White Nights" & "A Christmas Tree and a Wedding" (in honor of my father, who my mother loved right up to the moment she died, & maybe even after); McMahon's *Shakespeare's Christmas Gift to Queen Bess in the year 1596*; *The Christmas Books of Mr. M. A. Titmarsh* (William Makepeace Thackeray—love that name); & then, because I had time before writing this entry & setting my stocking beside the Christmas tree, I read "The Gift of the Magi" again. & cried again.

The Christmas theme of a star in the sky reminded me of research I've been doing to answer one of my big questions about the invasion: How extensive is it? Jefferson City is just a small town (pop. ~ 20,000) w/ a pretentious name. Hard to imagine invaders, whoever they are or wherever they came from, having anything against us in particular. Which suggests the invasion is bigger than what I can see out my window. I've assumed that it is, but my assumption was based on the scantiest bit of logic.

Turns out the little slice of the world visible to me offers some very important info. 1st, jet trails/chemtrails/contrails, or whatever you want to call them. No, I'm not talking trumped-up conspiracy theories about how they're part of a deep-state attempt to control reproductive rates or financial markets, conduct chemical or biological warfare, or turn us all into sheep-like creatures who believe anything the government tells us. Hey, I abhor the control of The People by self-serving Elitist Governments in the pocket of Big Money as much as the next person. But using jet farts to do it? I think not.

I'm talking the absence of jet trails. Jefferson City is located in a wide-open part of the country that stretches a couple hundred miles from the foothills of the Cascade Mountains to the eastern border of Washington State. Jet pilots—private, commercial, military—seem to love this area based on the rate they fly over it. We have ~300 blue-sky days a year, &, at any given time, I used to see at least one white jet trail crossing the blue. Until the invasion. Now, zip. I was so focused on my own survival & angst that I missed this for a long time. A complete lack of jets (I haven't seen or heard any other type of aircraft fly over, either) must mean the invasion is affecting other places in this country, big places, like major cities & military bases.

2nd (the "star in the sky" theme comes in here), I haven't seen any satellites pass over since I injured my ankle (I wasn't checking for them before that). Benji & I used to sit on a bench by the RAW after late-night choir practice, share a snack, & catch up on each other's news, & we always saw satellites going over. My narrow view of the world from inside the library became much narrower after I injured my ankle, which has kept me from climbing the ladder: The only part of the outside world I've been able to see for almost two weeks now is a small section of the sky. I've been upset about that constraint, which I considered a severe limitation. Turns out it forced me to focus on something of real importance, because the part of the sky I can see out the high windows while lying on my back on the floor is the same section Benji & I used to watch together. I've been looking for satellites every night, sometimes for hours at a time when I can't sleep, & nothing. I think that means the invasion is affecting other countries, too.

While these observations are disturbing, they put my situation in perspective. I still have the problems I've whined about before, but they seem less significant now. I'm guessing times are tough for any human still alive out there, probably much tougher than for me here in the relative comfort & security of the RAW. All we can do is hang on for now, hang on & follow the light we carry inside.

Day Twenty-Seven

Snow in the night! Six inches. &—best Christmas present ever—no pac tracks.

I used the bathroom only once last night because my period has already ended. All my bodily functions are slowing down, which is probably not a good thing in the long run but certainly makes nights easier.

Since I was wide awake & out & about anyway, & probably because I wrote about it yesterday, I tried climbing the ladder to watch the snow fall. The process was more painful than I'd thought it would be, & it set off a long coughing fit. But I went slowly, putting weight on my uninjured ankle & pulling myself up w/ my arms instead of pushing myself up w/ my feet.

What a treat to look out the window again. Big clumps of flakes drifting down, rocking back & forth. Quiet, peaceful. Even though I was cold & my ankle ached, I watched for ~ 10 minutes.

When I started back down the ladder, I saw a slight movement between two buildings. I tensed up. Bile & nausea churned inside me. I had been so sure pacz would not be active in the snow. Then three deer stepped out from between the buildings. I forgot everything else & watched them for ~ half an hour as they nibbled their way around the Quad.

I was in tears for much of that time. It was a relief to see deer instead of pacz. A relief to see something alive & familiar. I'm guessing most "worlds"—social, political, financial, emotional—are in chaos at this moment, if they haven't been destroyed already. But the natural world? Maybe, just maybe, it's doing fine.

Merry Christmas!

The 1ˢᵗ thing I saw when I woke up this morning was Bonnie, her tiny blue & silver stars twinkling. & then…. What's this? A lumpy stocking beside the tree? & a present w/ my name on it?

In the stocking, Santa left me a Scharffen Berger chocolate/candied orange peel bar, three Ghirardelli chocolate blueberry squares (sadly, the last three in his sack), & ten cinnamon hard candies from Quin's. Yes! The present was a box from Powell's w/ two books about my favorite artist: *Collected Works of Walter Crane: The Black and White Series* & *Collected Works of Walter Crane: The Color Series*. Also, two children's books Matilda & I love: *The Tailor of Gloucester*, by Beatrix Potter, & *Under the Window: Pictures & Rhymes for Children*, by Kate Greenaway.

"Hallelujah! Hallelujah!"

I ate my usual oatmeal for breakfast, but a whole package this time, & I added chopped cranberries for a festive touch. Drank half a glass of water w/ four mango juice ice cubes melted in it. Delish. For dessert: not just a tiny nibble of a chocolate blueberry square, but the whole fantabulous piece.

Be sure to maintain your exercise routine over the holidays to melt away those extra pounds. I was able to wear both shoes today for the 1ˢᵗ time since Day Fifteen. I did some careful hobble-stepping around the perimeter aisles w/ the aid of my trusty umbrella crutch, singing Christmas carols all the way.

"Angels we have heard on high
sweetly singing o'er the plains…."

My mother & I used to go caroling w/ the folks in her quilting group at church. We sang at the nursing home, the homeless shelter, the soup kitchen, &—when we were slumming—the mall.

"There's a song in the air!
There's a star in the sky!"

I loved those times. I feigned reluctance about going, since the average age of the quilting singers was probably seventy (my mother was one of the youngsters). But I knew my mother & I were never going to have enough time together, so I went.

"In the bleak mid-winter frosty wind made moan,
Earth stood hard as iron, water like a stone...."

No, no, no! Not that song. I needed happy songs today. Upbeat. Lively.

"& in despair I bowed my head,
'There is no peace on earth,' I said...."

"Seriously, Kaylee," I said out loud, "what part of happy, upbeat, & lively don't you understand?!"

"Joy to the world...!"

After getting warmed up by pacing, I was able to sit for a few hours & read something I found ~ a week ago & have been saving for a special occasion. *Galaxy Science Fiction*, a magazine that began publication in 1950. Complete set. Major score!

More exercise, this time w/ only one shoe on because my injured ankle swelled up after my morning session. As part of my exercise, I climbed the ladder again to see if pacz had been out on patrol. Only deer footprints in the snow. It will be much easier to track pacz w/ snow on the ground.

Then it was time for the big event: The Christmas Feast.

Appetizer: a lovely antipasto tray w/ one Kalamata olive, one stuffed green olive, three capers, & a large pickle chip.

Main course: A savory soup made by simmering together ketchup, sun-dried tomatoes, & a clove of garlic from the bottom of the pickle jar. I thickened the soup w/ crushed crackers, sprinkled six chopped macadamia nuts on top (livin' large), & served the soup w/ a smoked cheese biscuit.

Dessert: Lemon curd biscuit topped w/ a tart & tangy berry coulis made from cooked cranberries sweetened w/ honey.

I finished the feast w/ two cups of hibiscus flower tea, which I sipped while listening to music in Head Lib's office: Corelli's "Christmas Concerto," Vivaldi's "The Four Seasons,"

& then some Brazilian samba music. I had to set my tea cup down during that last part because I was chair-dancing like a wild (albeit wounded) animal.

I've been thinking about that Christmas during World War I when soldiers on both sides of the Front called a truce. They met, talked, ate, sang, exchanged gifts. Nice idea, but I guess it wouldn't work w/ the pacz.

Enough of that. I don't want to think about invaders at the moment. I don't want to think about anything negative. I want to think about what a lovely day it was here in the RAW. & now I say....

Merry Christmas to all (especially any humans out there who are still hanging on), & to all a good night.

Day Twenty-Eight

Fueled by relatively large meals for the past two days, & buoyed by Christmas cheer, I decided I had enough energy to tackle the task at the top of my "to do" list: deal w/ the smell in the con-lab. Took me three hours to break into Head Lib's office; took me three minutes this morning to break the lock on the con-lab.

When the door opened a crack, I almost keeled over from the blast of nasty stink coming out of the room. But there was only enough space for the smell to escape—the door wouldn't open wider than a crack.

I wrapped a dishcloth around my mouth & nose, then returned to the task, pushing against the door several times. No joy. The hinges looked fine; the bottom wasn't rubbing against the floor. Something was blocking the door from the inside. Keeping weight off my injured ankle, I pushed, rested, pushed, for ~ 40 minutes. When I had the door open far enough to fit my head through the crack, I peeked inside.

Pac!

Ran to the bathroom, locked the door, vomited before I could remove the dishcloth, then sat on the floor while I wiped my mouth & tried to breathe, while I tried to stop my heart from banging through my chest.

It must be dead, I thought. It was lying w/ its head against the door, & I had bashed the door into its skull every time I pushed, but it made nary a peep. Face down, not moving, no sound, horrible smell: It must be dead.

But maybe this is how pacz sleep. Maybe this is how they smell. Maybe there were other pacz, live pacz, in the room. It was no use hiding in the bathroom anyway—if there were other pacz in the RAW already, they could get to me easily. I tied a clean cloth around my face & peeked into the con-lab again.

The pac hadn't moved. I pushed the door open far enough to squeeze in, then did a quick check. No other bodies. One window was broken. When I looked closer, I realized the book repair project on the counter under the window was askew, a jar of glue was knocked over, & there were splotches of goo on the floor.

My theory: The pac was looking in the window, smacked against it, broke the glass, lost its balance, fell into the room. It was injured by the fall, but it survived. Couldn't go back out the window. Saw the door. Crawled toward it, scratching against the floor as it moved. Heard something (me) moving. Scratched at the door to be let out. Died.

What an awful thought. Me in the library thinking the barricades had kept the pacz out while there was a pac already in the RAW. If it had been able to stand & use its hands, it could have killed me instantly. Instead, it died a horrible death. I became aware of the scratching on Day Three & it continued, on & off, for ~ a week & a half, so it was a slow death, too.

If the pac was, in fact, dead. I still wasn't absolutely sure. I didn't want to touch it because it might be able to kill me even now. How to find out? I needed a poker. The umbrella. But what if the pac death ray could travel up through the metal shaft & bone handle into my hand? I put on my glove, added a mitten over that, then wrapped my hand in the XXL tee-shirt. Reached out w/ the umbrella & poked the pac.

I was still alive, & the pac didn't move, didn't make a sound. I jabbed it harder. Still no movement, no sound.

Then I kept jabbing the pac. Harder. Faster. I thought of the people who had died on the Quad, the most horrible moments of their lives playing out in public. No dignity. No sanctity of life. I recalled horrified faces. Howling. Writhing.

The irrevocable bloodstain on the library doorstep. The young man's hazel eyes....

I heard crying. It had been going on for a long time, & it was coming from me. But when I stopped—jabbing, crying— because a coughing fit made me double over in pain, the crying continued. From a different voice. A voice making an odd sound I seemed to recognize, even though I had never heard anything like it before.

Followed the sound. Up, up to the top of the wall. The tall pac was outside, head pressed against the broken window, arm reaching gingerly through the hole in the glass, hand waving toward the body on the floor.

No universal translator was needed to understand the sound the tall pac was making. It was the anguished cry of a sentient being, a being w/ emotions, who was mourning the loss & desecration of someone he loved.

Day Twenty-Nine

After finding the dead pac in the RAW yesterday, & after seeing the tall pac in intense emotional pain & w/ part of his body actually extending into the library, I was severely rattled & not sure what to do. So, of course, I wrote a journal entry. When all else fails…. (I always thought that keeping a journal was a way to say I believe in the future. True, but now I realize it is not necessarily a way to say I believe in *my* future.)

There is no way I can secure the con-lab door now. Not after breaking the lock. I thought about putting a barricade against it, but that would be a waste of time because the door opens into the room: I could pile up items on this side, but anyone inside the room could open the door & remove the items fairly easily from that side.

& since one pac came in through the window, it's possible others can, too. There's no way I can reach the broken window, let alone block the hole in it.

Like most women, I've felt vulnerable many times. Face it: we are vulnerable, even when we don't acknowledge it. Even when we don't hear footsteps behind us after dark as we walk alone from work to our car or bus stop & realize we have quickened our pace in response. Even when we don't hold a set of keys in our sweaty hand, the largest key extended, ready to gouge out an attacker's eyes. Even when we don't hear the doorknob turn as we lie in bed, half asleep, & wonder if it was turned by friend or foe.

I've never felt as vulnerable as I have during the past 24 hours. Illusions of safety & security, which all of us maintain to make it through the day, have vanished. Doors, windows, walls: Those things can't protect me. In truth, I wasn't really protected by them before the invasion. Windows can be broken. Locks can be picked or smashed (if I can do it, anyone can). Walls do not seem like much protection to people who have experienced a tree falling on their house or a car crashing into their living room.

We live in eggshells, ready to be cracked open or crushed w/ a tap.

Maintaining the illusion of safety, security, & invulnerability is a seductive but exhausting act of self-deception. I've been trying to maintain that illusion for a long time. I need to give it up.

The pacz are here, & they seem intent on staying. I can't imagine why. Certainly, the few pacz still on campus can't be hanging around just to kill me, even though they keep trying. That makes no sense. I wish they would go home. Why don't they go home?

But they're here, & I need to deal w/ them. Just like those situations & people that existed pre-invasion that were threats to my safety. Obviously, I can't keep the pacz out completely — the dead one in the con-lab is proof of that. & I can't avoid them completely because I need food & water, & the only sources for those will — very soon — be outside this building.

This morning I remembered a quote, possibly from Abraham Lincoln, about a friend being someone who has the same enemy you do. What I think he (or whoever) meant is that finding something you & the enemy hate more than each other can be helpful in decreasing hostilities, perhaps even in reaching a truce.

The upshot: I need to find points of connection w/ the pacz. Something we have in common. It could be an enemy — from the way the tall pac reacted yesterday, I think death is our common enemy. That's something I might be able to establish a connection around. But I don't think connections/ friendships exist only around shared enemies. At least I hope not. My task is to find other ways to show the pacz we are all in this together. Don't know if that's possible, but it's worth a try.

Other than that, all I can do is live as best I can in the bubble of now, the bubble that does not keep me safe or secure or invulnerable but that does keep me aware of the precious, fragile, fleeting nature of life.

Day Thirty

Slept under my bench last night, not for protection but because it is a small enough space to keep relatively warm w/ my body heat.

Got up this morning & began the day w/o focusing on my woes. Did my morning ablutions—I think that's the phrase Katharine Hepburn uses in "The African Queen." Ate breakfast. Exercised. Tidied up. Crumpled book pages. Read.

I didn't inspect the con-lab to see if another pac had squeezed through the window & into my life. I didn't peek into the SoDoc rooms or the library corners for lurkers. I didn't check under Head Lib's desk. I went about my business, enjoying the here & now, gratefully accepting the gift of another day of life.

Snow began falling in the afternoon. I climbed the ladder w/o too much pain, watched the snow, then, when the sun came out, watched birds flit about. A red-tailed hawk soared over the Ag Sci building. Deer came back to paw through snow.

I thought of another potential point of connection w/ the pacz. Tall Man was upset not just because his friend was dead, but because I was causing harm to the body. I can understand that. I felt the same way when I saw people in the hospital handling my mother's body like a piece of meat after she died. I know she was dead, not there, beyond caring. & I know they were just doing their job. But it bothered me.

I must deal w/ the body of the dead pac. But not today. Not today. After the stress of yesterday & the day before, I need a little calm, a little peace.

I need snow, deer, birds, sun.

I need (sniffs; sniffs again) to wash my clothes.

Day Thirty-One

I really need to wash my jeans, flannel shirt, & socks. It's gone way beyond a smell issue—I'm getting used to strong odors, what w/ the no-flush toilet, dead pac, & all. It's more of a crusty issue. But my water supply drops lower each day: Vases & bowls evaporate from the kitchen counter as I drink their contents & store them in the cupboard. I predict water will be the ultimate limiting factor in my RAW occupation.

Nights are quiet now. No howling sessions since that awful day when the hazel-eyed man died on my doorstep. The pacz in this area are down to the Final Four (The Twins, Pudgy, & Tall Man), & they don't patrol as often as before, either.

At some point last night I woke up long enough to realize it was snowing, then drifted back to dreamland. Snow = no pacz. Snow = water. Danger = pacz + go outside. Water = snow + go outside − pacz. Equations kept popping up in my dreams. In one I was standing at the board in trig class & couldn't figure out a problem. In another, I knew the answer but couldn't make my hand write it on the board. There was a short dream about dancing cosines that I can't explain. Bottom line: I needed to collect snow.

Right now!!! A bossy but melodious voice (Benji's) shouted that at me in my dream, zapping me awake. I sat up quickly, bonking my head on the bench seat.

I saw a five-gallon bucket in the con-lab the other day. I don't know what it was used for, but that doesn't matter because I'll use the snow I gather in it for washing clothes. I'll use the empty punch bowl as a scoop, then use the snow I gather in that for drinking. Good thing I can wear a shoe now.

To go outside. To make a conscious decision to leave the RAW. Not to run out in reaction to a gut-level instinct, like I did on Day Three. Going outside is a terrifying idea, but oddly thrilling, too. It's been so long....

Studying my enemy, as Sun Tzu recommends in *The Book of War*, makes me a bit more confident about the excursion. I don't know much about pacz, but I know they don't go outside when it's precipitating. Knowing this gives me power.

Going out the back door was the logical choice. There's a wheelchair ramp angling down to a narrow parking lot. Beyond that is a strip of grass w/ a row of tall birch trees, then the steep river bank, the Yakima River, & JSU's nature preserve on the other side. I know pacz visit the back side of the RAW: the maintenance ladder to the roof is next to the ramp. But I don't think they go often. & I'm sure they can't see anything on the back of this building from wherever they hole up when it precipitates because the nature preserve stretches for miles & has no structures.

Dark night—not much moon, many clouds. I climbed the shelf ladder, slowly, to check for pacz. None. I peeked into the con-lab, scanned windows for pacz, then put a hand over my nose & mouth & tiptoed past the dead pac to retrieve the bucket. While taking down the barricade on the back door (in the dark), I dropped a chair on my injured ankle. Had to put both hands over my mouth to keep from crying out in pain.

Then the door. The only thing between me & the invasion. I set the bucket & punch bowl on the table next to the door, closed my eyes for a second to visualize exactly what I planned to do, &....

Go!

Door unlocked, opened. Head poked out; look right, left, up. Bucket in one hand, punch bowl in the other. Hobble down ramp, cross parking lot to grass strip. Eleven, twelve, thirteen scoops w/ the bowl—bucket is full. One more scoop—bowl is full. Hobble back into building. Set down bucket & bowl. Lock door. Breathe.

I knew the snow would take a long time to melt because it's so cold in the RAW. Sure enough, the snow was still mostly snow this morning. But there's a portable heat lamp, used to dry gluing projects, in the con-lab, & the electricity still works. I wish I could figure out why pacz have kept the electrical system up & running: Knowing that would give me power, too. Anyway, if the snow doesn't melt soon, I'll....

Wait. What? Portable heat lamp? Port-a-ble? Heat?

(Slaps forehead.)

Would you excuse me for a moment?

I set the bucket of snow on the floor next to my desk. I set the miraculous heat lamp near the bucket (& my feet). Plugged in the lamp. Turned it on. & here's what I plan to do for the rest of the day: Read, warm my feet & other body parts (Yes!), & watch snow melt.

Day Thirty-Two

Amazing how little water there is in a five-gallon bucket of snow.

I know: I should have remembered that from 1st grade science projects. But, in the eighteen years since then, I haven't needed that particular bit of information, so the measly little puddle of water in the bottom of the bucket was a bit of a surprise. I did recall, however, that snow crystals form around particles (let's not call it dirt) in the air, so the dark specks were not a surprise. Surely I deserve a C+ for that.

The melted snow in the punch bowl increases my drinking water supply by two days under my new, stricter rationing plan. I am grateful for that.

Once the amount of water in the bowl is determined, it's easy to calculate the amount in the bucket: Not much × thirteen = still not much. But it was enough to wash my socks & flannel shirt (jeans will have to wait)—by focusing water & scrubbing on sections that needed it most. I gave Bonnie a sip, too, because I enjoy her company.

After washing clothes, I spent an hour warming my numb fingers by the heat lamp so I could write. The snow has melted, but the water is still mighty cold. The good news is that, w/ a little luck, I will have some clean clothes tomorrow.

Later—

I was at the top of the ladder hanging up the wash when I heard soft tapping. At 1st I thought it was the branch of a cotoneaster bush being blown against the building, but I peeked out the window, & everything was calm out there.

The sound came again. No panic—whatever happens happens. I climbed down the ladder slowly & looked around the library for the source of the sound, ending my search in the con-lab. Tall Man was outside the broken window. While I watched, he tapped on it. Very, very gently.

I thought: he is afraid of breaking the glass. I thought: he is afraid.

Then I realized he was tapping because he wanted to get my attention. There was a long pause while the ramifications of that sank in.

1st contact. Sort of.

Not how I imagined 1st contact w/ aliens might happen (if pacz are, indeed, aliens). Certainly not how it happens on old "Star Trek" episodes. I looked at him; I assume he was looking at me. We were statues for a long time. Then he extended an arm through the hole in the window, carefully to avoid the broken glass, & waved his covered hand in the direction of the dead pac.

Observe the enemy, Sun Tzu says. Watch & learn.

From the small, & rather strange, interaction w/ Tall Man today, I learned the following.

1. Pacz know broken glass can cut, & they fear it. Why they're afraid of being cut when being shot point blank does nothing to them, I have no idea.

2. Pacz honor their dead in some way.

3. If pacz could get into the library through the doors, they would have done that already, if only to retrieve the body of their dead friend.

4. If Tall Man, or any of the other pacz, could fit through a window, or felt safe squeezing past the broken glass, they would have done that already.

5. Most important, this pac wanted—no, needed—something from me.

I thought: An opportunity has presented itself.

As soon as I thought that, I knew another piece of the old me was gone. The old me—friendly, helpful, anxious to please—would have dragged the body to a door at once, removed the barricade (if it was the front door; I haven't rebuilt the barricade on the back door yet), & opened the door wide so Tall Man could retrieve the body. & would you like a side of fries w/ that, too, Sir?

The new me thought about how to leverage this to my advantage. I didn't mind getting rid of the body, of course, although that might be construed as giving aid & comfort to the enemy. But what would I get in return? That's what the new, manipulative me asked myself. & how could I give Tall Man what he wanted w/o putting myself in danger? That's what the new, pragmatic me wanted to know.

Unfortunately, the new me was so new at this dealing-w/-the-enemy thing that I had no answers. So, in a move that I realized, on reflection, was brilliant (although it happened totally by accident), I mustered my sincerity & then smiled, nodded, made random hand movements that appeared to communicate something important but meant absolutely nothing, waved at the body, smiled again, & left the room, closing the door behind me.

Tall Man seems content w/ whatever he thinks I told him—no more tapping today. Of course, he might be out there at this very moment rallying hordes of pacz from far & wide to storm the library & take the dead body, & my life, by force.

But I think not. Which is good, because I need time to think. Time to plan my next move. & that's exactly what the new, thoughtful-warrior me bought myself.

Day Thirty-Three

At dawn I heard tap, tap, tap. Pause. Tap, tap. Pause. Tap. Pause. Tap, tap, tap. Pause. Tap, tap. Pause. Tap. I hoped the tapping would end eventually, but half an hour of it was all I could take. I crawled out from under my bench & finished preparing for a confrontation w/ the pacz, one that would be, I hoped, mainly a battle of wits.

I'd spent most of the night developing a strategy for dealing w/ Tall Man & his chums (dead & alive). During my early musings, I liked the idea of getting something from him before I gave him the body. But all I really want, from him or any pac, is to be left alone, & it's not like I can make him promise to do that: Who knows if pacz understand the concept of promises, or, if they do, if they keep them?

I decided to make a gesture of good will instead. I thought again about the Christmas truce of 1914, about how someone had to be the 1st to climb out of a muddy trench, face the enemy, & indicate the desire to cease hostilities for a while. Of course, those fighters were of the same species, even if they thought of their enemies as animals. Some on opposite sides of the front line even spoke the same language. But, at some point, someone had to muster enough gumption to stand up— wearing a virtual target on the chest—& make the 1st move.

This is what a nice person (the old me) would do. Want something? Here, take it. But the more I thought about my strategy, the more I liked it: I wasn't going to do it because I am (or I used to be) nice; I was going to do it because it might work.

I took precautions. I set three weapons on the table by the back door: the umbrella; a large, vicious-looking piece of glass from the broken window; &—the pièce de résistance—a trash can filled w/ the contents of the toilet (unflushed since the water system quit), plus cleaning fluids I found under the sink. In addition to the awful look & smell of the concoction, it was wet, & I know pacz hate getting wet.

There was a 4th item on the table. Not really a weapon. It had seemed like a good idea in the middle of the night, but I felt uneasy about it this morning. I wasn't sure about my motives for making it. I wasn't sure I liked what it said about me. & I wasn't sure I would put it in play: everything depended on how the pacz reacted.

The plan was to let Tall Man watch me wrap a strap around the dead pac & drag it out of the room. (I brushed against the pac's brown suit last night—I did most of my preparations in the dark—& I didn't die, so pacz must lose their zap juice when they pass away.) I would drag the body to the back door, then open the door slowly, w/ the umbrella hooked over one arm & the piece of glass in my other hand. Tall Man understands the damage those items can cause, so my hope was that he would get the idea & take the body w/o making trouble. But if it looked like the pacz were going to attack, I would heave the trash can full of gunk at them before locking the door again. There would still be a dead body in the RAW in that case, but I would be alive.

Tall Man was at the window when I entered the con-lab. I waved, smiled, made gestures to signal my good will. He stopped tapping. I knelt beside the dead pac & wrapped the strap around it under the arms. He stuck his arm through the hole in the window & waved wildly. Still kneeling, I showed him I hadn't hurt the body. He calmed down. I stood, grabbed the strap, & dragged the body toward the door. Tall Man, agitated again, rapped on the glass. I pointed toward him then in the direction of the back door several times. He seemed to understand because he left the window.

Dragging that dead pac was one of the hardest things I've ever done. The smell made me stop four times to vomit, & the body was surprisingly heavy, even though this pac was shorter & more slender than the others. I had trouble maneuvering it around corners—I was glad Tall Man couldn't see or hear it head-bang the walls. & finding the perfect position for the body by the door was tricky: The body had to be far enough away from the door so I could open it, but close enough to the door so Tall Man wouldn't need to step into the RAW to grab the body.

When everything was ready, I opened the door enough to peek out. All four pacz were there, Tall Man at the foot of the ramp, the other three a few steps behind him. As soon as they saw me, they rushed the building. I slammed & locked the door.

Pause. Tapping on the door. Long pause. Tapping.

Now what? If I opened the door & they were all right there, they could push the door open w/ no trouble, touch me, & that would be that.

Tapping. An even longer pause.

Slight change in plan. I propped the body up into a sitting position, its left side leaning against the door jamb & its back by the edge of the door. While doing this, I noticed something strange about the body. Took a few seconds to process, but....

Baby bump. Or a bump where a pregnant human would have one. If this pac was pregnant, Tall Man had lost his mate & his unborn child. I felt a wave of pity &—

Stop that, Kaylee! Stop it right now! Don't you be having those kinds of thoughts. Not today. These beings murdered thousands of people, & that's just in this area. Think of the frightened faces of those people, their writhing bodies, the high-pitched howls.

Keep your focus! Stay sharp! Get a grip!

I took a deep breath & grabbed the strap. If I opened the door w/ my free hand, I could lower the top half of the body into the opening by loosening my grip on the strap. The dead pac would be the 1ˢᵗ thing Tall Man & the others saw, & they would have to actually step on the body to get to me. From the sound Tall Man made when I was poking his mate w/ the umbrella the other day, I was sure he wouldn't allow the body to be trampled.

No one is truly safe. Everyone is vulnerable....

I opened the door a crack, standing mostly behind it to use it as a shield. The four pacz were farther away now, huddled in the parking lot, & I was able to lower the top half of the body into the opening a few inches before Pudgy noticed the movement & alerted the others. There was a rush toward the ramp, w/ Tall Man in the lead, &....

Tall Man saw the body.

He skidded to a stop & flung out both arms to halt the others. The Twins ran into Pudgy, who ran into Tall Man, & all of them fell. I saw this out of the corner of my eye, but I stayed focused on what I was doing—slowly lowering the body. I wasn't thinking about dying, although my enemy was within spitting distance; I was hoping the body didn't drop suddenly & bang against the threshold, thus angering Tall Man.

The pacz regrouped while I lowered the dead pac's upper body inch by inch. Tall Man took a step forward at several points: each time, I pulled on the strap to raise the body, & he stepped back. The message was clear: You want this body? Then keep your distance! When the head gently touched the floor & I knelt to remove the strap w/ my free hand, Tall Man took a step forward again, but I showed him the piece of glass in my other hand, & he stopped. This was good. This meant we had established a minimal but seemingly effective non-verbal contract. Tall Man needed something; I needed something; we understood each other.

In appreciation for this, & to show pacz that humans also honor the dead (another point of connection), I put into play the non-weapon I had set on the table by the door. Keeping the piece of glass in full view, I picked up a wreath of colorful origami flowers (I made it last night using illustrations ripped from one of Matilda's books) & laid it on the dead pac's chest.

I didn't move. The pacz didn't move. There was a moment of perfect stillness, perfect silence.

Then Tall Man made a sound that wasn't a cry & wasn't exactly singing, either, at least not as I know it. The sound started on a low note & slid up the scale until it reached a note so high & clear it made the piece of glass in my hand vibrate.

The others joined in, starting on the same low note then sliding up to match Tall Man's high note. I could feel the sound. It created an odd vibration deep inside me that made my chest warm. The pacz held the note, w/o breathing, for over two minutes.

While the voices of the other pacz slid down to the low note then back up to the high note again, Tall Man stepped forward. I stepped away from the body. He walked slowly toward the ramp while the other pacz continued to hold the high note. He took small, cautious steps up the ramp until he was standing on the landing a few feet from me. I stepped back. The other pacz held the high note. Tall Man knelt & gathered the body in his arms as gently as I would have held Matilda, then stood, lowered his head briefly in my direction, & rejoined the others.

As I locked the door, I heard all four voices drop down to the low note again, then slide up to the high note. I leaned my back against the oak door & felt the vibration in my chest. I felt the sensation of warmth for a few seconds, too, but it faded as the pacz' funeral procession crossed the Quad, their voices becoming fainter & fainter....

The warmth in my chest cooled.

The silence returned.

Day Thirty-Four

Happy New Year. No exclamation point.

I was so focused on my encounter w/ the pacz yesterday morning that I forgot it was New Year's Eve day. After they took the body, I crawled into my sleeping nest & shook for what seemed like hours. All the danger involved w/ that interaction, all the ways it could have gone wrong, slammed into me full force. I felt beaten & bruised by the whole thing. In the late afternoon, I dragged myself out to eat & write a journal entry, then crawled back in & slept until the sun came out. Now it's New Year's Day, & I feel much better—sleep really can perform miracles.

I was happy when I went into the bathroom & saw the clean toilet—nice way to start the new year. I've decided to use a trash can instead of the toilet from now on, since it's easier to care for w/ limited water. When the next big storm comes along, I'm going to take the stinky trash can "weapon" I made the other day & toss it in the dumpster behind the RAW.

Side note: I'm amazed by how much ink I've spilled in this journal writing about the bathroom. Almost as much as I've used writing about food. I seldom wrote about food in journals I kept before the invasion, & never about the bathroom. I focused on lofty ideas, goals, dreams, deep feelings (which don't seem all that deep compared to those I'm experiencing in my present situation). Now, most of my focus is on finding things to put into my body & dealing w/ things that come out of it. Basically, the same focus as that of a toddler being potty trained.

What else am I happy about at the start of this new year? Ah, clean clothes. My socks & flannel shirt are finally dry. I did a little happy dance when I put those on. & the dead body is gone (never expected to use that phrase in a journal entry). Makes a huge difference in how the library smells. The wind blew yesterday—whistling through my dreams—& freshened the air in here. Still, the scent of dead pac will be stuck in my nose for a long time. It's almost as if I can taste it.

Another side note: Why could I hear Tall Man cry out the other day, & hear the pacz sing, when I can't hear what they say when they communicate w/ each other? I'm sure they communicate in some way: I've peeked through the hole in the front door a few times, & I've seen them gather on the porch, stand next to each other w/o making a sound, & then begin working together on a task that they would certainly have needed to discuss beforehand. Maybe they "talk" through mental telepathy or some other form of thought transfer but, for some reason, it doesn't work for emotional vocalizations. Maybe they have transmitters in their suits that they can turn on (so only pacz can hear what's said) & off (so their voices are audible to others). Maybe....

Actually, I have more important things to spend my limited energy on today, so let's move along.

"Count your blessings,
name them one by one...."

Even though it's not Thanksgiving, focusing on positive things keeps me going. Because it's not easy staying upbeat in my journal, in my life, during this captivity. I'm trying, although it might not seem like that to someone who hasn't had this experience. Trust me, if I wrote what I'm feeling most of the time, this journal would say "I'm going to die, I'm going to die" every day, day after day, & not much else.

So—although I'm not thankful for the invasion, of course—it helps sometimes to think about the up sides. & there are a few. For example, I'll never need to wear a bra again: I washed that little torture device for the last time early in the invasion & buried it deep in the LAF box. Earning money, paying bills, balancing checkbooks, filling out tax forms—most likely things of the past, & good riddance. What else? No more alarm clocks, robocalls, perpetual political campaigns, televised golf tournaments (or golf of any kind) (or televised anything).

All in all, I'm starting the year on a positive note. I wish I had more water & food. I wish this cough would go away; it's rattling around deep in my chest now. I wish Benji would show up & make me laugh, & maybe sing "Dalla Sua Pace," the aria that always made me feel so happy, so peaceful.

& I feel a little sad about ripping up Matilda's Greenaway book to make the dead pac's wreath. Matilda has—had—a nice collection of books by Greenaway & Beatrix Potter, including some very old copies I gave her that were my grandmother's. I thought about using a RAW book for the wreath, but I decided that while selectively "harvesting" book pages for my personal needs seems justified under the circumstances, destroying a rare book for a pac does not.

On the other hand, that bright & colorful wreath clearly meant something to the pacz, & it seemed to make a big difference in how they treated me. Bottom line: I am alive to see the new year, & I think I might owe that to a bunch of paper flowers.

Day Thirty-Five

Woke up at dawn this morning to the sound of insistent tapping on glass. Instead of slipping into a dark place, I just felt annoyed. Again w/ the tapping? Seriously?

I really, really did not want to crawl out of my nest. In general, I've been sleeping better lately because: I have a more accepting "whatever happens happens" attitude now & am not constantly on edge, as I was earlier in the invasion; I've become accustomed to sleeping on the floor; I use the heat lamp to warm up my nest before I crawl into bed, which makes a big difference in how fast I fall asleep; &, on the negative side, my body is slowing down due to the lack of food & water, & to my exposure to the cold.

But I dragged myself out of bed anyway. As I hobbled to the con-lab, where the tapping was coming from, I heard a thud. A very loud, very solid thud. Instead of feeling frightened or panicky, I felt even more annoyed. Another dead body? Really? Oh, puh-leeze, that is sooooo early invasion.

There was no dead body, or body of any kind, in the con-lab. Tall Man was at the window doing something odd w/ his hand. I think it was intended to be waving, his awkward interpretation of a gesture I had made the other day. When he was sure I was looking, he stuck an arm through the window very carefully & motioned toward the work counter below. Then he pulled his arm out, "waved" again, & waited.

I hobbled over to the counter. A book was lying there, one I hadn't seen on the counter before. *String Theory and M-Theory: A Modern Introduction*, by Becker, Becker, & Schwarz.

A physics textbook?

Um…. Okay….

I looked up. Tall Man waved a hand, raised the other, waved both. I suspected he might be waving a foot, too. Gesturing in a way I would understand. Communicating. Giving me this book, this gift, as a way of saying what? He was sorry for killing the entire population of my campus & town, everyone I knew, & the one person I loved? He was grateful for the return of his dead friend? He has always been a fan of origami? For all I knew, giving someone a book in his world was a pledge of eternal love, & we had just become engaged.

But he was communicating. That was a big deal. Sure, I would have preferred a roasted turkey breast sandwich on whole wheat bread, w/ garlic aioli, a schmear of lemon thyme cream cheese, cranberry sauce, & lots & lots of crisp romaine lettuce. But it was a start.

I picked up the book, smiled, waved, turned pages, pointed to illustrations (no clue what they meant). I held the book close to my chest, waved again. Remembering something he did the other day, I bowed my head slightly in his direction.

He bowed his head, too, then disappeared.

Day Thirty-Six

After Tall Man left yesterday, I read the book he gave me. I don't know why. It's not like I'm suffering from a lack of reading material. & it's a fizz-sicks textbook. But a pac gave me a gift, & I'll bet there aren't many humans who can say that.

Interesting read, especially for someone whose course work focused mostly on literature. I noticed a section on heteroerotic string, which seemed exciting, but I'd misread that: It's heterotic. I found the lingo appealing. As I hobbled around the aisles for exercise, I chanted some new favorite phrases: flux compactification, monstrous moonshine, space-time supersymmetry (unfortunately, this has little to do w/ the space-time continuum).

There was a quick rainstorm in the afternoon. I had high hopes for collecting water, but I could tell it wasn't going to last long enough for that. It did last long enough for me to get rid of the trash can "weapon" full of stinky goop, the smell of which had increased exponentially over the past few days.

I waited until rain was falling hard, then opened the back door & checked for pacz. The coast was clear. I looked up to make sure the storm would last for a few minutes. Yes. I wrapped the scarf around my face, not because of the cold but because the smell from the can was so intense. Grabbed the can, half-hobbled down the ramp & across the parking lot to the dumpster, & tossed the whole thing in.

There was a satisfying "splat" when the can landed. I had expected to hear that. What I didn't expect to hear were the coarse cries of a flock of magpies feeding, unbeknownst to me, deep in the dumpster. My deposit came as a huge surprise to them, & the birds made a noisy fuss while flapping away in a huff. I watched them fly south, over the river, over the nature preserve.

I tried not to think about what the magpies, which feed on carrion, had been eating in the dumpster.

I could tell the storm was winding down. I knew I should go back to the RAW. But I didn't want to. I really didn't. The rain felt good on my face & hands. The air smelled fresh. Outside the library walls: that's where I wanted to be. I walked back to the building slowly, feeling the rain, smelling the air, using all my senses to take in this world, which is alive, unlike the world where I exist, which is simply preserved.

So, yesterday was mostly a low-key day here in Invasion Land (after Tall Man left). I ate a little, read a lot, exercised, tidied up, crumpled pages, wrote a journal entry, & went to bed.

It wasn't until the middle of the night that I went totally ballistic.

Which, in retrospect, should have happened the second that Tall Man—the butcher of Jefferson City—gave me a gift.

Day Thirty-Seven

Still cleaning up my night-before-last mess.

The half-height shelves in Contemporary Literature are standing upright again, & the scattered books are back in their proper places & dusted (yes, I'm still cleaning up caustic residue from the bombs). Even though the shelves hit the floor hard when I slammed into them, I couldn't find any chips or cracks in the wood.

The broken glass littering the kitchen is cleaned up—I'm keeping the bigger pieces for weapons. The drinking glasses exploded in the most delicious way when I threw them against the stone floor. Shards ricocheted everywhere, like a combination of lightning, fireworks, & the best round of "Candy Crush" ever. Total, glorious, savage-soul-satisfying destruction.

I've collected the pages I ripped out of the string theory text. No qualms at all about destroying that book. The sound of pages ripping—one after another—was exquisite; the feel of paper at that moment when it starts to give, when the binding begins to let go of its hold on the page—there is nothing quite like that.

What else? Ah, yes, the windows.

No, I didn't break any: They're way too high for me to reach easily w/ a projectile while standing on the floor, &, while I could have stood on a ladder & thrown books at them, I've never had what you might call a good arm. Plus, somewhere deep in the primordial/reptilian part of my brain, the part that had complete control over me during the rampage, I realized two things: windows offer some protection, if only from the elements; & I really didn't want to spend the next 6 months cleaning up glass.

However, each window has a Roman shade. Tall Man had violated my space; he was the one I wanted to shut out. I ran through the RAW unwinding window shade cords from around their expensive fleur-de-lis tie-down fixtures, flinging cord ends into the air & watching them twist, spin, & fly when they were set free. I delighted in the rhythmic "thwump, thwump, thwump" sound the shades made when they cascaded down. The 1st shade I closed was on the broken window in the con-lab. Tall Man can make deposits through the window if he wants to, but now he will need to deal w/ both the broken glass & the shade. Anyway, I spent a few hours wrangling & untangling shade cords, making them straight & taut again, rewinding them around their tie-downs.

I'm still a mess inside. That can't be cleaned up as easily as overturned shelves, broken glass, & squiggly cords. My emotions are too scattered & shattered at the moment, too tangled to be straightened out.

Which is odd because I've been under great stress in the past—when I was caring for my mother, taking high school & then college courses, & dealing w/ a dining room table constantly littered w/ unpaid bills & bottles of her pills; when I was a research assistant & dealing w/ the many ugly & unfortunate complications of that experience—& hadn't gone on rampages. I had dark thoughts at those times, many sleepless nights, & a huge # of prolonged sighing sessions, but nothing like my outburst the other night.

In some ways, life in the RAW was easier early on, back when I could hate the pacz unconditionally, w/ all my heart & soul, w/ every fiber of my being. When I could think of them in the clear & simple ways I had been taught to think of enemies. Brutish. Ungodly. Deceitful. Twisted. Maniacal. Evil. The Dreaded & Much Despised Other. Nothing at All like Us.

But then my annoying nuanced view of the world began to creep in, muddying the waters. Sun Tzu came along, encouraging me to think about war & the enemy in completely new ways. & Lincoln (or whoever), w/ that "how to destroy the enemy by making them a friend" notion, blew the whole thing out of the water.

To survive, I need to pick my way along a narrow emotional middle ground. On one side is an inferno of hatred for the pacz. I feel that burning inside me, but I know it is unproductive & am trying hard not to plunge back into it. On the other side is an icy, calculated acceptance of them that goes against everything in my nature. I feel a bit of acceptance might work, but the slope on that side is as steep & slippery as the river bank, & if I slide down it too far, my life & soul will be washed away.

I had an instructor who said about every piece of modern art she discussed in class that the juxtaposition of opposing elements created a tension that bordered on rage. I don't know if that's true of modern art (the paintings seemed like random squiggles & splashes to me), but it seems to be true of my life at the moment. Case in point: the other night, when my feelings of hatred for the pacz collided w/ my need to find points of connection w/ them, and that juxtaposition of opposing elements led to my raging rampage.

Even my humming & singing have been affected by this feeling of being caught between two opposing elements. I've been humming rage-filled songs by the Ramones—Benji's favorite punk group—incessantly for the past few days (Benji renounced classical music for a while in high school & dove deep into the musical dark side). He played some Ramones hits for me now & then, but not often, so I'm surprised I remember them. They really must have hit a nerve. The songs I recall are all about pain, angst, & living on the edgiest of edges.

A lot like my days have become here in the RAW.

Day Thirty-Eight

Tall Man is a murderer. Absolutely. What he & the other pacz did on Day Three was genocide. A dream about that day sparked my rampage the other night. I jolted awake screaming, writhing, clawing at my covers, kicking the wall.

In my dream I heard the awful screams again, smelled smoke, felt ash burn my nose & eyes, tasted soot in my mouth & spat it out because the thought of where it came from made me sick. My head throbbed because of the particulates I took in w/ every breath, so many dark & ugly specks of sadness. The nightmare began in color, images of events outside my window oversaturated to the point of being lurid. As the dream went on, colors faded. Just before I woke, everything was gray on grey.

They say words we hear in dreams & remember after waking convey messages of two types: something we are trying to tell ourselves or something the universe is trying to tell us. If I recall, words spoken by other people in our dreams are messages we send to ourselves, whereas those spoken in our own voice come from the universe. I wish I knew if that's true, because in my nightmare, in response to the carnage, I heard a voice screaming, "Kill the pacz! Kill them all!" & the voice was definitely mine.

The number of howling sessions here on campus had decreased significantly by Day Three. I peeked out my window that morning & saw only a band of five pacz patrolling the area. The invasion seemed to be winding down. Maybe it would end soon. Maybe help was on the way. I thought the pacz might be retreating, returning to the slime pit from whence they had slithered.

I decided that morning to develop a routine to help me stay focused & strong until the cavalry (i.e. troops from the Yakima military training center southeast of Jefferson City) rode over the hill, rescued me & all the other sheltered-in-place humans, & put the world right again. (I've written about my routine elsewhere, so I'll skip that here.) I had chosen the books for my daily readathon & was 27 pages into the 1st book when the screaming began.

I climbed the shelf ladder, peeked out the window, & saw nothing. Not at 1st. But the screaming continued, & the voices sounded familiar.

Then I saw them. A cluster of little bodies, bundled in colorful winter clothes, scrunched together in a tight circle at the far corner of the Quad. A woman beside them: Tall, hatless, bootless, long hair flying in the wind, holding the two smallest children—just toddlers—in her arms. Those two were screaming, making the high-pitched, gut-gripping sound that comes from terrified children. No, I thought. No, no, no!

But I wasn't thinking it. I couldn't have been because I could hear my voice. I had never raised my voice in a library before, but now I was screaming.

No, no, no!!!

Children from the campus pre-school. Eyes wide w/ fear, cheeks bright red w/ the cold, each child crying, each holding the hand of one other child. I knew many of those children from my volunteer work at the school. I knew their teacher very well. What I didn't know was how she had kept the kids safe through almost three days of intense activity by the pacz. Now, for what I am sure was a very good reason, she was trying to herd them across the Quad.

They needed me. I slid down the ladder, tore apart the barricade, & rushed out the front door. Didn't stop to look for pacz. Leapt off the porch—didn't even use the steps. Kept my eyes on those little kids. Ran.

By the time I hit the ground, a patrol of five pacz was heading from the soccer field toward the Quad between the Ag Sci & Humanities buildings. One of the children saw the invaders, screamed, & pointed. The teacher hurried the children along faster. "Stay together; hold your partner's hand," she called as their quick shuffle became a jog. But when the pacz closed in, the tight circle of colorful bundles split apart, & the children took off in every direction, still two-by-two, still holding their partners' hands.

Then all of us—kids, teacher, pacz, me—were running. The pac patrol split, & each pac chased either the teacher or a twosome of children. There were five pacz, but there were six groups to chase—five w/ two children each, another w/ the teacher carrying the toddlers. She was an easy target: Carrying the little ones made her slow, & she kept turning to call out "Stay w/ your partner" to the other children.

The pacz were busy chasing the others; they didn't notice me. I ran toward the two children who were not being chased by a pac, waving to catch their attention, then motioning for them to head in my direction. They did. Those two little kids ran like the wind. I have never seen tiny legs pump so fast. They were running for their lives, &—this breaks my heart— they knew it.

Howling from the other side of the Quad when a pac reached the 1st group. I knew what the howling meant, & the children running toward me knew, too. One of them turned to look at his fallen friends. He tripped, fell, skidded several feet, then curled into a ball & didn't move, all the while holding tight to his partner's hand.

The other child tried to help him stand. He refused to move. I motioned for her to keep running toward me, but she didn't. Teacher had told her to hold her partner's hand, and that's what she intended to do, even though she could see a pac—the one that had just killed her other friends—heading in our direction.

At that moment I morphed from a sprinting human into a full-throttled speed machine, racing against the pac to reach the children 1st.

But the pac ran faster. When I realized there was no way I could reach the children in time, I stopped & made the heart sign: fingers curled, w/ fingernails touching; thumb tips pressed together. The little girl let go of her partner's hand, finally, patted his cheek to comfort him, then turned toward me & made the same sign.

Just before the pac touched her, she put her hands over her eyes & stood still. A perfect statue. I knew what she was thinking: if she couldn't see anybody, if she didn't move, she would be invisible.

I turned & ran for the RAW, the howls of dying children hounding me the whole way. There was nothing else I could do. I knew that. I knew that! & I expected the pac to reach me before I reached safety. My only comfort was in knowing that the last thing the little girl saw before she died was a sign of love.

I locked the door behind me a few seconds before the pac reached it.

& that afternoon, the afternoon of Day Three, the pacz burned down the town. Not the campus, but the rest of the town. To the ground.

Day Thirty-Nine

Is it possible to be in a coma & still be walking?

I don't know how else to describe the state I was in on Day Three after failing to rescue the two pre-schoolers. That I almost died was not a factor in my condition: It was caused by the grief & guilt I felt about what had happened to other people, especially the children—those beautiful, tiny humans—& their teacher.

I can't imagine how difficult it was for her to protect the children during the 1st days of the invasion, to take care of their physical & emotional needs in the midst of such horror. I don't know why she took them out into the open. I expect she had either run out of food for them or thought there was a safer place somewhere else. Turns out—other than the RAW—there was no safe place. Anywhere. If they had left the campus, they would have been incinerated when the town burned.

I heard sounds after my failed rescue attempt that day. I saw flames & smoke. I smelled & tasted the remains of the burnt town in the air. I touched the soot that settled everywhere. But I couldn't respond to any of those things. I was lost somewhere deep inside myself, separated from the world by a chasm of grief & guilt.

I remember singing, although it felt as if the sound was coming from someone else. Snippets from "Gimme Shelter" about fire & coals, over & over. My brain was burning.

I didn't eat on Day Three, or drink anything after those few sips in the morning. I rebuilt the front door barricade then sat, stood, paced. I spun in tight circles for hours.

"Here we go 'round the mulberry bush, the mulberry bush, the mulberry bush…."

Somewhere beyond my body there was bashing on the front door, breaking glass, sickening thuds. The sights, sounds, & smells of animals & people—dead & alive—burning. Flames turning the sky orange. Choking smoke. Things that should have bothered me. They didn't. Because "me" was not here.

There was light outside, then dark, then light. I heard scratching during the night.

Everything that happened on Day Three after the children died continued through the night, then happened again on Day Four. Horrible sounds, smells, sights, tastes. Soot. Nothingness. More sitting at the desk when it was light, sitting there in the dark.

I had a cracker in my pocket. I nibbled that, vomited.

When the light returned on Day Five, I was still sitting at the desk. I had no reason to move. Everything was burned, everything was gone.

In the late afternoon, as the light began to fade, I felt my mother's arms around me. I wasn't asleep: At the moment I felt her presence, I was rubbing a finger across the desk top, making a wobbly line in the soot, trying to remember why I was sitting at this desk in this library, trying to remember what had created so much soot.

She said what she always used to say when I was upset at the end of the day. "Go to bed, Kaylee. Life will seem better in the morning."

"No, it won't. It's never going to be better."

"Trust me. Go to bed."

"But I'm afraid. 'To sleep, perchance to dream.'"

"Dreams can't hurt you."

"Yes, they can, Mom. You don't know what I've seen. What I've done. & all of it is stuck in my head, & when I dream it spins around & around & hurts so much."

"You're my sweet girl. You could never do anything wrong."

"I could. I have."

"Sleep."

"But…."

"Sleep."

I stood up—legs shaky, existence shaky.

I crawled under my bench.

I slept.

Day Forty

People were always having epiphanies, back in what my mother called "biblical times," after they spent forty days & nights dealing w/ a difficult situation. I've put in my forty days & (almost) nights dealing w/ the invasion, & I am sooooo ready for an epiphany. Actually, I would settle for a sign: finding a box of crackers in Head Lib's cupboard; discovering a pair of sox my size in the LAF box; hearing a gurgle that means the water is running again. Seriously, I'm not asking for much.

Hello, God? It's me, Kaylee.

If I hadn't felt my mother's presence on Day Five, I might be hunched over this desk half-mummified at the moment, so I guess that might have been a sign. Making it back to the RAW after the failed rescue attempt could have been, too. & not being killed when I returned the body of the pac, of course.

Not to put too fine a point on it, but I expect theologians would classify those as blessings rather than signs. Plus, they happened before my forty days & nights were up, so they probably don't count. & they're not exactly a burning bush.

Wrapping up what happened before I began this journal: Day Six—forced myself to eat & drink, did a food inventory, developed a rationing plan, rested, began to feel better; Day Seven—ignored the rationing plan & ate three times my daily allotment (I was making up for lost time & burning calories big-time while cleaning the RAW).

Deep cleaning, I should say. How could so much soot get in when the only opening was the broken window in the con-lab (which I didn't know about at the time), & the door to that room was closed & locked? Whenever I tried to clean anything, soot swooshed into the air & floated around looking for someplace else to settle. At times my cleaning efforts seemed more like a perpetual redistribution.

Good thing the water was still running back then, because I rinsed out cleaning rags hundreds of times. & a really good thing the floor is covered by stone tiles instead of carpet because I was able to wipe up most of the soot w/ damp rags.

Wait, I've got it! I know what I want as a sign. NOT a burning bush. No, please, not that. Forget I even mentioned it. Nothing that creates soot. What I want is a rain storm. A snow storm could work, but, knowing me, I would quibble about whether or not it counted as a sign. I am in desperate need of water, & a rain storm would be perfect—clear, unambiguous, & welcome.

Since I've gone all religious-y today, I might as well share some good-&-evil thoughts I've had about Tall Man. I haven't seen him, or any pac, since the textbook incident. Having the shades down helps, but there has been no tapping, gift dropping, or other attempt at contact. No bashing on the front door. No footsteps on the roof. Five days of peace & quiet. I think he/they got my message.

This is the million-dollar question: sure, Tall Man is a murderer, but is he, & are the other pacz, inherently evil?

Tall Man complied w/ our contract the other day, BUT it was in his best interest to do so. He didn't kill me when we stood near each other at the back door, BUT I made it clear he would be injured if he tried. (The fact that Tall Man did not kill me when he had a chance doesn't make him a nice guy—I'm not ready to set the bar for niceness that low.) He reacted w/ deep emotion to the death of his friend, BUT it was one of his own kind. He has a beautiful voice, BUT so does the Devil, according to the women put on trial during the Salem witch hunts. He brought me a gift, BUT.... I can't factor that into the equation because I don't know what gift-giving means to him.

I don't have an answer to my question. Humans have killed masses of our own species in horrible ways: Are we inherently evil? I would say we are not (the minister at my mother's church would disagree, which explains why I stopped going). I think some humans are totally incapable of doing anything evil. I think many are capable but refuse. I think some commit evil acts when forced to by their family, friends, or nation, then regret it for the rest of their lives. & I think a few humans delight in evil & seek opportunities to do it. But I think we, as a species, are not inherently evil.

I don't know where Tall Man & the other pacz fit on the good/evil spectrum. I do know this: humans are very clever at coming up w/ reasons to justify, or excuse ourselves for, the evil deeds we do. Maybe pacz are clever at that, too.

Day Forty-One

No rain yet. Still waiting for that sign.

Thought I heard rain in the night. I crawled out of my nest, climbed the ladder (not too painful now), pulled the shade back from a window, & looked out. The moon was fairly bright, although it's a bit past full, so I had a good view. Everything was quiet in my little piece of the world. Quiet & dry. Sigh.

I did have a mini-epiphany today. Actually, a micro-epiphany in two parts. I had been looking through the remaining picture book I bought for Matilda & feeling miffed again about using the pages from her other book for the dead pac's wreath. I was fuming about that when I brushed against the pile of pages I'd ripped out of the physics text/gift during my rampage. The pages scattered across the floor &, while gathering them, I decided to use those pages to make a wreath for the man who died on my doorstep.

That's what I did today. The illustrations aren't as colorful as those from the children's book, but they'll do. I plan to place the wreath—which is larger & more elaborate than the one I made for the pac—over the blood stain on the doorstep. The front porch is covered, so the wreath will have some protection. I worried about it blowing away, then recalled the book conservation crew using bricks to weigh down repair projects. Tied the wreath to a brick & voilà! Now I need to wait to place it on the doorstep until a storm comes along to keep the pacz away.

A rain storm. Hint, hint.

While I was admiring the wreath, the 2nd part of the micro-epiphany struck. That part has two subsections, a sad one & a happy one. I will deal w/ the former 1st, because having sad subsections hanging over my head makes me nervous.

I fell in love w/ Walter Crane's art when I was a baby. Literally: My grandmother had several of his books (one from 1896) & let me "read" them when I was tiny. She believed books were made to be touched, not to remain pristine (& lonely) on shelves.

During a poli-sci class, I found out Walter was a socialist, so we became BFFs (I had to do most of the heavy lifting for our friendship because he died over a hundred years ago). When I discovered he was a feminist (in a Victorian-era kind of way) & had championed comfortable clothes for women, I fell head-over-heels in love. I focused on his work for my senior project, then continued that focus in graduate school. (The title of my Master's thesis was going to be: "Confronting the 'Catch-Penny Abomination': An Analysis of the Influence of Walter Crane's Art and Writing on Anti-Capitalism Movements in Australia and New Zealand." Catchy, no?)

Anyway, I bought the books on Walter Crane (my Christmas present) because I needed them for my Master's thesis & borrowing them through Interlibrary Loan took too much time & money. But now.... The thesis train has left the station. On the same track as humanity's other trains, I'll bet. Even if I survive, I don't think there will be universities around. (In which case, I'll be the expert on many subjects, which is sad.)

Yes, that's the sad subsection. Now the happy one. Since I won't need the books for my thesis, I've decided to use some of their pages as illustrations for my journal.

Whoa! I know: they're beautiful books, elaborately bound, filled w/ gorgeous photographs of stunning art. But if/when I leave the RAW, I can't take them: I could carry a hek-a-lot of food & water in their place. Of course, I could leave the books here, intact. My name would be engraved on the donor plaque someday, if/when the world is better again, & I would be invited to every donor reception. & since the invites are for "You & a Guest," I could bring Benji along. Which would totally irritate Head Lib, especially if she had to watch him gobble all the fancy hors d'oeuvres.

But.... This journal is the only writing I expect to give to the world. It's not much. In fact, it's pretty measly. I was hoping to write weighty tomes on important subjects during my illustrious academic career, plus toss off a few dazzling creative works, the kind that spark bidding wars for screenplay rights. Never gonna happen.

Since this is the only work I'll leave behind, I want it to look good. It's not like I'm going to destroy Crane's art, just relocate it. & only the black & white photos: I'll leave the book of his color prints intact. So my project for the next few days will be deciding which pictures of Crane's art to include in my journal. Now that I've discovered a dizzying variety of tapes in the con-lab, I think I'll tape some journal pages back to back, too, so the growing stack will be easier to handle.

Here's the thing: I can write on only one side of the printed pages I rip out because Sharpie ink soaks through the paper, making a mirror image on the flipside. I tried writing on an ink-soaked side—no matter how hard I tried, I couldn't decipher what I wrote. I've been bothered by this, but I couldn't think of a way to make the process less wasteful. Now, those flipsides will serve a purpose, too.

I'm going to have illustrations! I'm going to have illustrations! (Does several clever, but clumsy, hip-hop steps across the library floor, w/ ABBA's "Dancing Queen" playing loudly in head.)

Side note: As my time in captivity increases, I am becoming more & more easily amused. If this goes on much longer, I'll break into giggles every time I sneeze.

Day Forty-Two

I was drinking the last watered-down sips of hot cocoa this morning when....

BAM! Thud. BAM! Thud. BAM! Thud.

Gunfire. Had to be. Very loud. Very close.

The cavalry was on the way! Or some type of human liberator, anyway. Pacz don't use guns: Why bother w/ a smelly, noisy gun when you have a highly effective & silent death touch?

I scrambled up the ladder, yanked aside the shade, & scanned the Quad. Nothing moving out there yet, but liberators would probably congregate in the foothills of the Cascades, just beyond campus (I couldn't see the foothills from this angle), before launching a full-scale attack. Plenty of cover for them up there, & they would have a great view of the whole area.

Today we take back the world! Let's hear it for the human Home Team—w00t, w00t! I was so excited I almost fell off the shelf ladder.

No sign of humans yet, but I didn't give up hope. I kept watching. & then.....

Tall Man sauntered to the middle of the Quad, just as casually as could be, turned around, looked up at me, & waved.

I cried. Full on ugly cried.

If humans were on the way, Tall Man would be worried or hurried or irritated or agitated in some way. Clearly, he was not.

In fact, he was doing something odd. An interpretive dance? Maybe the "Macarena"? I wiped away tears to get a better look. Yep, that's exactly what it looked like.

Wait. It wasn't a dance so much as the strange movements of a crazed creature. That's it! Tall Man had lost it. & why not? They say the only thing harder than being a prisoner day after day after day is being in charge of a prisoner day after day after day. The monotony had finally made him crack.

He was walking quickly in big circles, one hand out in front, the other waving randomly. Then he sat on the bench in front of Ag Sci w/ arms extended. He crawled under the bench, crawled out. Walked in circles, one hand in front, the other waving. Sat on bench, arms extended. Crawled under it. Crawled out. Circles. Sitting. Under the bench, out again. Circles.

My persistence had paid off. I had driven Tall Man—my nemesis—bonkers.

Except there was something familiar....

Oh, no. Walking around in circles w/ one hand out in front? That must be what I look like when I'm doing laps while reading journal entries out loud. Waving an arm around in what appears to be a random fashion? That must be me writing. Sitting w/ arms out? Reading. Crawling under a bench? What I do every night.

Communication through imitation.

He looked up at me & made a movement w/ one hand to the place on his face where I assume his mouth is located, then pointed toward the RAW. Hand to mouth; pointed toward building. He did that several times, waved w/ both hands, & left.

In the con-lab, a section of the counter was smashed to smithereens, & there were three huge cans on the floor. The blasts weren't gunfire: They were the sound of institutional-size cans of food hitting the counter (BAM!), then falling to the floor (Thud). Cans of....

Lima beans.

Hmm. I'm going to go out on a limb here & postulate that pacz feel the same as ~ 99% of humans do about this particular vegetable.

In the midst of my despair about not being rescued, I recall thinking this: I refuse to view lima beans as a sign.

Day Forty-Three

I'm stuffed. Didn't take many lima beans to accomplish that: My stomach has definitely shrunk because of all the not-eating I've been doing lately.

Feels good to be full. & energized. Each of those beans is like a little power-packed protein pill. My body is buzzing, my mind is zipping along at a bazillion miles an hour, &, for some reason, my sprained ankle doesn't hurt so much.

When I glanced at the can label yesterday, I missed one very important phrase: "Packed in butter sauce."

Butter. Want. Now.

Sure, it's fake, a margarine-like substance mixed w/ artificial flavors & colors & other chemicals I'd rather not think about. I'll probably die several seconds sooner than I would have otherwise because I'm eating gunk. But, hey, chemical-laced lima beans taste pretty amazing, especially to someone who is starving. I take back every bad thing I've ever said about them.

Also, I take back what I said about the beans not being a sign. They are. A sign that crunch time is coming for the home team here in the RAW, & I'd better get my butt in gear & start planning for it now. Because, barring a tragedy or a rescue—I don't want to think about the former, & the latter seems less likely w/ every passing day—I will run out of food at some point. It will happen. Sure, this new supply of protein pushes back that date by several weeks. But someday the food will be gone.

I must decide if I should stay in the RAW & starve, or if I should leave & deal w/ the dangers beyond these walls.

There could be a 3rd option. I think I've become the pacz' pet, a creature they keep alive for amusement or some other purpose. I'm sure there are many cans of food on campus, & I assume the pacz also collected supplies from town before destroying it. Probably lots of odd tidbits they could toss into my cage. But while Tall Man might consider pet status an option for me, I do not.

So, it's stay & starve, or leave & deal w/ who knows what.

I should have recorded how much food I ate each day & how much I had left. I keep a running tally of food supplies in my head, of course, but information of that sort might be useful to others. It's too late to start recording that now. Suffice it to say, I had very little food left before those lima beans flew through the window.

I know the days of pre-invasion food are numbered. There are only so many canned goods out there, & I'll bet pacz are hitting them hard. It's a safe bet there won't be pizza places, cafés, or gelato stands out there, either, so I've been reading books about wild edibles. Amazing how many of the weeds I used to pull up in my mother's garden can be eaten. This area is fairly rich in wild foods (berries of all sorts, camas roots, etc.), & I intend to learn which plants are edible & which are not.

However, my main concern is the same as it has been for days: water. I'm down to a few cups of drinking water & enough bucket water to give Bonnie one more sip. I say hello to her every morning, stroke her leaves, set her near the heat lamp now & then so she'll be cozy, sing to her. Lately, she's looked distressed, & she seems much more standoffish than before.

"If all the world were paper,
& all the sea were ink,
& all the trees were bread & cheese,
What should we do for drink?"

If rain or snow doesn't come soon, I will either shrivel up & die of dehydration or I will need to leave the RAW to haul water from the river at a time when there is a high risk of running into a pac patrol. My choice.

Day Forty-Four

Okay, deep breaths & a great big drum roll. I have made a decision: I am leaving the library.

Not today. Too many things to do 1st if I want to have a chance of surviving out there. But soon. Maybe on my birthday, ~ a week away. I can hold out that long, I think. I don't expect a major assault from the pacz, since I'm such a cute little pet. I will still have food at that point (lima beans, odds & ends). Water could be a problem, but I hope to resolve that issue soon. If not, I will leave earlier.

Now that I've written the words "I am leaving," the decision sounds like a total no-brainer. But it wasn't. Not for someone like me who agonizes over even the smallest decisions. This is huge; this is life & death. I took my time.

Before the lima beans arrived, I wasn't thinking much about what I would do because there didn't seem to be anything I could do. If I stayed here long enough, I would starve: I tried not to think about it, but I knew starvation was waiting, hunkered down & licking its lips, somewhere out there on the event horizon.

But, but…. There was always a chance I would be rescued. I mean, the Yakima military facility is not that far away. If anyone else survived the invasion, it would be someone at a place like that. If I just held down the RAW fort, took care of the books and myself, & kept hope alive, someone from that place would show up &….

Bam! Bam! Bam! The sound those cans made when they broke the counter also made me wake up. I realized my hopes of being rescued didn't amount to, well, a hill of beans. The cavalry is not going to charge in. A band of human hold-outs is not going to launch a commando-style raid, destroy the pacz, & take me w/ them.

Turns out that, in this situation, I'm the It girl. Strange, but true. The only person who can save me is me.

I had given some thought, early in the invasion, to what I might do if the pacz broke into the RAW or burned down the campus & I was forced to leave. All I came up w/ was to grab what I could & run. Not exactly a plan. Grab what? Carry it in what? Go where? Etc., etc., etc. Many questions, zero answers.

Go where? That was the important question, the one that made me throw up my hands in despair every time I thought about leaving. The other questions didn't matter if I had no place to go. At 1st I thought I could hide in town, but that idea went up in smoke on Day Three. Then I thought about going into the foothills, but I would need to traverse the entire campus, plus a long open space, before reaching cover, & my chances of being caught were high.

The town was to the north & east of here, the hills are to the west. That leaves south, the area behind my building. I'll go that way. I'll follow the river, which flows into a lake surrounded by holiday cottages. Or, if I can cross the river, I'll follow paths in the JSU nature preserve: No buildings & lots of cover, plus it extends all the way to the lake. Either way will be a long, soggy trek, but they're both doable.

On the far side of the nature preserve, in the hills above the lake, is a safe place: a fallout shelter from the 1950s that was upgraded during the Great Recession into a swanky survivalist home. It is well hidden: in fact, since I've only seen a map to the place once (courtesy of Benji), I'm not entirely sure I can find it. Benji said it's stocked w/ food & other necessities. Should be comfy no matter what the outside temperature is because it's buried deep underground.

Also, it's the only place I can think of where Matilda might be if she is alive. Not that I think she is alive, you know, but....

Many questions still to be answered about my trip. I was getting agitated by that today. Then I reminded myself I don't need to figure out everything all at once. Focus on one task until it is done, then focus on the next task. One step at a time.

Today, my task is making food for the trip, something super nutritious & easy to carry: mashed buttery lima beans mixed w/ wasabi mayo & cheese biscuit crumbs, shaped into patties, & baked slowly in the oven (but not for more than thirty minutes at a time due to the weirdness of this appliance, which requires at least three hours of cool-down time between baking sessions). I did this to dry out the patties so they won't spoil & so they will be lighter to carry. Not haute cuisine, but not bad.

Day Forty-Five

I've written as honestly as possible about the invasion, sharing my weaknesses & uncertainties along w/ my experiences. Day Five, for example. Do I think my mother—as apparition, angel, or actual being—was in the library, putting her arms around me & talking to me? No. But I felt her presence, heard her voice, & recorded that. I guess my survival technique for dealing w/ infernos is: self-induce a semi-coma for a few days, dredge up the most comforting thoughts & feelings possible, move on. Good to know.

So here's a caveat about what happened last night: some of what I recall might have been a nightmare caused by hypothermia. I believe my recollections are real, but I mention the hypothermia thing up front because I hate stories that end w/ the discovery that it was all a dream. When that happens, I feel used, hoodwinked, badly bamboozled.

Back story: the water situation has been bad. Really bad. After writing about having only a few cups left, I knew I had to do something. I didn't want to go outside until a rain/snow/hail/sleet/drizzle storm could give me cover, but I had been waiting & waiting, getting thirstier & thirstier. W/ a river no more than 50 feet from my door.

Before I went to bed yesterday, I checked the weather. Flakes of snow, but not a storm. Just large, lazy bits of white taking their own sweet time meandering to the ground. Not enough to scare away pacz.

I fell asleep hoping for a blizzard, for drifts of snow plastered against my door, for piles of crystallized water I could scoop up fast w/o leaving the building. For…. Okay, I had drifted off at that point, & it really was a dream. A dream from which the sound of sleet tapping on the windows woke me.

Sleet—not the best precipitation, but okay. After all, the water I wanted was in the river, not falling from the sky. I was ready to go in a flash. The bucket was by the back door, w/ the red sweatpants cord tied around its handle. The plan was simple: open door, scan for pacz, run to river bank, hang on to tree branch w/ one hand, use cord to lower bucket into river, haul up water, run to building, lock door, fill vessels. Repeat until all vessels were full or the storm stopped. I said each step of the plan out loud several times, giving myself plenty of time to be fully awake. Piece of cake.

Not.

By the time I opened the door, the sleet had turned to freezing rain. The snow that fell earlier was covered w/ a slick crust & glazed w/ a skim of water. Walking on it was like crossing an ice rink full of ball bearings while wearing a pair of KY jelly shoes.

I fell more than once, starting w/ a spectacular tumble right outside the door that sent me skidding down the ramp— on my butt & backwards—all the way to the parking lot. Maybe I should have returned to the RAW, but I really needed water. I picked my way across the parking lot & grass to reach the river bank. I grabbed a tree branch, lowered the bucket into the river, & started to haul it back up. Then something about the bucket's weight & the way I put oomph into my effort by digging in my heels—through rain skim, sleet crust, & snow—made me slip. Into the river.

Pain. Oh, pain, pain, pain. Who knew cold water could be searing?

Shock. My head explodes w/ the worst brain freeze ever.

& I am counting.

My mother told me a story about my father falling through the ice as a child while skating on a river in Russia. She said he almost died because the human body can survive for only so many seconds in water this cold. I can't remember how many seconds she said, but I keep counting. I can't stop counting. Seventy-two, seventy-three….

The rain stops. Oh, drat! Now the pacz will come out.

One hundred one, one hundred two….

Holding tree branch w/ one hand, cord w/ the other. I must hold on to one & let go of one. Tree branch? Cord? Tree branch? Cord? I can't remember, so I hold both.

The bucket is in the river. The river wants the bucket to go downstream. The bucket wants to take me w/ it. I want to go down the river. To the lake. Then up the hill to the safe place. If I let go of something, I can leave right now. The river will take me. It will be easy. & fast. Very fast. But which hand should let go?

"Shall we gather at the river
where bright angel feet have trod…?"

Snow by tree turns brown. Brown snow slides down bank. Just like me! Who knew snow could do that? So many new things to learn at school. I can't learn them all. Not now. I am busy. I am going down the river to the safe place.

One hundred sixty, one hundred sixty-one…. Those numbers are too big. They hurt my head. Little numbers are good. One second. Two. Three….

Brown snow has a hand. Very funny! Something about brown snow…. It's bad. Like yellow snow, only more bad. Don't touch it! Don't touch me! Brown hand turns tan, grabs me. I let go—no tree branch, no cord. I float down, down, down….

Into nothing. For a very long time.

Bits & pieces from my past & present blur together. I am a child, & my father is carrying me. He is warm. He smells good. Like cinnamon? Ginger? He's tall, w/ a beard & brown hair. I call him Bear, & he makes an odd sound, maybe a laugh, maybe a growl. He helps me take off wet clothes & put on a lab coat. He holds me until I stop shaking, then holds my hand as I fall asleep.

Later. I open my eyes & see someone. Not my father. Tall Man is wandering through the RAW. I try to scream, but my voice won't work. He isn't wearing a head covering: Tan skin, beard, brown hair. He chooses a book, sits at a table, & runs his fingers—six on each hand—along the lines of text. He looks older than I had imagined. & weary.

Later. Tall Man is near my bed. I scream so loud my eardrums ache. He holds a hand out toward me; there is no covering on it. He takes both of my hands in his, rubbing them gently. He gives me sips from a small amethyst bottle. I don't want to drink it, but I can't push it away. I fall back into a deep cushion of nothingness.

Later. The pac stands by my bed wearing its brown suit. I whisper, "Tall Man." He waves both hands, & then leaves.

Later—

It is late afternoon as I write this. I woke an hour ago—achy, bruised, head throbbing, feet feeling like I'd stepped on a porcupine.

Since waking, one question has buzzed in my head: What happened last night?

I was wearing a lab coat & nothing else when I woke. I wear lab coats over my otherwise naked body when I do the wash, but I always wear clothes under them when I go to bed (& I'm the kind of person who comes up w/ routines & sticks to them pretty closely). But it doesn't prove Tall Man helped me undress/dress. My many large & colorful bruises, however, confirm the falls I took on the ice last night.

All containers in the kitchen were filled w/ water, which must have come from the river (last night's precipitation wouldn't fill a tea cup). I don't recall gathering the water, so I believe Tall Man did. Once again, no proof.

The clothes I wore last night were soaking wet & hanging on the pegs by the con-lab door. They couldn't have gotten that wet from precipitation, & I would have draped them over the clothes line if they did. I don't recall dealing w/ the wet clothes myself or seeing Tall Man deal w/ them.

The back door was locked. I don't recall doing that. Tall Man could have turned the lock while still inside the RAW, then, when he left, pulled the door closed behind him sharply to set the lock.

Summary: I went outside last night (bruises) & fell into the river (soaking wet clothes). Such a fall at this time of year would almost certainly result in hypothermia, which can cause extreme confusion, so events after that are open to interpretation.

Except this one: There was a book lying on the table where I recall Tall Man sitting last night. A signed 1st edition of *Traveling through the Dark*, by William Stafford. I haven't read that book in several years, & there is absolutely no reason why I would expend energy searching for it & setting it on that particular table while experiencing the debilitating effects of hypothermia.

Only Tall Man can confirm what happened, so I might never know. & I can't think about it anymore at the moment—my brain feels like a ball of clothes dryer lint. But if even half of what I recall happening actually happened, last night could change everything.

Day Forty-Six

I just took the last of the lima bean patties out of the oven. When they're cool, I'll pack them in tins—the ones that held fancy biscuits—so they're ready to travel. The RAW smells wonderful: earthy, buttery. I'm leaving some beans unbaked so I'll have something to eat during the next week. I've eased up on my rationing of water & food because I want to increase my energy in preparation for the trek.

I'm going to carry water in the glass jars from the mango juice. Not ideal, but I'll wrap them in the huge crimson sox from the LAF box so they don't break. Not many plastic containers in the RAW except my honey bear (going) & the glue pots (not going).

I might have ended up eating glue if I'd stayed here longer. & boiling leather book covers to gnaw on for protein. I'm happy I haven't been reduced to that: Even for someone w/ Russian heritage, it would be way too Dr. Zhivago-esque.

One week from today is my 25th birthday. On that day, I will leave the library & begin my quest to discover what happened to Matilda. Notice I didn't say "find Matilda"—don't want to get my hopes up. She wasn't on campus on Day Three, so there's a chance she's alive. One percent, maybe. Either way, I need to know.

So much to do in a week. Like figure out how to haul my supplies. The little bag I carried w/ me everywhere before the invasion is just big enough to hold my wallet, cell phone, sunglasses & case, comb, travel toothbrush & toothpaste, dental floss, & golf-score pencil. The wallet & cell phone have no purpose now & will remain in the LAF box, & the toothpaste & dental floss are history, so I have extra room for needles, thread, & other small items. But what about extra clothes, food & water, etc.?

The gym bag from the LAF box was a logical choice, but it's awkward to carry using the handles. Also, because the handles don't fit over my shoulders, I can't carry it on my back. Not in its present state. But, clever girl that I've become, I'm turning it into a backpack using linen thread & bookbinder's needles from the con-lab, plus the sharpest scissors I've ever seen—I'm definitely taking those along for a weapon.

I still don't know what to think about my non-dream experience w/ Tall Man the other night. It's clear he doesn't want to kill me. Not at this point. Maybe I really am a pet to him, an amusing, harmless, live-action trinket to add to his collection of species he has exterminated. If that's the case, pacz take good care of their pets. I mean, he risked falling into the river to pull me out (I believe), & pacz hate water. He (I believe) took off parts of his brown suit for me, comforted me, warmed me w/ his body, held my hand. Yes, he saw me naked, but I didn't get a creepy feeling from that: I never sensed I was in danger of being spirited away to the mother ship to be probed.

As a way of saying thanks, I've opened the window shades. I don't know if that means anything to Tall Man, but it might. &, seriously, what do I have to hide at this point? He's seen it all: if he wants to look, let him. I'm just going about the business of getting ready to leave. If he figures out what I'm planning & wants to stop me, I need to goad him into making that known now so I can factor it into my get-away plans.

In preparation for leaving, I'm spiffing up the RAW. Today, I focused on the freezer, which was basically one big mound of frost. Or so I thought. But underneath the frost was—wait for it, wait for it—most of a pint of Häagen-Dazs coffee ice cream!

Now the happy tailor, who is zipping through the day on a serious sugar high, returns to her needles, thread, & crimson weather-proof nylon.

"A fair little girl sat under a tree,
sewing as long as her eyes could see...."

Day Forty-Seven

The backpack is done! I like everything about it except the color—no way to be inconspicuous w/ that splash of bright crimson on my back. If only JSU's colors were moss & sage…. But it works. I packed some items in it, & there's plenty of room for necessities. It's a trade-off, really: I could take more items in a bigger pack, but then the pack might be too heavy & the seams might rip out. In the end, I think I achieved a

Later—

News flash!
Several times this morning, while I was finishing the backpack, I noticed Tall Man looking in the window. I didn't acknowledge him. I knew he was there; he knew I knew he was there; I ignored him & kept sewing.

After I finished the pack, there was enough nylon left over to make simple mitts to keep my hands a little warmer & drier. Back to needle & thread. As I worked, I caught more glimpses of Tall Man at the window. He didn't try to get my attention, but he wasn't hiding, either. Odd. Like everything about pacz.

I finished the mitts, ate, began my entry, & heard tapping on the back door.

He's baaaack!

What to do? I didn't panic, which was nice. After considering the situation, I decided I didn't want Tall Man in here again. He was kind the other night, rescuing me & helping me recover. & I haven't coughed once since he made me sip that stuff in the amethyst bottle. But too many things could go wrong. I ignored him.

More tapping. Twenty minutes of it. Forty. An hour (he is seriously persistent). The tapping became louder & faster as it went on. Clearly, Tall Man would not be denied. My resolve to keep him out dissolved. I put the glove & mitten on my hand, picked up my trusty piece of razor-sharp glass, & cracked open the back door.

He was alone. Good. Standing at the bottom of the ramp. Good. No brown coverings on his hands, both of which he was waving. Good. I opened the door a little more; he took a step up the ramp. We continued this pattern, this pas de deux, until he was standing fairly close, his covered feet on the threshold.

Seeing a pac so close started the cauldron of hate simmering inside me again. For a second, I thought about slamming the door in Tall Man's face. I wanted to humiliate this murderous creature. To hurt him as much as he had hurt me. To make him agonize later over what a fool he'd been to think he would be welcome here after the horror & death he'd caused.

But my rampage a week or so ago must have served as a safety valve, a way for me to let off enough steam to keep hatred from reaching the boiling point. Now, I had the presence of mind, & enough control over my emotions, to remind myself that pacz seem to be here to stay & that, to survive, I need to find—& find ways to communicate to them—our points of connection.

I let him in.

He nodded as soon as he entered. I nodded at him. Then we just stood next to each other by the back door. For a longish time. Awkward.

While I tried to decide what to do next, I noticed the scent of that unusual spice I'd smelled after the river rescue. So he was in here that night! I wondered if pacz smell like this naturally, or if it's the soap they use. Or maybe something they spray on to attract humans?

I motioned for him to enter the library's main room. He took a step in that direction, & his suit brushed against me. I jumped back, terrified. He jumped back in surprise at my reaction. More seconds of awkward. It occurred to me then that we might be the most socially inept members of our respective species. I wondered if "ironic" was the correct word to describe the fact that two misfits were serving as lead negotiators for inter-species détente.

When all else fails, try books. Beatrix Potter had kept me happy the day before w/ *The Tailor of Gloucester*—one of the books I'd bought for Matilda—& it was still on the front desk. I retrieved the book & sat at a table, motioning for Tall Man to sit. He did—at the far end of the table (I think he was afraid to brush against me again). I moved my chair closer to him (but not too close), opened the book, & read aloud.

After a few sentences, I was immersed in the story, & I could have been reading it to anyone—my dying mother, who loved to sew & who loved this story; the children at the campus pre-school; Matilda. Whenever I stopped to take a breath, Tall Man waved both hands. I interpreted this action to mean, "It's all good. Please continue."

Which I did. When I reached a page w/ an illustration, Tall Man ran all six fingers of his hand over it slowly. He hadn't taken his head covering off yet, so I couldn't tell if he was smiling, but I'm guessing he was. He lingered longest over pictures of mice wearing clothes & doing human tasks. Probably confusing, but fascinating, too—as a child, I had wanted to believe such things could happen.

His strongest reaction was in response to the songs. At a few points in the story, mice sing as they work. When I reached those parts, I sang the songs instead of reading the lyrics. Tall

Man turned in my direction. I had the impression that, under the head & face covering, he was staring at me.

His action made me self-conscious. I stopped. He waved both hands. I sang another song. He took off his head covering & stared at me. Unnerving, to say the least. He waved again, but by then I was too flustered to sing.

So he did. At least I think that's what he did. He took a deep breath, then filled the room w/ his voice, which slid up & down an odd scale. There were trills. There were parts that were more like whistling than singing. There were long sections that sounded like Tibetan throat music. & between those, there were repeated sequences of three or four notes (I think they're the pac equivalent of a chorus, but that's just a guess).

The sound created that strange vibration inside me again, like the mourning song had when the pacz carried away their dead friend. I felt warm, invigorated, comforted all at once. Tall Man sang for ~15 minutes—must have been an epic ballad. When he hit the last note, the sound echoed in the building, reverberating for several seconds.

Beautiful. Moving. Addictive. The song, if that's what it was, touched me on such a deep level that my eyes teared up. I waved both hands quickly, like a 1st-grader overcome by excitement when responding to a question. I waved again. He put on his head covering, nodded slightly, & left. Just like that.

Here's the question I've been pondering for hours: What is going on?

Day Forty-Eight

Can't believe I've spent 48 days observing pacz & still don't know, beyond a shadow of a doubt, what they are. I've made progress: I know they're not zombies—that was pretty much a given from Day One. I know they're not creatures, by which I mean trained animals. So that leaves people, robots, or aliens. Even after seeing the head & hands of a pac, though, I'm still not sure which of those they are.

I thought the mystery would be solved w/ Tall Man's unveiling. But his tan skin is like that of many humans. His hands have 6 fingers, but that runs in some human families, especially from areas—Japan, Utah, Nevada—exposed to nuclear explosions. His hair looks like human hair. His face is not quite like the average human's (if there is such a thing): forehead higher, nose narrower, chin more pointed, eyes.... They're shaped ~ like human eyes, but the pupils are an intense shade of indigo, almost electric. I remember thinking, when I saw his face for the 1st time, that his ancestors probably never mated w/ a Neanderthal-like species, either by choice or force, as ours did.

If I had to decide, I would say pacz are aliens/andro-aliens. The way they showed up out of the blue in overwhelming #s; the way they kill; their odd behaviors: All of these point to an alien invasion rather than one carried out by humans.

Basically, it comes down to this: is there a group of humans—from another country, a terrorist organization, or a radical faction in our own country—w/ the means to carry out such a rapid & (apparently) effective genocide w/o the use of nuclear weapons or other WMDs? I would say no.

But whether he's a human, a humanoid alien, an android, or a non-corporeal being who has taken control of a human body, I enjoyed Tall Man's visit yesterday. I was awake much of the night thinking about him. That has happened often during my time in the library, but this time the thoughts were pleasant instead of charged w/ fear.

If Benji were here, he would give me a long, loooong lecture about the Stockholm Syndrome—the emotional state that causes people to "fall in love" w/ their captors. He would explain slowly & patiently, as if to a child, that it wasn't my fault if I was drawn to Tall Man, because that was just human nature. & then he would promise to kick my butt all the way around the perimeter aisles if I ever allowed Tall Man to enter the library again.

But this is not Stockholm, & I am most definitely not Patti Hearst.

No, this is an art of war/understand your opponent/keep your friends close & your enemies closer type of situation. I believe the odds of my survival will increase as my knowledge of pacz increases. Plus, I can't view humans as totally good & Tall Man as totally evil. The universe is not that simple.

Enough about pacz.

My escape preparations are coming along great. Most items I'm planning to take are stashed in the backpack already. It's a load, but I'm sure I'll be able to handle it for my relatively short trek to the safe place (crosses fingers, toes, & eyes, hoping for the best). &, if I can't find (or am not welcome in) the safe place, I could continue on from there for a long distance/time w/ the items I can carry in this pack. I could follow the Yakima River until it joins the mighty Columbia, then follow that all the way to the Pacific Ocean. I've always wanted to live....

"By the sea, by the sea,
by the beautiful sea...."

While deciding what to take, I found the shard of mirror I'd saved after the bathroom was bombed. Caught a glimpse of my reflection. Yikes! My face looks so different now. Skin color more yellow than pink, cheeks hollow, circles under my eyes darker & puffier than the last time I saw myself. My eyes have a look in them that borders on frightening. I smiled to see if that made my face look better, but it just made me look a bit ghastly, like a pale & slightly evil jack-o-lantern.

Then I made the mistake of taking off my knit hat for the 1st time in, well, I can't remember how long. Whoa! My long hair, which I've kept tucked inside the hat for most of my stay in the RAW, was one big super-size snarl, a tangled mess resembling what I imagine the butt of a bear looks like when it emerges from hibernation.

Time for a change. I grabbed the sharp scissors in one hand, a bunch of matted hair in the other, & hacked away. Slash, slash. Snip. Slash, slash. Snip. Five minutes later I had the strangest, punkiest hairdo ever. Rebellious-Benji, & the Ramones, would be proud of me. But I…. If I'd had any tears left, I would have cried great big ones when I saw my reflection in the mirror shard. I didn't. I pulled my hat on & went back to my escape preparations.

No need to map a route for my trek: I either follow the river to the lake, or I cross the river here & traverse the nature preserve to reach the lake. I can take the 2nd route, which is safer, if the river freezes over. That hasn't happened yet, & I won't know if it's an option until the day I actually leave.

Once I reach the lake, I need to make my way up one of the hills above it to the safe place. I saw Benji's map to the place only once, but I've been to the lake many times: I'm hoping familiar landmarks will help me figure out the correct dirt road to take. My mother always said I have an unfailing sense of inner direction. Hope she was right.

I continue to spiff up the RAW—wiping up the last of the soot & bomb dust, putting things back where they belong, etc. At my present rate of cleaning/preparation, I can read a few hours each day & still be ready to leave on my birthday, as planned.

I took a break while cleaning the con-lab today to admire some old books w/ bindings in need of repair. Started me thinking that my journal needs to be bound in some way. I'm using the shipping box from Powell's to hold the journal-page stack at present. The stack has grown quite tall. Even though I've taped pages back to back, they slip around in the box whenever I move it & their edges are getting all bashed & crumpled. Plus, I'd like the journal to resemble a book, at least a little, & it doesn't at present.

The pages are all different sizes, which will make containing them a challenge. But there must be a way to do it. The RAW has many books on book making/repair, of course. Those are what I'll be reading when I take breaks from (sigh) cleaning.

Day Forty-Nine

Life in the RAW is getting curiouser & curiouser.

It was dark outside this morning. Low, heavy clouds. Storm on the way. Probably rain instead of snow because the library felt a little warmer. Good. I needed water to wash clothes before heading out for the safe place, I needed to dump my bathroom can, & I needed to lay the wreath on the doorstep to honor the man who died there. The wreath was ready over a week ago, but I was so busy trying to turn myself into a popsicle by falling into the river that I never got around to holding the memorial service.

Everything was set; I could jet as soon as the storm began. The plan: put the water bucket under a rain spout & set the bathroom can a few feet away; place the wreath on the doorstep, say a few words, sing; deposit the contents of the can in the dumpster; retrieve the water bucket. I could stop at any point if the rain let up, but I hoped it would last long enough for me to fill the bucket a few times.

Why do I even bother to make plans?

The rain started; the storm seemed to be settling in for the long haul; I took off. I set the water bucket under the rain spout & dropped off the bathroom can. Then, holding the wreath under my unzipped coat to protect it from the rain (brick in my coat pocket), I ran to the front of the building, rounded the corner, &....

Tall Man & Pudgy were on the porch. Under the roof, of course. Tall Man: Sitting on the porch, back against the door, chin on chest, eyes closed, head covering on the floor beside him. Pudgy: Sitting cross-legged (crisscross, applesauce) a few feet from Tall Man, awake, head turned away from me.

Trapped in the R.A.W.

I froze. I was on their turf, & both pacz were wearing the hand coverings that seem to be the source of their killing power. I became a statue: If I hadn't been carrying the wreath, I might have put both hands over my eyes so the pacz couldn't see me. "Back away, back away!" My brain was talking to me, but my body wasn't listening. I couldn't move.

Pudgy stood & shook Tall Man to wake him, then turned & saw me. He hurried to the edge of the porch, being careful to stay under the roof, & made a gesture I think was intended to be both insulting & threatening. Tall Man—groggy—looked toward the Quad 1st, scanning it for trouble. Then he turned & saw me. He fumbled for a second putting on his head covering, then was on his feet.

What followed was the strangest argument ever. It was carried out in total silence, at least as far as I could hear. Clearly, the pacz were "talking" to each other (Telepathically? Using devices in their suits?), & each was gesturing wildly. At one point, Pudgy tried to pick up a metal beam (Ah ha! That's what they've been using to batter the door!) to hit Tall Man, but TM shoved it away. Any being from any species on any planet in any quadrant of any galaxy would know they were both upset.

It was all mime to me.

My body came back on line. I backed away until I reached the corner of the building, then ran, the wreath still under my coat. Heavy rain was falling, so I knew I would be safe for a while. I deposited the contents of my bathroom can in the dumpster, grabbed the water bucket (almost full), & dashed into the RAW. Locked the door. Then collapsed on the floor, laughing uncontrollably, which might seem strange, but, hey, that's just the way I roll.

But wait, there's more. Later, after I washed my clothes & was cleaning the RAW in the raw, so to speak (but w/ a lab

149

coat on), I heard knocking on the back door. I'd been so busy I hadn't noticed the break in the storm.

"Come, tell me, blue eyed stranger,
Say, wither dost thou roam....
Hast thou no friends, no home?"

I was humming that old song when I went to the door. I was distracted: thinking about getting ready to leave, about binding my journal, about Tall Man's singing. & I knew the drill at this point: I put on my glove, pulled the mitten over it, picked up the piece of glass, opened the door a crack, &....

Pudgy shoved an arm through the opening.

I slashed at the arm while slamming my weight against the door. It's a heavy door & must have hurt when it smashed Pudgy's arm. No sound. Not even a whimper.

Pudgy's arm was still in the opening, w/ the awful covered hand clawing around, almost touching me several times. I slashed again at the arm, cutting through the suit. Again, no sound, but Pudgy began pushing against the door rhythmically & w/ great force. Whomp! Pause. Whomp! Pause. Whomp!

It was just a matter of time before Pudgy touched me or broke in. I waited until there was going to be another hard push, &, at that moment, took my weight off the door & ran. When Pudgy pushed & there was no resistance, I'm sure the door flew open. I didn't turn to look, but I heard a thud & figured Pudgy fell. The few moments it took for the pac to regain footing gave me time to reach the bathroom & lock the door.

I expected Pudgy to start slamming against the bathroom door. But no. Instead, I heard noises that seemed to indicate the library was being torn apart. Heavy objects falling. Something breaking. Thuds. A sickening crack, as if a watermelon had been split open. The back door slamming. Silence.

No way was I going to leave the bathroom, not until I was absolutely sure the coast was clear. I sat on the floor w/

my back against the wall for a long & very scary time. I was prepared to sit there for the rest of the day & night. For days, if necessary.

I guess the stress of the situation wore me out because I drifted off into half-sleep. & woke to the sound of a pac song that sounded like the one Tall Man sang the other night. My 1st reaction was relief because I assumed it was Tall Man. Then I reminded myself what had happened earlier when I made a false assumption. For all I knew, it was a song pacz learn in pre-school. For all I knew, it was the pacz' national anthem.

Then I heard a tune that mice sing in *The Tailor of Gloucester.* No words, just humming. Perfect rendition. Only one pac would know that.

Tall Man was waiting when I opened the door. His head & hand coverings were off. He looked older & much wearier than he had the other night. & he was standing in a puddle of blood.

As I write this, he's sleeping in Head Lib's office. I put the two chair cushions on the floor end to end, &, although the bed they make is long enough for only the top half of his body, he seems comfortable. I showed him how to use the iPod. He smiled when he heard the 1st notes of Beethoven's 5th, then fell asleep listening to it.

Took forever to stop the bleeding from gashes on his head & a puncture wound in his side. The side wound was nasty— deep, w/ ragged edges, & w/ fibers from his suit embedded in it. I boiled rain water to clean it out, sutured it as carefully as I could w/ linen thread & a bookbinder's needle (which is blunt, so it must have hurt), & cut a freshly-washed lab coat into strips for the bandage. Head wounds always look worse than they are, so I expect they will heal just fine. But the wound in his side worries me.

Tall Man was surprised when I took my hat off before beginning the cleaning & suturing process. It had soaked up a lot of blood while I was helping him lie on a table so he would be at a good height when I worked on his wounds. I'd forgotten about my new haircut. He reached out & touched my hair w/ his uncovered hand. I stood still, a little afraid of what was happening. Then, as his hand drew away, the back of it brushed against my cheek. Slowly. Gently. If I hadn't been shaking already, I would have started then. Different reason, same effect.

His blood is red, & that makes me happy. Another point of connection between humans & pacz.

It seems more than a little strange having a pac here in the library w/ me. After so many days of doing everything in my power to keep them out. Tall Man won't hurt me: I don't know why I feel confident about that, but I do. But now, most likely because of me, he is in some kind of blood feud w/ the other pacz, one that could lead to more violent confrontations. I think the other pacz would zap me dead in a flash w/o giving it a 2nd thought.

I'm going to crawl into my sleeping nest now, but I'm planning to sleep w/ one eye open.

Day Fifty

Busy, busy, busy.

Light is fading, so I'm writing fast. I've already written a note w/ ID info so whoever finds the journal (if there is anyone left to find it) might be able to figure out who I am/was. I'm sure most records are destroyed, so I'm noting as many people/ place connections to myself as possible in the hope at least one will be traceable.

While Tall Man slept, I bound the journal. I considered punching a hole in the corner of each page, using donut sticky things to strengthen the holes, then connecting the sheets using the library key ring. Two problems: No hole punch, no donut stickies.

I found some big pieces of hunter-green cardstock behind a file cabinet in the con-lab when I was cleaning. According to a book I read, that's what I needed to make a modified four-flap book wrap/tuxedo box. Take two long pieces of cardstock, set one over the other to create a cross, stack journal pages in the middle of the cross, crease around the stack, fold the four flaps over the journal, & tie something around the bundle (I'm using the crimson cord from the XXL sweatpants). Voilà! A container w/ enough layers to provide heft & protect the pages.

My other project was cleaning the mess from the pacz' confrontation. Shelves, books, tables, chairs all over. Must have been quite the fight. I'm glad Tall Man won—he's in rough shape, but you should'a seen the other guy (I'll bet Pudgy got trashed). Tall Man saved me from Pudgy's wrath: cleaning is a small price to pay for that.

Tall Man slept all night & most of today. I thought he might have a concussion, although I checked his indigo pupils after the fight & they were equal & reacting properly to light. But I got up twice in the night & tiptoed into Head Lib's office to make sure he was breathing. I did that many times for my mother when she was ill, especially near the end. &, of course, I did that for Matilda, too.

Late this afternoon, Tall Man stood (wincing from the pain), hobbled to where I was working, sang the mouse song, put on his brown suit, & left. I have no idea if he will return. It's almost too dark to write now, & he's still not back. I tell myself whatever happens happens. No matter what, I am leaving.

Day Fifty-One

I couldn't sleep last night. I was worrying about my trip & about Tall Man, but mostly I just couldn't get warm. My nose (the only part sticking out from under the covers) was freezing. I'd set up the heat lamp near Tall Man's bed the other night. Since he wasn't here to use the lamp, I decided to retrieve it.

When I crawled out of my nest, the RAW felt colder than ever before. I grabbed the lamp, stopped to use the bathroom, closed the door, flicked the switch, & no light. Used the facilities by feel, but, when I tried to wash my hands using the puddle of water I keep in the sink for that purpose, discovered the water was a solid block of ice.

No worries: I had a heat lamp. I took it to my nest, plugged it in, & no heat. Tried another outlet. Nada. The electrical system had gone down.

I fumed about that for a while until it dawned on me this could be good news. Maybe even a sign. If it was cold enough to freeze water inside the RAW, it might be cold enough to make a crossable layer of ice on the river.

I needed to find out. The only windows facing the river are in the con-lab &, because that room doesn't have tall book shelves, it doesn't have ladders. It would have been nice to watch the river during my stay here, but I didn't have access to the windows in there. Now it was critical that I see the river w/o going outside.

I took a few gentle laps around the perimeter aisles in the dark to limber up my ankle, get my blood flowing, & think. There's a cabinet against the river-facing wall, & it's wide, deep, & tall. Plus, it's next to a counter. If I set a chair on the counter, I could climb onto the counter, stand on the chair,

& then climb from that to the top of the cabinet. Then, if I dragged the chair up, set it on top of the cabinet, stood on the chair, gripped the bottom of the window opening near the ceiling, & pulled myself up, I might be able to see out the window.

There aren't enough preface pages in this library to write about all of the trials & tribulations I went through to reach that window. Suffice it to say that now—many hours, bruises, goose bumps, abrasions, & contusions later—I have seen the river.

Yes! The river is frozen over. Couldn't tell how thick the layer is, of course, but I'm guessing the temperature is below zero, so the layer could be solid.

By the time that fiasco was over, it was dawn, when pacz tend to be active. I had planned to leave on my birthday, two days hence. Now I wanted to leave right away; the ice could thaw at any moment. I wanted to grab my pack & go. But it would be foolish to leave when pacz are likely to be around, it would be foolish to leave in broad daylight, & it would be foolish to leave at dusk, the pacz' other active time of day.

I decided to finish my preparations properly & mindfully, write one last journal entry, take a nap to make up for my body-bruising & sleepless night, & then, after dark—really dark, because it's the new moon—leave. For good.

Last day in the RAW. Last journal entry. Now that I've made up my mind, I am anxious to be off. To be outside for longer than a dash to the dumpster. To be moving forward. To see what happens next. To search for my dear Matilda.

Yes, I know I could be dead before tomorrow morning. Even if I cross the river before the pacz reach me, there are many ways I could die: drowning, freezing, starving, bleeding to death, or being eaten by humans who have turned to cannibalism to survive. & that's just the "Top Five Ways to Die" list. But such is life in the new world.

I've cleaned the library. The barricades are down; the tables, chairs, & shelves are back where they belong. The book wall that I constructed around my writing desk is deconstructed now, & the books—even the most disgusting romance novels—are back on their shelves in their proper places. The heavy books I kept in the rolling cart in front of my sleeping area have been put away, too. Shelves dusted; staff kitchen cleaned. I am particularly proud of the bathroom: What's left of the sink, toilet, & floor are sparkling, which was not easy to accomplish because the place has been grubby for a long time.

The locks on Head Lib's office & the con-lab are destroyed. There's a broken window in the con-lab, plus a counter splintered beyond repair. A hole in the front door. The bathroom—what can I say? A bloodstain on the front porch. Deal w/ it.

I wanted to leave this place as I found it. To the best of my ability, I have. A patron who frequented the RAW pre-invasion & walked in now would think not much had changed.

There is a small stack of books on the table nearest to this writing desk. Those are books from which I tore printed pages for my journal. I didn't want to put them back on the shelves because—if there is another human out there who cares about such things—maybe they can be restored in some way. After this entry & my ID note, I have included a list of those books—an annotated bibliography—to make that process easier.

I had trouble deciding what to do about Bonnie, my faithful companion. If I leave her in the library, & if it's not liberated soon, she will die. I had resigned myself to that. Then I gave her what I thought was her last drink of water today, & she looked so sad. I realized I couldn't let her suffer an inevitable death. "Inevitable" being the key word.

So, when I leave, I will set her outside against the south wall near the rain spout, dump my last bathroom can next to her (for fertilizer), & pile all the rags I can find around the pot to protect its roots. I told Bonnie my plan, & her blue & silver stars spun w/ joy. Beautiful. She will probably be dead soon, but I am giving her the same thing I am giving myself: A chance.

It would be foolish to take this journal w/ me. I expect it would be destroyed by the river, snow, or pacz in no time. Also, if I do manage to survive, & if I do find Matilda, my plan is to hide us away where we will never be found. Then the journal would not be available to others, & that's not right.

There must be a record of the invasion—an accessible record—because, for me to survive after I leave here, I need to believe in my heart that humans still exist. Humans who will make this world right again. I believe books will play an important role in reconstructing the past, building the future. My journal about the invasion might be helpful for both of those purposes. It will be waiting here on the writing desk.

Later—

Tall Man came back while I was writing the previous sentence. He had an odd hard-shell rucksack thing on his back & was carrying the brown hand coverings he had worn, along w/ those of the other three pacz. He tried to give me the coverings w/ a great deal of ceremony, but I refused to touch them. Then it became clear the act of giving me the coverings meant something very important to him. I took them. No zap. I don't know why they no longer have killing power. I don't know what he had to do to take them away from the other pacz. &, really, I don't want to know.

Apparently, I will have company on my trek. Not sure if that's good or bad, but that's the way it is. So be it.

There was an important task to complete before leaving: honoring the man who died on my doorstep. Tall Man was here to protect me, so I felt safe taking the wreath to the front porch for the ceremony. W/ him looking on, I knelt, set the brick on the blood stain, & placed the wreath over it. Then I stood, said a short prayer, & began to sing.

"Amazing grace, how sweet the sound
that saved a wretch like me.
I once was lost but now am found,
was blind but now I see."

Tall Man was humming along by the 2nd verse—hard to believe he could pick it up so fast. We continued to hum the song together while I tossed strands of my cut hair off the porch & watched the wind blow them across the frozen ground. There is death, then there is life again: I am hoping birds will line their nests w/ my hair in the spring.

When we came back inside, I realized it would make sense to leave behind samples of my blood & Tall Man's blood, along w/ the sample from the young man. There were some small plastic bags in the con-lab. I took two bags, two blank book pages, & my piece of broken glass into the kitchen. Tall Man followed. I held out my hand & indicated I was going to cut it. He was horrified. I sang a song to assure him it was okay. For better or worse, the only one that came to mind was "Let it Go."

I cut my hand, let blood drip onto the paper, & put the paper in a plastic bag. I took Tall Man's right hand & indicated I wanted to cut it. His eyes told me he was afraid, but he hummed the song to say it was okay. I will write our names on the plastic bags, seal them when the blood is dry, & place them in the drawer in my writing desk, next to that of the young man w/ hazel eyes.

While I finish this entry, Tall Man is using a piece of miraculous plastic-like material from his rucksack to fix the hole in the con-lab window. I watched him fix the hole in the front door w/ it a few minutes ago: He kneaded it several times, stretched it out, pressed it on, &, in a few seconds, the stuff sort of melded w/ the door, filling in the hole & taking on the color of the wood. I showed him the bombed vent pipes, & I think he's going to use the plastic stuff to fix the holes up on the roof they used to pass through, too.

Using plastic to repair the RAW. Ha! Head Lib wouldn't know whether to laugh or cry.

There are things I've done during my time in the RAW for which I could be criticized. There are things I've done that I regret. All I can say in my defense is this: I did my best.

May you do the same.

To anyone who finds this journal

I have been trapped in the Jefferson State University special collections library, commonly known as the RAW, since Day One of the invasion. I stayed at first to protect myself, then to protect the books. Now I am running out of food & water, & I can't protect either. I must leave.

I've kept a journal during my time in the library, something to help me stay sharp & to provide others w/ an account of the invasion as it played out here on campus. My journal is not great literature: It is just what happened.

The purpose of this note is to provide identifying information to anyone interested in finding out more about me. In addition to the journal & note, I've left my blood sample & two others (one from another human, one from an invader) in the drawer of this desk.

My name is Kaylee Bearovna. I was born on January 19th, 1996, here in Jefferson City. (I should add, in case my note &/ or journal are moved elsewhere, that JC is/was a small town located at the eastern edge of the Cascade Range, just ~ smack dab in the middle of Washington State, w/ only one real claim to fame—JSU.)

My mother, who died before the invasion, was Mary O'Halloran, born in 1958 & a fourth-grade school teacher for most of her life. She was the only child of Michael & Annie O'Halloran, who emigrated to the U.S. from Ireland in 1950 & settled here in JC. My grandfather worked at the lumber mill & died in an explosion there before I was born. Annie died when I was a child.

My father, who was Russian & whose name was Bear (hence my patronymic last name), was born in Vladivostok not long before World War II began. Even though he was married to an American, he had trouble obtaining U.S. citizenship (this was back in the old days, when every politician distrusted Russians & railed against the "communist threat"), & he had returned to Vladivostok in search of documents to support his citizenship application when he died of a heart attack. I was four at the time of his death.

Our house was the light blue one w/ white trim on Maple Street. It's gone now, of course, burned down by the pacz, but perhaps someone will remember it. It was the one w/ the enormous apricot tree in the front yard. My mother used to give away baskets of fruit to anyone who stopped by.

I attended JC High, graduated a year early thanks to AP courses, then took on-line courses (while caring for my mother, who was in the final stages of ovarian cancer) for my Bachelor's degree in Literature, which I completed in three years.

I had intended to continue my studies immediately after obtaining my BA degree, which I received a few months after my mother died, & was accepted into the Lit graduate program at JSU. However, Professor Gulick contacted me during the summer before my grad studies were to begin. He had a Fulbright to teach & conduct research in Australia for the coming year, & he needed an assistant.

I could go into great detail about the consequences, almost all negative, of my acceptance of that assistantship. I won't. In a world as messed up as ours is at the moment, the devious ploys I was subjected to by the professor & his wife are, as my Grandmother Annie would say, small potatoes.

In a nutshell: I was sexually attacked by the professor while we were in Australia; the attack resulted in a pregnancy; my daughter—Matilda—was born after I returned to the U.S.; not long after her birth, I was tricked into giving up custody of her to the Gulicks; they allowed me to babysit my daughter occasionally in exchange for my silence about these events (a silence I no longer need to keep); &, as a sort of compensation for my loss, the professor pressured the Head Librarian into giving me a job in the RAW.

The important thing is that Matilda came into this world. I am comforted by knowing that, when the invasion began, she had a chance—maybe a good chance—of escaping. She wasn't w/ the group of children from the campus pre-school, those beautiful little children who died on Day Three, so she must have been at the professor's house that day. I can only hope he, his wife, & Matilda were able to reach his underground shelter near the lake before the pacz burned their house.

I have survived the invasion so far by telling myself that Matilda, the one person I love, is dead. I had to do that so I wouldn't think of her still facing the awful agony of death by pac touch. Now that I am leaving the library, now that I have come to the end of this stage of my life, I hope she is alive. In fact, I absolutely must believe she is alive. That is the only way I will survive the next stage.

I say this to Matilda: I love you. I have always loved you. I will always love you. You were a perfect baby, the sweetest toddler, & now the most amazing little girl. I remember your smile. I remember your laugh. Your eyes are so bright. You are the most beautiful thing I have ever seen.

I will try to find you. I will search for you for as long as I am able. Please understand that there is nowhere I would rather be than w/ you.

My hand is on my heart right now, my heart is beating fast, & every beat it makes is sending my love to you.

Remember me.

Afterword

by Pearl Larken
Editor, "We Survive" Series

Thirty-six years after Kaylee Bearovna wrote her last journal entry, locked the doors of the JSU special collections library, and walked into the winter night with an invader she called Tall Man, ten members of the Northwest Expeditionary Team (NWET), Unit 22, entered the area searching for survivors.

They had covered a great deal of territory during their deployment, all in areas remote from those that had been major or secondary population centers before the invasion. Their mission was four-fold: Distribute food and supplies, map locations of inhabitants, add information about them to the census, and begin the process of restoring the rule of law in places that had been subject to the cruelest human and invader practices for decades. For many survivors, a visit from Unit 22 brought not only life-giving supplies but also a ray of hope, the first indication that the world was on the path to recovery. In some cases, members of the unit were the only people a survivor had seen since the invasion began.

Each deployment is a major challenge for people who volunteer to serve with expeditionary teams, but this tour had been especially hard for the U-22s. Some members of the group had been killed by survivors who did not understand the peaceful nature of the mission. Some had been killed by survivors who preyed on others, knew they would be held accountable for their cruelty if law and order were restored, and tried to quell that restoration by killing the harbingers of justice. About one

167

quarter of the group had contracted a strange new illness that made it necessary for them to evacuate to the closest mobile health clinic, which was almost one hundred miles away. Several of the unit's pack mules had lost their footing on a narrow trail high in the Cascade Range and had tumbled into a deep and inaccessible ravine, taking a significant amount of the unit's food and other supplies with them. The area around the old town of Jefferson City and the JSU campus was the last place the unit was scheduled to survey on their deployment, and the ten remaining members of the group were anxious to finish their task and go home.

Ishi Kenai was the senior member of the U-22s when they entered the area and, thus, the de facto leader. He had been shot earlier in the deployment while rescuing several ambushed unit members, including the unit's original leader, and his wounds caused him excruciating pain. He should have evacuated with the others, but he refused to leave until the mission was finished.

When Ishi stood on a hill above JSU and scanned the campus and burned town, he saw a place similar to many he had surveyed while volunteering with the NWET. He thought he knew exactly what his unit would find. There would be human skeletons, many of them gnawed by animals, and too many of them gnawed by cannibals. There would be signs that roving bands of survivors and invaders had used burned-out basements and other structures for shelter over the years. There might be a few textbooks or other usable items on campus, depending on how long the initial invasion force had stayed there. Ishi would have bet a week's rations that a thorough search of the town, campus, and five-mile radius around them would reveal minimal post-invasion use and no survivors. He would have lost that bet.

Finding Kaylee's journal, dusty but otherwise in good condition, changed Ishi Kenai's life. He was impressed by her honesty, tenacity, and ability to negotiate what she called an "inter-species détente," a difficult process that has stumped many experts, both human and invader, over the decades since I-Day, that dark day when the invasion began. He was most deeply moved by the identification note Kaylee added at the end of her journal. It was a powerful plea for someone to take the time to help her connect, if only through memories, with anyone who knew her. Ishi felt she was speaking to him.

He understood her longing for connection. He had given food, supplies, and basic medical care to thousands of people during his twenty-five years of volunteer work with the NWET, but the first request most people made was not for those things. Even when people were starving and in need of care, their first request was for news about loved ones. "Have you seen…?" "Did you ever run into…?" "Has anyone heard anything about…?" Ishi dreaded those questions because, almost invariably, he had no answers. From his own observations, and from the limited information that ham radio operators provided about other regions around the globe, he knew that our world was deeply fractured by the invasion, and it felt as if most of the population had fallen into fissures and disappeared.

Ishi retired after that tour of duty. While recovering from his wounds, he amassed the trade goods, supplies, and support crew necessary to search for Kaylee and for those who knew her. He returned to the JSU area three years later to begin his quest, and he spent about seven years searching before he felt his quest was finished. He had heard about our little book group, here on the coast of what used to be called Washington, and he shared with me Kaylee's journal and the information he had gathered about her.

I was as deeply moved as Ishi was by Kaylee's account of her experiences during the early weeks of the invasion. Most of us were forced to make the transition from pre-invasion world to new world within a matter of seconds on I-Day. The moment we saw invaders heading our way we gave up our relatively safe, orderly, and peaceful lives and began new lives as desperate, calculating, brutally realistic survivors. There was no time to process the change, to think about the consequences and ethics of our actions, or to consider what kind of people we wanted to be in the frightening post-invasion world.

After reading the first few entries in Kaylee's journal, I asked myself: Were any of us ever that innocent? I wanted to believe we were not. I wanted to believe humans had not changed much due to the invasion. I told myself Kaylee was not like most people at that time. However, as I read on, her words reminded me of who I had been before the invasion. Reading about her transition from the old world to the new brought back memories of how I felt during my own much faster transition. By the end of her journal, I had to admit that most of the people I knew before I-Day were indeed decent, caring, and, by today's standards, innocent. I felt conflicting emotions: despair at how much we have changed for the worse, and gratitude because we have Kaylee's journal to remind us of what we could be again.

I was moved, too, by Ishi Kenai's dedication to finding Kaylee and anyone who might have known her. I am sure there were many times over the years when his quest seemed quixotic, both to himself and to those around him. I know he continues to struggle with feelings of guilt about the people who died while helping him on his quest. And yet, I am thrilled by what he discovered: An intact trove of "rare and wonderful" books, a journal written by the brave young woman who protected them, and a story that reaffirms the power, and the necessity, of interpersonal connections.

Our book group was looking for the perfect manuscript to publish in commemoration of the fiftieth anniversary of I-Day. This was it.

Afterword

Book publication has presented challenges throughout history, and publishing what might be the first post-invasion book in the world almost killed a few of us (but that is another story). We are a small band of book lovers, only a few with any pre-invasion experience in editing and publishing. Our main activities have been salvaging books, caring for them, reading and discussing them, and sharing them with others. Some of us are elderly; some of us are blind. Taking on the task of publishing a book was ambitious, perhaps overly so in hindsight, but everyone in our group agreed it must be done.

Our location in an area that has many of the resources necessary for book publication made the project seem feasible. One of the large summer homes in our village was owned by a couple who, before the invasion, created letterpress poetry chapbooks when they vacationed here. I knew the place well because my mother was the couple's housekeeper. The basement was filled with antique printing equipment, and several pieces were still functioning before the invasion, including a large Chandler and Price press, a small Kelsey press, and an etching press. There was some old bindery equipment, too. The couple had not been seen since the invasion, and I still had the key my mother used to let herself into their house. Our group decided that the couple would want the equipment to be cared for and used rather than to rust away.

A printing press is of little use without paper, and blank paper has been a rarity for decades. Many people born after the invader die-off have never seen a piece. Once again, our location proved to be ideal. A storm blew down a shorepine about ten miles up the coast from our village the winter before we heard about Kaylee's journal. The tree fell next to a storage shed that hadn't been ransacked after the invasion, most likely because it was overgrown by blackberry bushes. Branches on the falling tree ripped aside the vines, exposing the building. As it happened, one of the sailboats that carries trade goods up and down the coast had taken shelter from the storm in a cove near the shed. When the storm blew over, the crew spotted the building and hauled away the contents. Our village was the next stop on the trade route, so we had first crack at the goods: thirty-seven cartons of high-quality paper, all in perfect condition. We weren't sure what we would do with it at the time, and I had to trade my brother's beloved Redden-style catboat for it (he made the small sailboat by hand before the invasion, and it became mine after he was taken by human traffickers), but the paper was too good to pass up.

Even though we had the necessary equipment and paper, turning Kaylee's journal pages into an easily readable and reproducible book was difficult due to three key factors: She wrote entries (1) in cursive, (2) on previously printed pages, and (3) with a permanent marker, the ink of which soaked through pages. Those three factors give her journal its unique appearance, a look we hoped to maintain for the book, but they presented major challenges, too.

Factor 1: Cursive font. Initially, the group decided to use a cursive font similar to Kaylee's handwriting for pages in the book written by her. This was one of only two unanimous decisions during the publication process (the other was to skip a preface, and anyone who has read the journal will understand why that decision was unanimous). We realized the cursive font might make the book less accessible to those who learned to read after the invasion, due to the bare-bones curriculum of the few schools that exist, but we thought it would provide an important reminder that a real person, someone like us, had managed to survive these experiences.

Included with the old printing equipment were containers that held many types of fonts, including some cursive styles. However, only one of the cursive styles had enough letters to create a full page of text, and that style wasn't easy to read. In the end, we used a simple print font for most of the book, relying on cursive fonts only for titles or headings and for words that Kaylee underlined in her journal.

Factor 2: Previously printed pages. We assumed, at the beginning of the publication process, that we would print the book on blank paper because that is how books have always been printed. Also, that would make entries easier to read: Kaylee's journal requires time, effort, and sharp eyes to decipher because entries are superimposed on previously printed pages; when her hand-written words blend with printed words, they tend to morph into something quite different.

Then Ishi Kenai met with our group to share what he had learned from close readings of Kaylee's journal. He pointed out many passages to support his theory that Kaylee had chosen with great care the printed pages on which to record specific entries, selecting those that contained words or ideas that added layers of meaning to her writing. Ishi argued that the journal tells a compelling story and the story becomes fuller and richer when entries are considered in conjunction with pages on which they appear.

After this discussion, the group became excited about the possibility of printing Kaylee's journal on copies of the same pages she had used. We were sure the opacity of the background pages could be reduced enough to make her words stand out clearly while still allowing people who had the time and the inclination to read the original text.

The sticking point, of course, was finding copies of the books from which Kaylee had ripped pages so we could use the unaltered text in them as a starting point. One member of our group had a copy of Walt Whitman's *Leaves of Grass*, but, after an extensive search, we tracked down only three of the remaining books in this region of the continent. (Anyone who doubts the importance of what Kaylee did to protect the books in the JSU library should read the previous sentence again: some books in her library might not have been rare and wonderful at the time, but they are now.) None of the caretakers for those three books had access to copying equipment, none had the time to transcribe the original text, and none would agree to send their books to us, via expeditionary units, on what was sure to be a perilous journey. In all honesty, I would have made the same decision.

Enter the microscope. A volunteer with NWET, Unit 18, found it in the science room of a ransacked high school and, when she heard about our book project, passed it along to us. The plan was to put every inch of every page in Kaylee's journal under the lens so the printed words beneath her entries could be read. Then we planned to recreate the original text based on what we found. We tested the accuracy of this process by using a page she had ripped from *Leaves of Grass*, the text on which she recorded her annotated bibliography. After weeks of painstaking work, the text we created by scanning that page of Kaylee's journal under the microscope was compared with the same page from our copy of *Leaves of Grass*. On one hand, the results were encouraging: our accuracy rate was over 96%. On the other hand, a quick calculation of the time needed to recreate every original printed page in Kaylee's journal was discouraging: if we did that, many members of our group would be dead by the time this book was published.

Once again, lofty ideas were squelched by the realities of the post-invasion world. Our group decided we could not afford the time it would take to recreate the printed pages. We have included in the appendices Kaylee's bibliography of the books from which she tore pages. The brief annotations add to her story and are a must-read, even for those who usually skip such sections. It is our hope that a brave bibliophile will, in the not too distant future, spend a few years at the JSU library (where Kaylee's journal and the microscope are now housed) scanning and recreating all of the pages on which Kaylee wrote her journal so that the added layers of meaning in her entries can be made known to those who are fascinated by her story.

Factor 3: Marker ink. The writing implement Kaylee used to record her journal entries contained ink that soaked through paper. For this reason, she wrote on only one side of the pages she tore from books. She was bothered by this: she mentions feeling guilty about not being able to take full advantage of those ripped pages by using both sides. Also, for someone who was inclined to be a perfectionist, as Kaylee was, those messy, ink-blotched backs of pages would be a source of constant irritation.

Near the end of her time in the library, Kaylee decided to rip out drawings from her own book of black and white art by Walter Crane and tape those drawings to the back of entries as illustrations (she taped journal pages back to back, too, to make the journal neater and easier to handle). Ishi believes Kaylee chose drawings for specific entries or time periods during her captivity, either to deepen the meaning of her words or to make the reader laugh through quirky juxtapositions of text and image. We have included the drawings and, whenever possible, kept them following the same pages Kaylee chose. The black and white Crane artwork Kaylee did not include in her journal was given to us by Ishi to use as illustrations in the appendices. The bibliography section in this book includes drawings by someone else, but the artist and the reason for including those drawings will be obvious to readers when they reach that point.

In addition to those three key factors, there were other challenges during the publishing process: injuries; close calls with death; four years of tedious work, day after day; questions about the ethics of devoting so much time and effort to this project when we could be using that time and effort to help people in need. At least every other day we asked ourselves the big question—

Why are we doing this?

When I wonder why, I walk through the building that holds the books our group has gathered over the years. Some were gifts from NWET volunteers, who find books while deployed on survey missions. Some came from people who found the books wedged between walls for insulation. I remember years when we received dozens of books. Those years are gone. As time goes on, and as more books are destroyed by the elements and by people who use them for purposes other than reading, the flow of books has slowed to a trickle.

Our group decided that, no matter what the risks, it was time for a new book to be published. Time to add a book to the few libraries that survived the invasion. Time to provide NWET units with a book they can make available to communities. Time to create a book that speaks to people living in the post-invasion world.

This book is the first in a series focused on people who survived the invasion, especially those who are working to rebuild the world, the people who believe the future will be better than today. Kaylee believed the future would be better: her journal is a testament to the power of that belief in the face of what seemed like total annihilation. Ishi believes that: no one spends years searching for a person and connecting that person with friends and loved ones if they do not believe in a better future. Our small band of book lovers believe the future will be better, too. This book, this labor of love, is the substance of our belief.

Appendix One: Where Were You When…?

by Ishi Kenai
Unit 22, Northwest Expeditionary Team (retired)

My dad always said he didn't like crybabies. The man was solid military, right down to the shrapnel in his bones: short hair, staccato voice, straight back, and that look in his eyes, as if he knew trouble was out there somewhere and it was his job to watch for it. He fought in Afghanistan and Iraq, had half a leg blown off by an IED, and never complained about the pain of his prosthetic, the medical care he was promised but did not receive, or the low-wage job he ended up with due to the injury. He ran our house like boot camp because he wanted us to be prepared to follow in his footsteps. Or, as my oldest brother used to say when my father wasn't within earshot, his "footstep."

I was six years old on I-Day. My dad's work shift was over at 3:00 p.m., and it was pay day, so the family went Christmas shopping. He gave each of us kids twenty dollars to add to the allowance money we had been saving. We felt rich, excited, and happy. The three older kids didn't want to visit the store's Santa Claus, so my mother went with them to pick out gifts. I thought they were crazy to pass up such a great opportunity. My dad took me to the North Pole, at the back of the store, where Santa was talking to kids and giving them treats and trinkets from a huge box.

The line was long and, right before we reached the front, Santa went on a break. When I saw him disappear into the stock room, I lost it. I began crying so loud that everybody looked at us. My dad was upset. "Are you a crybaby, Ishi? Are you, Son?

Because you know I don't like crybabies." He turned around to tell people I was okay, and he saw something my tear-filled eyes could not. Then I was sailing through the air like a paper airplane. I landed in Santa's box and heard my dad shout, "Close the lid." I did.

I remember thinking everybody was sad about Santa leaving because they were crying, screaming, and making an awful sound I had no word for at six years old. I wanted to eat one of the candy canes in the box, but I didn't. That would be stealing. There was a stuffed bear in there and, after the horrible sounds went on for a long, long time, I decided it would not be stealing to hug the bear.

When the store was quiet again, my father opened the lid. He was covered with gooey stuff that smelled bad, and he was in a big hurry. He grabbed me, pulled the hood of my coat over my face, and ran out of the store. I reminded him that we should wait for Mom and the other kids, but he kept running. Later, when we were hiding in a dumpster behind a bakery, I saw my father cry for the first and only time.

I tell my story now, as I have many times before, because this is how people who survived I-Day begin conversations when they first meet. This is how we reassure each other that, no matter what differences there might be between us, we have shared a defining moment in our lives and, because of that, are connected.

My father said each generation has a "Where were you when" story. For his grandparents, it was the bombing of Pearl Harbor during World War II. For his parents, it was the assassination of President Kennedy. His generation shared stories about the attack on the Twin Towers. My generation shares stories about I-Day.

It was many years after I-Day before my father shared with me in its entirety his story about that day. He told me details about trying, and failing, to rescue the rest of our family, and about watching children die who had been standing in line with me. He explained how weak and helpless he felt because he could not save our family, how guilty he felt because he had to leave behind other children in his effort to save us, and how ashamed he was of crying in front of me.

I cried when I found Kaylee Bearovna's journal. It was wrapped and tied like a Christmas present. After months of witnessing illness, starvation, death, depravity, and destruction with my unit, I had finally found something whole, something humorous and heartfelt, something that reminded me of life before the invasion: the love my father and mother had for each other and for their children; the kindness our neighbors had shown my family when my father was deployed with the military; the joy I had felt as a child in simply being alive. I sat at Kaylee's writing desk and cried as I read her journal.

A member of my unit entered the library while I was reading the journal and was shocked to see me crying. I was going to blame it on the medication for my injuries, but I didn't. I told her this was the first time since I-Day that I had cried. I told her I was crying for everything we had lost because of the invasion, for the horrors I had seen during twenty-five years as a U-22, and for the times I had felt as weak, helpless, and guilty as my father. I told her I had lied about my age so I could volunteer for an expeditionary team at sixteen years old, back when units were just beginning to form after the invader die-off. I told her my story, she told me hers, and we cried together. I felt reborn.

The special collections library was the only building on campus that was locked and intact when my unit reached JSU. Solid doors, high windows, and a lack of food and supplies (obvious to anyone looking through the windows) probably discouraged roving bands of humans and invaders from trying to break in. Buildings that haven't been burned, ransacked, or destroyed by the weather are extremely rare. I wanted to do everything I could to preserve this one, if only to honor Kaylee. Our unit's lock picker opened the library doors without harming them, which allowed us to lock the doors again when we left.

I took Kaylee's journal and blood samples with me when our unit trudged back home. I read the entries many times during the months I spent in the Vancouver Island NWET hospital having multiple surgeries to fix the damage caused by my wounds. I retired from the NWET on the day I was released from the hospital, and I devoted myself to developing a plan to find Kaylee, or information about her, and to share what I found with people she knew. A doctor I met while in hospital had access to a relatively intact lab capable of doing DNA testing, and he agreed to test the three blood samples Kaylee left behind.

I took the blood sample results and a pile of notes with me when, three years after finding the journal, I began my search for its author. I was fortunate that Klaratee of Arcadia, a good friend and an excellent qualitative field researcher, agreed to come along with me to conduct interviews. Four retired U-22s provided security for us and cared for our horses and other pack animals. Thanks to the many donations we had received, we were well stocked with food and supplies, both for us and for those we hoped to meet.

The U-22 survey of a five-mile radius around JSU had found no survivors, but our unit was understaffed and rushed at the time. Our new group had more information and a different focus. Kaylee had planned to head south, toward the lake, then east into hills above the lake. Instead of searching in concentric circles, we broke into two search parties, one to do a three-mile-wide sweep from the library southward, the other to do a three-mile-wide sweep from the lake edge up into the hills.

Ishi Kenai

Any sign of Kaylee would be welcome, but finding the underground home was our main goal. We knew that wouldn't be easy. If someone living in an underground shelter does not want to be found, it is very difficult to find them. If they leave no sign of activity around the outside of the place, the only clue that might give them away is an air vent.

So much death and destruction. So much ground to cover. The words "tedious" and "depressing" come to mind often when I am conducting a search of this type. Looking for bright spots becomes a necessity: a locket with pictures someone might recognize; a teacup in good condition; a packet of waterproof matches (finding these is more exciting than finding gold); a pocket knife without too much rust; an unbroken mirror. Our group met in the library twice each week to compare the information we gathered and the objects we found. Items we couldn't use and those with potential sentimental value were stored in one of the few rooms on campus that still had a door with a working latch. We gained a pair of binoculars in good condition early in the search through this process, and the binocs came in handy later.

I have never overcome my unease about using items that once belonged to someone else. Even though I know the person is dead, I still feel like a thief. This was an ethical issue that sparked heated debates when expeditionary teams were beginning to form, here and elsewhere, and volunteers were trying to decide what to do with found objects. I remember long discussions about it in our unit, discussions that were hard to sit through for a kid of sixteen who just wanted to get going, have an adventure, save the world, and skip all the chitchat. Some members of the U-22s thought items should be left in situ for survivors who might come back in search of their past. They argued that taking items was like robbing a grave and that places destroyed by the invasion should become historical monuments. Some members argued that meeting the desperate needs of the living was more important than making monuments to the dead.

Other groups like ours were grappling with the same issue, a fact we discovered in a roundabout way. As far as we can tell, our group was one of the first to form on this continent, but it was based on groups that had formed elsewhere. The earliest might have been a handful of survivors in Namibia: they emerged from hiding when it was clear that most of the invaders had died, and they decided to give thanks for their survival by dedicating themselves to finding and helping others. A ham radio operator from that area of Africa, also responding to the increased safety that the die-off provided, began reaching out to other radio operators around the world, sharing stories of the group's experiences. From the news that radio operators passed along about far-flung groups, we gained ideas about preparing for and carrying out successful expeditions, meeting the needs of survivors, dealing with resistance, and other important information, including how to handle ethical issues.

Results from the early expeditions that we heard about indicated around three percent of the world's population survived I-Day and the ten-year period that followed. Most survivors lived in areas with heavy snowfall or rainfall for much of the year, for those were the areas that invaders tended to avoid. In temperate zones, which had some of the largest populations before the invasion, groups were discovering that less than one percent of the population had survived. This was worse than anyone had expected. Based on these estimates, most groups that eventually became expeditionary teams, including our unit, decided that the needs of the living were so great, and the hardships they continued to suffer so extreme, that members should distribute useable items to survivors but leave items of sentimental value either where they were found or in a protected area nearby.

The binoculars we found early in our search for the safe place were of no use on our first sweep from the lake edge up into the hills. It was April, but an unusually late and heavy spring snow storm happened to cover up all signs of activity on that day, and we came close to but never saw the safe place Kaylee mentioned. But in mid-July someone spotted a slight movement on a hillside. The binocs confirmed that it was a person moving around.

We did not try to make contact immediately: too many members of my unit had been injured or killed by frightened or opportunistic survivors. We watched the location for a few days to determine how many people were there. When we were fairly certain only one person was there and his main activity was gardening, we decided to make contact. Our interview with him is included elsewhere in this book.

Slowly and cautiously: That is how the search went for seven years. We spent months searching an area for signs of Kaylee or someone who might have known her. We found objects, kept some of them, stored others, and gave most of them to people with whom we made contact. Usually, the survivors we met had no information that would help us with our search. We gave them food and supplies anyway. When we received a tidbit of information, no matter how small, we followed up, which meant moving our operation to a new area and starting over. Due to harsh winter conditions in the areas where we were searching, we could spend only about six months of the year on our quest. During the months when I was home, I sought donations of trade goods, food, and supplies, and I tried to convince people to volunteer for the next season of the search.

We didn't find everything we had hoped for during our search for Kaylee and those she had known, but we found enough to feel that we had honored Kaylee's request.

In the years since I handed Kaylee's journal and my research results to the book group that will publish them, I have continued to search for survivors. I do this as a member of a private organization focused on helping people connect with one another. The ten members of the organization interview survivors to find out more than the cursory information gathered by NWET units, then we use any solid leads they provide to connect them with neighbors, friends, classmates, loved ones, or others who might have known them. I took blood samples from anyone who would allow it while searching for Kaylee, and I had the doctor analyze the samples. We have continued the practice of taking blood samples with the new organization. In these few years, we have helped nineteen people find an acquaintance or loved one. Nineteen doesn't sound like many, I admit. That was the number of children in my kindergarten class before the invasion, and the class was just one of at least twenty-five in our school. However, I view the work we have done so far as one small step in a journey that will take the rest of our lives, and as the amount of information grows so does the possibility that we will help a person find someone they know.

Some people are reluctant to provide information about themselves, or to provide a blood sample, because they believe anyone out there who knew them pre-invasion will not want to see them again. Perhaps they quarreled with that person. Perhaps a word was spoken at the wrong time or in the wrong way. A child became a gang member and left home, a parent was too busy to provide emotional support, a wife cheated on her husband, a husband drank too much and did things he has regretted for over forty years. The list of reasons to fear that someone from the past will not want to reconnect goes on and on.

In every case in which we have been able to find a connection, the person we contact wants very badly to see the person we interviewed. Old wounds, slights, infidelities, feuds, and personal short-comings from the past mean nothing now. What people want most is to find someone who remembers them so they will no longer feel completely alone in the world.

Every generation experiences a major event, something they share with each other through "where were you when" stories. In the past, those events have involved death.

The goal of my work is to change that. I want stories the next generation tells to be about life. My hope is that the next generation will share stories about where they were when they first realized our world was going to be okay again.

Appendix Two: I Remember Kaylee

Benji Edelstein

Interviewer's Note (Klaratee of Arcadia)

When Ishi Kenai and I first saw the safe place Kaylee Bearovna mentions in her journal, an older man was working in the garden. As soon as he noticed us, he hid in his underground shelter and refused to come out. We spent over a week camped near the shelter before we saw him again.

Ishi spoke to the man through the door several times a day. Ishi told him he had found Kaylee's journal, wanted to know more about her, and was willing to exchange food for information. He talked about how he had survived the invasion as a child, and what he had seen during his many years serving with the NWET. He told the man what had happened, in this country and in the rest of the world, in the years since the invaders had mostly disappeared. One day, when Ishi was discussing the topic of the invader die-off, the door opened and the man said, "They're gone?"

The man was Benji Edelstein, who had been Kaylee's co-worker at the library. He was fearful and furtive, behaviors typical of humans who survived the first decade of the invasion, when invaders tended to kill any human they found and always seemed to have the upper hand. He had the pained expression common among humans who remember the pre-invasion world.

Benji Edelstein

Immediately after Benji stepped out of his shelter to talk to us, Ishi tried to hand him a box of food. We have learned that there is a correlation between the speed at which food is offered to a potential respondent and the amount of information they provide. It became clear to us during that interaction that Benji was blind. Ishi asked how he knew we were approaching the place on the day we arrived if he couldn't see us. Benji said, "Nose and ears."

Benji told us little during that exchange, but he was grateful for the food, and he promised to talk more "some day." Ishi did not give up. Each day, he spoke with Benji through the door, telling him how important Kaylee, the library, and the journal were to those who survived the invasion and to those who were born later and needed to understand what had happened. We could hear Benji mumbling inside his shelter, as if arguing with himself. After several more days, Benji began to question us. He wanted to know why so many of the invaders had gotten sick and died. He wanted to know if there were any of them still around. Most people I interviewed while serving as Ishi's assistant wanted to know about other humans: Benji was focused on invaders.

One day, he asked to feel our faces and hands. We knew why he asked to do it, and we couldn't refuse. His fingers moved slowly and carefully over Ishi's forehead, nose, chin, and hands. Then he nodded and turned to me.

It is an odd sensation when the blind feel your face. It tickles, and it feels incredibly intimate. I have had that experience many times during my research due to the high incidence of blindness among human survivors. Humans gave invaders some diseases, and invaders returned the favor. My chin, nose, and forehead, which I inherited from my father, a human, passed Benji's inspection. However, as soon as he touched my hands, which I inherited from my mother, who was an invader, he dropped them and returned to the bunker, shouting "six pac" over his shoulder.

Ishi and I heard him mumbling that night. We were awake, too, trying to decide what to do next. Our hope was that Benji would agree to talk with us about Kaylee even though he might be uncomfortable interacting with me. If not, we would be forced to start our search over from square one. Ishi and I experience this type of reaction often during our research, and we understand why people react this way, but it is frustrating.

When Benji opened his door the next morning, we realized we were mistaken about the reason for his response. Benji explains that reason, and more, in the following, which I compiled from seven interview sessions.

Benji Edelstein

I remember Kaylee. Kaylee Bearovna. We worked together at the RAW. She was my best friend. I was her only friend, I think. Not because there was anything wrong with her. She was great—funny, sweet, sincere. She had a beautiful voice, too. She just never had time for friends, not in a hang out and goof off kind of way. She took care of her mom all through high school and during most of her undergrad studies. Then she took a mega load of grad classes, worked in the RAW, had a part-time job at the YWCA to pay for her room there, watched Matilda, volunteered at the pre-school. After a lot of effort on my part, I was able to convince her to join the campus choir so we could spend some time together outside of work and because she liked music as much as I do.

She was way too busy all the time. It was like a big hand was shoving her so fast she couldn't catch her breath. Like she had to do everything Right Now. Like she knew she wouldn't be able to fit everything she wanted into her life.

She was kind of lost, too. And hurt really bad emotionally. Who wouldn't be? Professor Gulick treated her awful. Used her. Dumped her. Like he did to me. Well, not quite like with me. He didn't steal anything from me. Except my dignity.

I knew when Professor G came into the library to have a little one-on-one with Head Lib that another of his "special friends" was going to start working at the RAW. Most of his love interests were slutty and ditzy. I hope there's nobody alive who takes offense, but that's how I saw it. They'd never been in a special collections library, or, for some of them, any library. Some of them didn't seem to read much. Or at all.

Kaylee was sharp. Way sharper than me. And she looked about twelve years old: short, slender, cute. Like a little pixie. I was hoping she was underage so I could get Prof G busted for what he did to her. She could have had his butt thrown in jail so fast. I know why she didn't do that. I mean, I don't like it, but I understand. He played his games with me, too, and I didn't call him on it. Nobody messed with a Gulick in our town.

Kaylee and I had a lot of fun working together. I used to wake up happy on days when I was going to work with her at the library. It wasn't like she was a comedian or anything. She didn't go around telling jokes. We just had a good time. Quietly, of course, since it was a library and Head Lib was a real fascist about sound. We called her the soundanista. Wow, I haven't thought about that word in, like, forty years. Still funny.

Kaylee could make me laugh with just a look. I was up on a ladder one day shelving books, and she gave me a look, and I laughed so hard I farted. Not a silent-but-deadly one, either. It was so loud! And I did it right over the head of one of the old professors who came in every day to do research on some musty-dusty subject or other. It wasn't silent, but it was deadly. Bean burritos for lunch, lots of hot sauce. Smelled like a dead rat, but everybody in the RAW went about their business pretending that nothing had happened. I thought Kaylee was going to pee her pants she laughed so hard. I don't know how she did it, but she could laugh without making a sound.

Maybe she could do that because she'd spent a lot of her life being quiet. I don't know if she mentioned this in her journal, but her mom was sick for a long time. Years, really. I guess Kaylee got used to being quiet so she didn't wake up her mom.

It was really hard to get Kaylee to talk about anything that had to do with her life. I'd get little bits and pieces now and then. That's about it. I had to work hard to get to know her, but it was worth it.

She would never have opened up about what happened with Prof G, about Matilda, and all that. She'd made some kind of deal with him so she could spend time with Matilda, and she kept her lips sealed. But I knew what happened, and I finally told her I knew. After that, she must have figured it was okay for us to talk about it, but she swore me to secrecy.

She didn't know how Professor G had treated me. I sort of told her, but I made it sound like I was talking about somebody else. Which I could have been. I'm sure there were lots of Prof G conquests running around campus. Male and female. I knew some, and I tried to fill Kaylee in so she wouldn't feel like she was the only one.

The weird thing is that I had a huge crush on Professor G for the longest time. I would have been happy if he had decided to, you know, woo me. I wasn't cheap and easy, but I was already halfway there. He didn't have to drug me and take me like he did. It was all about power. Being in control. Taking what he wanted.

Weird, isn't it? I'm getting agitated thinking about it. Something that happened maybe forty-five years ago. Pre-invasion. Ancient history. After everything that's happened since. I've almost starved or been killed so many times. But it still hurts. It still makes me mad. People say you get over that kind of thing, but I'm here to tell you that's not true. The pain is always there.

I digress. Sorry. I know you're here to talk about Kaylee. I brought that up because some people might think she led Professor G on or something. Teased him, flirted. No way. I'm that kind of person, and it still wasn't right for him to take me in that way. But Kaylee was not that kind of person. Not for a minute. She was the kind of girl who waited for the right guy to come along. She was not into Netflix and chill [casual sexual encounters]. Not even into kissing a lot of frogs while she waited for her prince.

She was a good mom to Matilda. Really good. I liked when Kaylee picked Matilda up at the pre-school, and the weather was nice, and they'd play out on the Quad before Kaylee had to return Matilda to her owners, the Gulicks. I'd make an excuse to leave the library, then go out there with them. There were times when I wished I was straight so Kaylee and I could be more than friends. I wanted to have kids. Wanted that a lot. But I never expected it to happen. Gays could get married, but having kids took lots of money. It was a big issue for many of us. Or, as Kaylee and I used to say, the problematicality of that situation was too great. We had so much fun together....

I'd just left the RAW when the invaders came.... [To me] Will it hurt your feelings if I talk trash about invaders? [I say no.]

Okay, then. I was working at the RAW with Kaylee, but I wanted to grab some food before we went to choir practice. It was almost closing time anyway, so Kaylee said I could take off. She would close up and meet me in the auditorium later.

Nothing weird going on when I walked over to the union. I got my beloved veggie dog [a sausage-like food made from ground vegetation instead of ground animals] and was eating it on my way to the auditorium when the pacz showed up.

It was a regular day, then it was a nightmare. People screaming. People running toward me like a human stampede.

I get out of the way. I turn off the main path and take one that leads to the river. There's a bridge over the river. Kaylee couldn't use the bridge when she escaped because it was too far from the RAW. She could have been seen really easily. But for me, it was right there. People going the other way. Pacz going after people going the other way. And nobody going to the river. I take off for the bridge, cross it, and hide in the bushes in the swamp. Yeah, the place JSU public relations people liked to call a nature preserve. Let's compromise and call it wetlands.

And it is wet. Like up-to-my-ankles in freezing cold water wet. I hide there for maybe an hour. Standing on one foot while I wiggle the toes of the other so they don't freeze. Then I switch feet. I fall once when I switch feet, so my butt and pants are wet.

I can see some of what's happening over on campus. I stop looking after a while, but I hear a lot. Too much. It's like the night is angry. Or the world is angry.

I keep thinking I'll go back for Kaylee. I tell myself I should. I know I should. But I don't. I don't. I am a coward. Wouldn't have done any good anyway, but I should have tried. I know that. That's my shame. That's what I live with.

Finally, the water is so cold and the sounds are so awful that I start slogging through the swamp toward the lake. To Prof G's love cave. This place. Yeah, he brought me here. Of course he did. More than once. After my first un-consensual encounter with him, I felt like, okay, sure, he's a creep, but I might as well see how this thing plays out. Which made him feel great, I'm sure. I'm sure he thought what he did to me was not really bad because I came back for more.

That's the game abusers play. My dad hit my mom. Every time he did that, she threatened to leave. He told her he'd kill her if she left, so she stayed. What else could she do? Then my father told himself and anybody who would listen that he must not be all that bad because she was still with him. That's the way it goes, you know. It's all about power and control.

I digress. Sorry. I was a Social Psychology major at JSU, and I have never fully recovered.

Anyway, it takes me all that night and most of the next day, but through some kind of miracle I make it to the love cave in one piece. It wasn't really a miracle because pacz hate water. But it seemed like one at the time. The road around the lake is clogged with cars, with people trying to get out of town. And here comes another wave of those things in brown suits from the other side of the lake. Pacz everywhere. Death everywhere.

I come into the area the back way so I'm not on the lake road. I take one look at what's going on down there, turn around, and start scrambling up the dirt road to this place. Like a maniac. I'm sure pacz saw me before I ducked into the woods. Probably why I had trouble with them later on. But I'm not thinking about that at the time. I'm running. My feet feel like chunks of concrete, but I'm running. I reach this place, find the key under the Buddha statue around the side, let myself in. And then sit here. Wet. Cold. Happy to be where it's quiet.

I'm calming down, warming up, when I think maybe Prof G will show up. With the wife. Yuh-oh. I remember the spy hole. A sweet little retrofit the Professor never told his wife about. [To me] I'd show you, but the place is a mess inside. Anyway, the spy hole is a tube-and-mirrors thing. Like a periscope. Prof G used it to spot people coming up the road in time to hide signs of his nefarious deeds. I should know: I spent hours hiding in the pantry once when his wife showed up out of the blue during one of our sessions and he had to think of an excuse to send her to the store so he could smuggle me out while she was gone.

When you turn the spy hole just so, you can see long stretches of the lake road. I couldn't stop looking through it during the first month or so I was here. It was like watching a TV show. Cars ramming into cars. People climbing over each other to get away. Pacz touching people, then moving on. People dying in that awful way when pacz touch them. Fascinating.

Makes me sound like some kind of monster, doesn't it? Watching people die? It wasn't that, really. It was.... I guess you had to be there, back in the early days of the invasion, to understand. The absolute incomprehensibility of what I was seeing, the feeling that what I was watching wasn't really real. Those things made me feel like I wasn't a total voyeur.

So it's about the middle of the third day of the invasion, I'm wearing a pair of Prof G's silk pajamas, I'm eating a bag of organic blue corn chips with some spicy hummus dip, and I'm watching the lake road through the spy hole. And here come the Gulicks. In their Tesla. Which really stands out in a sea of local low-end vehicles.

Prof G is ramming cars off the road to get through. Running into people in his way. He and his wife are almost to the turn-off by the dirt road when a guy rams them hard and the Tesla stalls. That's it: he and Mrs. G make a run for it. Dragging their baggage. Real and emotional. But not Matilda. She is not in the car or with them, so I think she is either at the pre-school or with Kaylee. Anyway, the pacz reach the Gulicks, touch them, and they die a horrible death, just like commoners.

Funny thing is, the guy who rammed them gets in the Tesla and drives off. Poetic justice? Don't ask me. I wasn't a Lit major. But I admit it made me laugh.

This place had everything. Lots of food. Really good food, too: I ate better when I first got here than I'd ever eaten before. Plenty of heat and light thanks to a bunch of solar panels embedded in fake boulders on top of the hill, plus a room full of batteries to suck up all that sun-juice. Prof G hadn't skimped on the sound system or the music collection, either. I used it all. Hey, I was only going to be here a week or two until things got back to normal, right? The way I saw it, Prof G owed me big time. For services rendered.

I watched the Road Show (that's what I called it) for hours every day. Things got pretty murky for a while after the third day, when the invaders burned the town. After the first week, the show really slowed down.

Slowed down, but didn't stop. There was always some human or bunch of humans trying to evade the pacz by hiding in an abandoned car or in one of the cottages around the lake. Watching them was like watching a show with different stories and characters each week. Sometimes there would be a two- or three-parter, but that kind of show never lasted long.

I liked the one about a big bald slob who hid for three days under a tarp in a dinghy docked by the store. I saw him now and then peeking out from under the tarp or creeping around like a Norwegian wharf rat to make food raids on the store. He used to pick his nose and hang his rear over the side of the dinghy to take a dump. Disgusting. This sounds horrible, because I'm sure I would do those same things if it was me trying to survive out there, but I was rooting for the pacz to get him near the end. Which they did.

That story happened early on, when I was still in shock. It felt like I was stuck in a nightmare, and by that I mean actually stuck in a real nightmare. I could not wake up. Honestly, I thought I was dreaming. Nothing that was happening made sense. It didn't seem real, so it didn't matter if I was a real jerk about things.

My favorite show happened a couple weeks after I got here. It was more like a soap opera [a televised story with an established set of characters in which most conflict involves difficult interpersonal relationships and emotional struggles]. It was cold and stormy, no human sightings through the spy hole in days, when I see a white sail go up on the other side of the lake. There's a bunch of pacz on shore, and the person in the sailboat is trying to get away from them. Not that the pacz would have followed the boat because of their fear of water, but nobody knew that then.

The person sails to the middle of the lake, hauls in the sail, drops anchor. Takes a while because of the rain slicker, but I see it's a woman. I watched her for weeks. I was at the spy hole, bowl of oatmeal in hand, at first light every day. Stayed there, with minor breaks, until dark. Mostly she sat on the deck, even in the rain and snow. Always looked calm. Maybe even happy. One day she pulls anchor, cuts the rope, cradles the anchor in her arms like it's a baby, and jumps in. I cried for days. That was the moment when things got real. When I woke up and realized what was happening out there was not a dream. When I went back to being my old irritating but compassionate self.

I digress. Sorry. Anyway, pacz patrolled around this place every couple days. I didn't go outside for weeks, but I could see them through the spy hole if I angled the mirrors just right. Probably looking for me. But, other than pac patrols and a few humans now and then down on the lake road, it was just me.

Until one night in January that first year of the invasion. Super cold out, I'm guessing way below zero. Probably only seven o'clock and I'm already sound asleep because, hey, the Road Show ends at dark. Unless there's a full moon. But it was dark that night. Out of the blue, there's a knock on my door.

I wake up right away. Listen. More knocking. I'm shaking, scared. More knocking. Then that knock everybody, every human, knows: dah, dah, ta-dah dah, (pause) dah, dah. Repeat. Repeat. Repeat. Finally a voice, faint because the door is thick enough to survive a something-or-other megaton blast. Takes a while to be sure, but it's Kaylee's voice.

I let her in, we hug, and she passes out. Right by the door. I reach down to help her, and suddenly there's a pac reaching for her, too. We have a stand-off. A squat-off, I should say, because we're both bent down about half way when we see each other. Tense. He shows me his hands, which doesn't mean a thing to me because I don't know about their suits yet. I make a move for a flashlight by the door, one of those things that can fry eyeballs and crack skulls. He grabs my arm. I don't die. I do make a mental note to change my underwear later.

Kaylee came to and told me her invader friend was okay. I did not like him being there. Not one bit. But if Kaylee gave him the thumbs-up, I wasn't going to make a fuss.

Then she took off her hat. I was shocked. Her long, beautiful hair was gone, and all that was left were patches of ragged spikes. I didn't say anything about it because I didn't want her to feel worse. Also, I could tell from her face that what she really needed was food. Lots of it.

I gave her juice and cookies: gone. Can of lentil soup: gone. Bag of pretzels: gone. That girl was starving. And, as she said later, she'd been much hungrier than that before Tall Man gave her the lima beans. The guilt I felt about leaving her behind got multiplied about a million times right then and there.

Tall Man didn't eat or speak. Slept on the couch. I was nervous with him there. Very nervous. I had seen too many people die, you know? And here's one of the guys or things that did all the killing sacked out in my living room. Of course, I didn't know then that he was falling in love with Kaylee.

Kaylee slept in the little bedroom. Actually, she stayed in there with the door closed and cried all night. The minute she showed up at my door, I knew I had to tell her about the Gulicks, but I put it off as long as I could. When she asked if Matilda was asleep, I gave her more food and took a bite myself. Can't talk while you're chewing, right? She asked which bedroom the "happy couple," which is what we called Prof G and his wife, was sleeping in. I gave her more food and took a bite myself. I kept putting her off like that. Finally, she gave me one of her looks, and it was not intended to make me laugh. She stood up, stomped through this place, banged open every door, checked every room, looked under the beds. Then, without another word, she closed herself in the little bedroom and cried.

The next day was her birthday. I'd forgotten until I checked the calendar. It's a perpetual calendar, which, by the way, is a very handy item to have when the world comes to an end. Anyway, I'd bought her a present long before the invasion. A poster of Walter Crane's painting of horses galloping in from the sea. She loved that painting. She saw it when she visited New Zealand. Something to brighten up her tiny space over at the YWCA. I even bought wrapping paper and a ribbon, which I'd never done before. I wanted something special for Kaylee. I hid the present in my dorm room. It's probably still there.

Weird day. Kaylee's pac friend was gone when I got up. He wasn't gone for good, just wandering around outside. I made pancakes for breakfast; she didn't leave her room. I made soup for lunch; she was a no-show. For dinner, I whipped up a brownie mix, baked a lasagna, and lit lots of candles. I thought I might have to eat all the food myself, but I guess the smells lured Kaylee out, and she brought Tall Man back inside.

Quiet dinner. Kaylee ate like she was starving, which, of course, she was. The pac took a few bites, but that's all. I was a chow-hound, as usual. Nobody said anything until I brought out the brownies, with cream cheese frosting and chocolate chip decorations. I lit the candle and started singing the happy birthday song. Just about fell over when the pac hummed along. Kaylee had taught it to him.

They stayed here a couple weeks. We sang or hummed a lot, because that's the only way we could all communicate at once. Tall Man had a great voice. Amazing range. He could have sung bass or tenor in the choir. Maybe even soprano. He picked up tunes in no time. We even managed some nice three-part harmony on a few songs. He did laugh at me when I used my opera voice, but Kaylee said it was because he'd never heard music like that before.

Speaking of opera, you're gonna wanna see this. [Benji enters the underground shelter, then returns with a picture to show me.] This is Kaylee. Didn't I tell you she was a little cutie-pie? It's from when we were both in JSU's production of *Carmen*. I snapped it with my phone backstage during a rehearsal, so the light wasn't too good. She kept telling me I should delete it, but I didn't. I couldn't. And she was really surprised when I printed a copy for my wallet. I told her it was because I might never see her again with her hair curled, wearing jewelry, wearing a dress. I mean, Kaylee was a no-frills kind of gal. Plus, the only picture I had in my wallet before that was the one it came with when I bought it, so I needed something.

Anyway, it was not all song and dance when Kaylee and Tall Man were here. It was a rough time for each of us. Matilda wasn't here, or with the Gulicks, or at the pre-school, so Kaylee had no clue what had happened to her. Hard for me to watch my friend deal with that loss, that awful sense of not knowing. Really, it broke my heart. It was years later before I experienced the same thing first hand. It was obvious the pac, Tall Man, was between two worlds and very unsettled about it. I'm sure he'd burned his bridges with the other pacz. And he knew he was not going to be welcomed with open arms by other humans. He was in real pain.

Kaylee had to keep searching for Matilda. I knew that, but I still felt bad when she told me they were leaving. I gave them everything I could. Everything they could carry. I waved goodbye, and they took off. But I knew Kaylee wasn't mad at me for not coming back for her when the invasion started. She told me that many times. I could drop some of the guilt I'd been carrying.

And go back to my quiet non-life.

Pac patrols came and went. I almost got killed a few times by them or by humans passing through. It got to the point where I was more afraid of humans than pacz. There were some very scary people around back then. It was like a bunch of paleo types were taking things to the next logical step. I swear, when they looked at you, you could tell that all they saw was steaks and chops.

The vegetarian food ran out, then the carnivorous food. I ate stuff that grows wild. Started a garden, which got raided by everything—humans, pacz, animals, bugs. Almost starved to death three of the first seven winters. The solar panels got destroyed. I don't know if humans or invaders did it, but that sure made my life a lot darker and colder.

Yes, I thought about killing myself. Of course I did. Who didn't back then? I'd remember how peaceful that woman on the sailboat looked at the end, and I'd think maybe I could feel that way if I decided to do myself in. I'll bet everybody had those thoughts at one time or another. Those times I was close to starving and it was winter, it would have been a cinch. Go for a walk, sit down to rest, fall asleep. That's it. Easy peasy lemon squeezy.

Why didn't I? Because, like I said, I'm a coward. Seriously, I am. All that stuff about how it takes more courage to keep on living than to die is ridiculous. I never believed it for a second back then, and I don't believe it now.

Kaylee came here one more time. It was about the eighth year of the invasion. Nice day. Sunny. I'm working in the garden, and I hear singing from way far away. Old show tunes. Human songs, you know. Two voices. I run into the place to check through the spy hole, and there's two people coming up the dirt road. Looked like Kaylee, but it wasn't Tall Man with her. The other person was short, a child, probably Matilda, but I couldn't tell because of the hat.

Long story short. It was Kaylee, and it was not Matilda. Tall Man had been killed by a mob a few months before. An ugly death, from the little I could get out of Kaylee. A real torch-and-pitchfork kind of thing. She was badly injured trying to save him, and she wasn't getting any better. I still had some medical supplies here. The one good thing about Mrs. Gulick was her hypochondria. If she sneezed, she thought she was dying. Lots of medicine and other stuff in this place.

None of it helped. It must have been some kind of internal injury. Maybe a broken heart. She really loved Tall Man, even after everything he did as an invader. They'd been on the move since I saw her before, always searching for Matilda, always trying to evade the worst of the humans and pacz. A hard life, but she said it had made her happy. That's all I wanted for her.

She'd run into a guy who'd lived near the Gulicks, and he said he thought he saw Matilda riding in a bright yellow Humvee the day pacz burned the town. He said Matilda waved at him. It was total chaos that day. People who'd been hiding in basements and safe rooms scrambling to get out when the blaze headed their way. So he wasn't completely sure. But he thought the couple who owned the Humvee had a cabin fifty miles north of here. He drew Kaylee a map. She was going to check it out.

I was pretty sure she couldn't make it that far in her condition. Neither of us said that out loud, but we were both thinking it.

I also knew there was nothing I could do or say to stop her, so why argue about it? I gave her whatever I had that she'd take, which wasn't much. She gave me her son's hand. Then she kissed both of us and walked down the road singing Christmas carols. Christmas carols in the middle of the summer.

That's the last time we saw Kaylee.

I got a great gift that day. The only one that could even begin to make up for losing my best friend. It's meant everything to me to have Trekker Tim here. I see Kaylee in him, and that makes me laugh and cry at the same time. I'm going to sound like a silly old fool when I say this, but he is amazing. Brilliant, strong, big-hearted. Great voice, great sense of humor. Great gardener and hunter. I can't say enough good things about my son. It's like he ended up with the best of everything humans can be and the best of everything pacz can be. I loved his mother. I love him.

You see? I really am a silly old fool. I'll probably start drooling any minute. Funny thing is, I'm about the same age now that my grandfather was when he died. My head feels like it's going to explode when I think about that. I look in the mirror, and I have to remind myself that what I'm seeing is me. My first reaction is always who's that old fart? My grandfather never looked this old, this wrinkled and haggard, before he died, so I'm guessing sixty-five is the new ninety.

I can't explain this, but inside I'm still that guy going out for a veggie dog. So much of what's happened since then has felt like I'm putting in time until I can go back to being that guy. It's like a lot of what I've been doing is waiting. Not living. Not really. It's like I've been in a cryogenic state or something. Waiting for you guys to show up here singing that old song, "Safe at last, the danger's past," so I'll know the world is okay and I can go back to being me.

Benji Edelstein

I'm never going to be that guy going out for a veggie dog again. I mean, the Benji who I think of as the real me died that day. Gone. And it's only taken me about forty years to figure that out. Talk about a slow learner.

The Benji I am now, the one I've had to be to survive and to care for my son, that Benji is not such a bad dude. A little weird. Okay, a lot weird, and getting weirder every day. But I've gotten used to him over the years. He's a much better me than the old me ever was. And, according to my son, he's a great dad. That's all I ever really wanted to be.

Appendix Three: Singing Past the Graveyard

Trekker Tim

Interviewer's Note (Klaratee of Arcadia)

When Benji Edelstein agreed, finally, to be interviewed, he came out of his underground shelter (the "safe place" Kaylee Bearovna mentions in her journal) with another man. Ishi Kenai and I were surprised by this for two reasons: we had not realized anyone other than Benji was in the shelter, and the man was of mixed heritage. That last fact would be obvious at first glance only to those of us who have seen many offspring of human-invader unions. Most people would think the man was human: light tan skin, curly light brown hair, regular facial features, deep blue eyes. However, scars where the sixth finger on each hand had been snipped off proved he was indeed of mixed heritage.

The man was Trekker Tim, the child of Kaylee Bearovna and Tall Man. He was in his mid-thirties and had been born about three years after I-Day. He was tall and strong. During one interview, Benji stumbled over a piece of our equipment, fell, and cut his head, and Trekker Tim picked him up and carried him back to the shelter as if the older man weighed nothing. Another time, Benji persuaded him to perform their special song and dance for us. It was something called "Uptown Funk," and the dance required Trekker Tim to toss Benji into the air and catch him. He did this with no problem. It was clear from this and from other interactions between the two men that they had a good father-son relationship.

Trekker Tim was quiet, but he observed everything we did, and he remembered everything we said. After interviews, he made meals for the crew and kept us busy answering questions. He asked Ishi about places he had seen while serving with the NWET. He asked me about the ocean. Also, he was very curious about my experiences as a person of mixed heritage. He called me a "six pac," short for "six-fingered pac," but he did not use the term in a derogatory way.

He was surprised to hear that some humans and invaders were co-existing in harmony, perhaps because his family's quest to find Matilda had ended on a terrifying note with the death of his father and the injury of his mother. He wanted to know about my parents, the settlement where I grew up, the education I had received. As soon as I mentioned the word "professor," he cringed and stopped talking. As Kaylee's child, he had heard that word used many times, and never in a positive way. I explained that most professors had been good, not like the one who hurt his mother.

I compiled the following from five interviews with Trekker Tim. His speech patterns were not easy to capture. Like many people who know multiple languages but have had few opportunities to say the words out loud, he spoke haltingly during our first interview. He was speaking and translating in his head at the same time, and he was unnerved by the sound of his voice. As we talked more, both formally during interviews and informally over meals, his speech became more fluid and much easier to follow.

Trekker Tim

I am Trekker Tim, son of Kaylee Bearovna and Tall Man. I speak, read, and write Tzngwaneezahan, the language of Tall

Man, who is my [unpronounceable word], which means "father who gave me life." I speak, read, and write English, the language of my mother and of Benji, who is my [unpronounceable word], which means "father who took me in." I read and write French and Spanish, too. Benji taught me those languages from books in our house. I don't know how those languages sound, so I don't say the words out loud unless I want to make Benji laugh. I like to hear him laugh. Sometimes he laughs so hard that he farts. Then we both laugh.

[To me] You are Tzngwaneeza, what Benji calls "six pac." I see from scars on your hands that your small fingers have been cut off, like mine. You should know these words. [I explain that my mother died when I was a baby, and my father, a human, did not know her language well enough to teach it to me.]

Yes, Tall Man said he learned my mother's language much faster than she learned his, and she was a smart human. Very smart. He said the Tzngwaneeza have two ears on the outside of their heads, like humans do, but their ears work much better, so it is like they have extra ears on the inside of their heads. He said humans use their eyes the most, but his people use their ears the most. I can teach you the language of your mother, if that would make you happy. [I thank him and tell him I will consider his offer.]

My sixth fingers were cut off when I was given my name, which happens one month after Tzngwaneeza children are born. My mother told me they cut off my fingers with her scissors because she was tired of knitting six-fingered gloves. I think this was a joke. She always laughed when she said it. I think cutting me was a hard thing for my parents to do. My mother tried to keep me safe from harm, so why would she hurt me in this way? My father was proud to be Tzngwaneeza. He was who he was. Why would he make me different by doing this to me? I ask you these questions, but I know the answers. I am sure my parents thought a long time before they cut me. I am sure it was difficult for them, but they knew I would be safer if I looked like humans.

One day when I was little, I cried because my hands did not look like my father's. He said it is not our sixth fingers that makes us who we are. He said who we are is on the inside, and it shows itself in the things we do: how we treat other species and our own, how we take care of plants and animals and the world around us, how we love our family and our friends. Those things are what make us good Tzngwaneeza and good humans.

My mother was a good human. She was better than any of the other humans we met on the journey that was our life. When humans or invaders did not try to hurt us, she was kind to them. She shared food with them. We had more food than others because Tall Man was a good hunter and my mother knew which plants we could eat and which plants would make us sick. She learned that from books in her library.

She loved the library. She lived in other houses before my father came to this world, but she said she thought of the library as her real home.

She said she had three best friends before she met my father: Matilda, Benji, and books. After she met Tall Man, she had four best friends. After I was born, she had five best friends. I begged her to have another baby so she could have six best friends, but she said we can only have as many best friends as we have fingers on one hand.

I think it was very hard for my parents to have a baby, to have me, and keep walking. Walking is what we did. It was our life. That is why they named me Trekker, because we were always on a trek someplace. When I was little, my father carried me on his shoulders while we traveled. I liked that. I saw everything from high up.

It is hard to find shoes. I am sure you know this. It was very hard for us to find shoes my size when I was little. My father said I would need to start working when I was three years old, as Tzngwaneeza children do on the world where he was born. Our work was walking, and that is what I would need to do when I was three.

There were times when we would find a place with food growing around it, with a cave or building to keep us dry, and with no bad humans or others to hurt us. When we found a place like that, my mother would say, "Welcome home!" That meant we could stop walking for a while. Then my father would hunt and my mother would gather plants and berries. We would eat and eat. We dried meat and plants and berries to carry with us on our travels. My father turned the skin of animals into leather; my mother turned the leather into shoes and other things we needed.

For my third birthday, she made me my first real pair of leather shoes. They were just the right size and they were very comfortable. She used berries to color them. They were beautiful. On my birthday, I ran all around the place where we were staying to try them out. That is when I started working; that is when I started walking.

When we were traveling from place to place, we told stories, played games, and learned family history. Some days we told silly stories, and some days we told serious stories. We played games with English and Tzngwaneeza words while we walked. When we stopped to rest, my mother liked to play a game called "Statues." That game was fun, but it was hard for me when I was little because I didn't like to stand still. My father liked to play a game called [unpronounceable word], which means "Death is looking for you." In that game, we had to think about what we would do if very bad trouble suddenly appeared in front of us. Sometimes we played the game silly and made up funny things we could do, and sometimes we played the game serious and told each other real things we could do.

My father said it was important to remember who we were, so he would recite the history of his people. He knew their history for over two thousand years, so he only recited that on days when we had a long, long way to walk.

What I liked best was when we sang as we walked. Mostly we sang human and Tzngwaneeza songs, but my father knew some Ilquanoochin songs, too. He said the Ilquanoochin were beings from his old world who sang when they drank something called [unpronounceable word]. Benji says the drink might be like whiskey. I don't know. I don't drink alcohol. My mother said bad things happen when you drink alcohol. I have seen some of those bad things on our travels. I don't know what all the words mean in the Ilquanoochin songs, but my father would laugh and laugh when he sang them. Most are about peeing, I think.

We sang when we were happy. We sang more when we were sad because it made us feel better. There were many things that made us sad. You have seen some of them, as you say in your stories. We were safe from most bad things that happened because my father's ears could hear trouble coming. He would say, "Death is looking for us," and we would know by the sound of his voice that it was not a game. He would find a place for us to hide. Then my mother would say, "Let's play Statues." I would be very still. We would be safe, but many times we could see what was happening. We saw humans and invaders do many terrible things. There was screaming, blood, and death.

I always won Statues when bad things were happening. I would not move. I had learned to breathe without making any movement or sound, but sometimes I didn't breathe. When the sad things were over and it was time to go, I could not stop being a statue. My feet would not move, even when my father, mother, and I told them to.

That's when my mother would say, "Let's go singing past the graveyard!" She picked my favorite songs, the ones that made me happy. She said everyone has times when they must do something that makes them happy to get past something that makes them sad. It was hard, but I would hold my father's hand and my mother's hand and we would start walking again. We would walk past blood and death. We would start the journey again that was our life.

I know that Tall Man heard death coming on the day it was looking for him. He heard it first, then I did, then my mother did. My father found a place for us to hide, so I was not too afraid. It was a very good hiding place. I thought we would be statues for a while and then start walking again, like we always did.

There were many angry humans in the group that came looking for us. They had sharp weapons. They should have gone down the road past where we were hiding without stopping. We had left no sign we were there. Then my mother pointed to a woman in the group. She had given food to that woman a few days before. Now that woman was with the angry group. That woman must have told them where we were.

My father told me to take our packs and run, and my mother said I should run until I was far away and then I should play Statues until she and my father came for me. My father and mother went to fight the group. I couldn't see what was happening for a while because I was running up a hill. When I reached a good place to hide, I sat behind a bush so I could peek between the branches and see the group down below but they could not see me. I became a statue.

I watched my father die. They cut him into pieces with their sharp weapons. They didn't cut my mother too much. They threw her on the ground and tied her hands to a tree. They did things to her that made her cry. I was a statue all through that night and the next day while they hurt her.

They would leave my mother alone while they ate, then they would come back and do bad things to her again. At first, she cried every time the humans came to hurt her. Later on, they would hurt her but she would not cry. She wasn't dead. I knew she was alive because I could see her looking at them. It was a terrible look. It made me scared to see that look on her face.

I was a statue one more day, then the bad humans left. My mother was not moving and her eyes were closed. I climbed down the hill and untied her hands. She didn't open her eyes. I dragged her into the woods, far from the tree. This was hard because I was only about five years old. She didn't open her eyes. I covered both of us with leaves, then I fell asleep. When I woke up, my mother's eyes were open. I asked if it was time for us to go singing past the graveyard. She shook her head and went back to sleep for two more days.

We gathered my father's bones and buried them. My mother sang the mourning song of the Tzngwaneeza by his grave. She let me use her sharp scissors to cut her hair short, as women do on my father's home world when their beloved dies. Then she took my hand and we started walking again. We walked very slowly until we reached this safe place. Then she gave me a new father and left.

This is a good place. Benji is a good father. I love him very much and hope I am a good son for him. I miss my parents and pray for them every day, but I have been happy here. It felt strange at first not to be walking. It felt strange to stay in one place. I am used to it now, but it was strange for a while.

When I was about ten years old, I felt like my insides would burst if I did not go walking. I had walked for the first half of my life, and I had stayed in one place for the second half of my life, and I wanted to go back to walking again. I decided to go to the library, the RAW, so I could see the place my mother loved so much. I knew if I told Benji where I was heading he would say I couldn't go, so I told him I was going for a walk. I told him the truth, but it was also not the truth. It was not right to fool him in that way. I know that now.

I was gone for five days. When I did not come home the first night, Benji thought I might be dead. When I did not come home the next morning, he was almost sure I was dead. He was not blind yet, but he could not see very well. He went searching for me anyway. He searched for me all over these hills. Then he went down to the lake and searched all around it for me.

When I came back, he was not mad at me. He was sad. Very sad. He cried. He hugged me and cried. Every time he saw me for many days after that, he cried. He thought his son was dead. Every part of my body hurts when I think about how sad I made Benji.

I would like to see the library again, and I would like to read the books inside it. I will not do that because I do not want to make Benji sad. It was good to see the place where my parents met. It was good to be in a big building with so many windows. It was good to take a nap in the beautiful room where my mother took a nap and where my father slept after he was injured by another invader. It would not be good to go back because it would make Benji sad.

I left everything in the library the way I found it. When I took a book off the shelf to read, I put it back in the same place when I was done. I didn't read the journal my mother left on the desk because I knew I would not be able to tie the nice bow on it again. It didn't matter about not reading her journal because she had told me many stories of her time in the library. I was little, so she didn't tell me everything that happened during the invasion. She told me stories I could understand, and she said she would tell me more stories when I was older. Then my father died, my mother was hurt, and she left to find my sister. Someday I would like to read her journal. Then I will know all of her stories.

I said I left everything in the library as I found it, but I did take one thing. I found the book my mother tore apart so she could put pictures in her journal. Illustrations, I should say. What was left of the book was lying on a shelf near her desk. Most of the pictures were gone, and there were some ragged pages that must have torn when she tried to take the pictures out. I brought what was left of that book back here with me.

Benji said it was okay for me to do that. He said he thought my mother would want me to have those pictures. He let me hang the pictures on my wall. I will give those pictures to you now. Maybe you can use them in the book that will include my mother's journal and the words I say to you.

[I ask him how he was able to go inside the library.]

My mother gave me the key to the library before she left to look for my sister. See? I keep the key on a cord of braided leather made from the hide of a deer my father killed. I keep the cord around my neck so the key will be close to my heart. My mother said I should keep it with me for the rest of my life because it is the key to the library and also the key to her heart.

When I was older, Benji explained what the angry human men were doing to my mother when she was tied to the tree. He said many of the good things people do for each other, the nice things they do, can also be bad things if they are done in the wrong way. He said it is a good thing when he gives me food to eat, but if he gave me food that made me sick, or if he stuffed so much food in my mouth that it made me choke, that would be bad. He said it is a good thing when he hugs me, but if he hugged me so tight that it crushed my ribs and then he kept hugging me when he knew it caused me pain, that would be a bad thing. He gave me some other examples, too. Then he gave me a book on human anatomy and told me I could ask him anything I wanted about my body.

I hope my mother is alive. Benji says it is possible she is alive. He says Kaylee is a trooper, which means she can put up with many difficult things and keep going. I know she is strong in spirit, as my father used to say.

Sometimes I wonder why she doesn't come back to see us if she is alive. Maybe she has not found my sister and is looking for her far away. I don't think my mother would stop looking for my sister until she found her or until she died.

My mother said she never wanted to be trapped in a building again. She never wanted to spend much time inside even if she wasn't trapped. When I think of her, she is always outside. She is walking and singing. She is gathering berries or sitting on a rock watching birds while she makes shoes for us. I imagine her dancing in the rain. My father liked to be in the rain with my mother after he gave up his brown suit. They danced in the rain together. I like to be in the rain, too. When I go outside in a rain storm, Benji tells me I'm nuts, whatever that means.

I would like to see my mother again. I would like to meet my sister. If you find my mother and sister, please tell them I love them. Please let them know there are two empty places in my heart that can be filled only by them.

216

Appendix Four: Tall Man and the Big Picture

by Lakshmi Nyquist
Cultural Historian, Northwest Center for Invasion Studies

Introduction

There is an old story about six blind people who try to describe an elephant. The first person grabs the tail and says an elephant feels like a rope. The second person, who touches a leg, says it is shaped like a tree. The third, holding the trunk, says elephants must be related to snakes. The fourth, feeling the elephant's side, says the creature is built like a wall. The fifth strokes an ear and says the animal resembles a fan. The sixth person raps knuckles against a tusk and says elephants are like spears. Then the six people argue loudly, defending their own descriptions and belittling those of the others.

I ask people to consider that story when they talk about their experiences with invaders. It is common to use the term "invader" in a monolithic sense, as if all beings in brown suits who came to our planet on I-Day were the same. However, as suspected by some humans even before the invader die-off, which occurred about ten years after I-Day, and as confirmed by examinations of dead invaders, there were four distinct species inside the brown suits.

Complicating things further was the rigid three-level hierarchical social system adhered to by one of the invader species. That social system is complex and fascinating, but Tall Man was not of that species so it will not be dealt with here.

Simply put, members of that species treat humans differently, and often in opposite ways, depending on their position in the lower, middle, or upper stratum of the hierarchy.

In effect, the term "invader" refers to six very different groups of beings. These are the Ilquanoochin, Frakyllo, Tzngwaneeza (Tall Man), and the three castes of Glaz: Glazeltak, Glazelrang, and Glazelbean. Each of those groups has unique customs, norms, moral codes, views about life and death, etc., all of which affect how they respond to humans.

Driven to the brink of extinction by events of I-Day and of the following decade, when invaders not only continued to kill humans but also used fear, especially the fear that humans had developed about being touched by an invader, to scare them away from food and other critical resources, desperate humans became obsessed with observing their mysterious brown-clad enemy. They hoped that gaining and applying information about invaders would improve the odds of human survival. The strategy worked well for Kaylee Bearovna. For example, her observation that invaders did not go outside when there was precipitation allowed her to complete critical outdoor tasks in relative safely. However, the strategy worked for her only because of a specific set of factors, which will be discussed later.

In most cases, the strategy did not work. When humans applied information gathered from observations of one invader to interactions with other invaders, the most common outcome was death by invader touch ("d-bit," as it is known in the vernacular). Also, humans were killed by other humans when they passed along information about invaders that, when applied, appeared to be inaccurate. We know now that the information was correct, but it applied only to invaders of the same species or of the same hierarchical stratum within a species. Brown suits hid the distinctions between invaders, blinding us to the big picture.

Imagine the disastrous results of a blind person interacting with an elephant based on one piece of information about the animal. For too long, that was the human condition.

Given that the book in which this summary will be published might be the only source of accurate information (see caveats below) about invaders, their descendants, and mixed-species beings that many people will have access to for years, I feel it is important to address not only Tall Man but also some repercussions of the invasion that continue to affect us. I will use nomenclature and spelling recently adopted by the six members of our research center and by other research organizations with which we have contact: Human = offspring of two human parents; Survivor = a human who was alive on I-Day or was born in the ten-year period following that day; Invader = a being who came to this world from another on I-Day for the task of killing humans; Ilquanoochin, Frakyllo, Tzngwaneeza, Glazeltak, Glazelrang, and Glazelbean = names of the six groups of beings who came from another world (used when referring to a specific group or to the heritage of a specific individual); person/people = any human, invader, invader descendant, mixed-species being, or group of these.

I have used information from many sources for this summary, giving more weight to information provided by sources deemed to be more credible. Here are the source rankings I used, listed from most to least credible: (1) direct observations (i.e., experienced in person) by any member of our research center; (2) direct observations by a member of NWET—shared with us in person; (3) direct observations by anyone else (human, survivor, invader, invader descendant, mixed-species being)—shared with us in person; (4) direct observations by a member of NWET or of an expeditionary team or research organization located elsewhere in the world— shared with us via letter or radio; (5) direct observations made by anyone else anywhere in the world and corroborated by at least one other source who also observed the event— shared with us via letter or radio; (6) information about an event not observed by the person sharing the information but corroborated by at least three other sources who heard about the event at the time it happened; and (7) hearsay, by which I mean information that, for whatever reason, is not sufficiently corroborated. For the last two rankings, the method of sharing the information with us (in person, letter, radio) did not matter.

This ranking system is useful but not perfect. For example, the mother of one of our researchers shared with us (in person) information about a disturbing and significant event, but she did not witness the event herself or tell anyone else about it at the time it happened, and the only person who observed the event was her sister, who died soon after. Thus, her information could not be corroborated, and I treated it as hearsay. Another example involved members of a South-Central Expeditionary Team unit. They say they saw a community of Ilquanoochin, which is highly unlikely based on the other information I have gathered about this species. Each SCET member sent a letter describing the observation, so their information was ranked higher, and given more weight, than I believe it deserved.

Also, the fact that I ranked as more credible the information given to us in person means I have relied more heavily on sources in the northwestern region of North America, where our research center is located. This creates bias, of course, which could make the summary less applicable to other regions. However, I felt this was necessary. Even with extensive research, verifying the identity of someone who has sent a letter often is not possible. As for radio contact, we have all heard stories about those times, in the months following I-Day, when an invader or human with malicious intents took over a ham radio and sent out false information, thus leading to more death and destruction.

I hasten to add that I have great admiration for the ham radio operators around the world who risked their lives to gather and share news on I-Day and during the early months of the invasion. Without them we would not have known that government and military centers were the first targets of the invaders, that almost all personnel in those centers were killed within the first hours of the invasion, and that we should not wait for help from those sources but go into hiding immediately. Clearly, radio operators have saved many lives over the past decades. Also, my research would be limited to one region if not for the "hams" who make new parts and cobble together power sources for their radios to keep us connected today.

Research in the post-invasion world cannot be carried out as rigorously as I would like due to constraints on travel and communication. I ask you to bear in mind that evidence could reach me tomorrow that calls into question some of the information used for this paper. However, what follows is the most accurate summary possible based on the information available to me at this time.

My primary goal for this paper is to enhance the reader's understanding of, and appreciation for, Kaylee Bearovna's story by explaining the actions of Tall Man. Beyond that, I hope this paper will dispel myths about invaders, especially myths about the highly charged issue of humans mating with both invaders and the descendants of invaders. Finally, it is my sincere desire that this paper, and the book in which it is printed, will encourage people to see the big picture and work together so we will be prepared to deal with critical issues that are certain to affect all of us in the future.

Tall Man: Why he was here

Kaylee Bearovna was fortunate the invader in charge of the occupying unit in her area was Tall Man, a Tzngwaneeza. Other than an additional finger on each hand, some variations in the size and shape of internal organs, and more refined facial features, the species is quite similar to humans, both in physique and temperament. According to his son, Tall Man passed as a human a few times during their search for Kaylee's daughter, but only when he felt it was necessary for the safety of his family. Unlike many of his species, Tall Man did not cut off his small fingers, or break and flatten his nose, to look more like a human. By all accounts, he was extremely proud of his heritage.

Tzngwaneeza have an expression that translates, roughly, as "I am what I am." Humans say that apologetically or with resignation. To a Tzngwaneeza, the phrase means something very different. To be what you are is to personify the essence of the Tzngwaneeza, to manifest all that is good about your species. Tall Man was what he was. While his species is not pacifistic in nature, neither is it blood thirsty, aggressive, or confrontational. A Tzngwaneeza would never conquer a world or subjugate another species. They are intelligent, creative, strong (physically, emotionally, and spiritually), and empathetic, with a solid work ethic, amazing aural skills, and a highly developed sense of loyalty that extends to their family, community, and owners.

I repeat: Tzngwaneeza are loyal to their owners. For they, like the other invaders, were slaves. Their relationship with owners differed in some ways from that of most human slaves on this world. One Tzngwaneeza described it as more like working for a large company, one that regulates many aspects of life for you and your family, has done that for generations, and from which you cannot quit or be fired. By law, owners must treat their slaves fairly, be sincerely appreciative, and offer generous benefits. They must provide health, dental or tusk, and mental health care for slaves and their families, and must support them when they cannot work due to illness, injury, or advanced age.

On the other hand, owners can force slaves do any job necessary, such as helping to conquer a world by killing as many of the inhabitants as possible.

Tall Man and the other invaders were cannon fodder, transported here (technical aspects of that process are proprietary and never shared with slaves, unfortunately) by their owner because she wanted this world. Perhaps she needed raw materials for her manufacturing endeavors. Perhaps she wanted a defensive location from which to fend off hostile take-overs by other owners. Perhaps she intended to give this world to her offspring as a playground. She did not share her reason with the invaders, and it would have made no difference if she had: they were given a job, and they had to do it.

The brown suits

As Kaylee rightly observed, invaders were the shock and awe, the means by which the owner "softened" targets, in this case humans. The brown suits, those mud-colored outfits that have inspired so many disparaging names for invaders over the years, were critical in accomplishing this task. The suits served a psychological purpose by creating the appearance of an indivisible "one," which fostered unity among invader species and tended to overwhelm the humans they were sent to kill.

However, the primary purpose of the suits was to meet the physical needs of invaders. Suits provided protection from heat and cold by a device that regulated body temperature. They included urine and feces collection systems (hence the bagginess). They contained equipment that allowed invaders to communicate with each other without being overheard by anyone without a suit (some humans believe invaders are telepathic because of this, but none of the species possess telepathic abilities) or to communicate with non-invaders with the blink of an eye. In these aspects, the suits were similar to those worn by astronauts.

The suits differed from those of the astronauts in at least two important aspects. The first difference was the role they played in killing the enemy. The ability of invaders to kill with a touch, which seemed like a form of black magic to many humans, is easily explained: hand coverings included devices that channeled and magnified electrical currents to a hot-spot that delivered a lethal jolt. This is why invaders kept the electrical grid intact whenever possible: the suits needed to be recharged periodically to maintain their killing power.

The second important difference was the way in which suits protected invaders from guns and other explosive weapons. The brown suits were woven from fibers that included nano-circuitry designed to detect force. When more than the normal level of force expected in day-to-day life was detected, fibers instantly hardened to create an impenetrable shell around an invader. When the force level returned to normal, the fibers softened again. This explains why the "Good Guy with a gun" Kaylee saw on I-Day could not kill an invader when firing at point-blank range.

According to an invader who survived the die-off and who was privy to talks between his owner and her confidants, the decision to use this fiber, a recent invention not yet tested in combat situations, was based on pre-invasion analyses of human societies, which found that guns and explosive devices would present the greatest danger to invaders. Although the owner knew the fibers might not perform as described, she decided the benefits of obtaining this world as soon as possible outweighed any potential risks to her slaves.

The force protection aspect worked well, but only if the cloth remained intact and fairly dry. The invaders surprised us on I-Day, but they were surprised that day, too, when they discovered that the fiber nano-circuitry could be damaged beyond repair if a suit was cut or became too wet. Their fear of broken glass and precipitation began then, and it increased as their access to undamaged suits decreased. However, the initial phase of the invasion was carried out so quickly that most humans did not have time to use guns or bombs. Also, invader forces were transported rapidly in and out of areas around the globe to take advantage of optimal weather conditions. For these reasons, the number of invader deaths attributed to the fiber glitch was relatively small. Slaves were advised to avoid sharp objects and to take shelter during inclement weather, since each had been issued only one suit for the initial phase, but the overall invasion plan was not altered due to suit malfunctions.

The invasion plan

The initial phase of the invasion was expected to last three to five days, and that phase was carried out as originally planned. Pre-invasion estimates indicated that eighty percent of the human population would be eliminated by then: the estimates appear to have been accurate. The second phase would be a period of four to six days, during which invaders would spread out from population centers to kill at least fifty percent of the remaining humans. Before that phase began, additional brown suits and supplies were supposed to arrive for invaders. They did not. The slaves began the second phase anyway, achieving half the estimated kill rate due to the lack of supplies.

Phase three would be a mop-up operation of six to eight months, during which most, if not all, remaining humans would be killed. Before that phase began, three-quarters of the invader slaves were scheduled to be transported back home or to work locations on other worlds. That group left on schedule about two weeks after I-Day. The remaining twenty-five percent of the invaders, scattered around the world in small groups, were supposed to receive supplies on the day their comrades left. The supplies did not arrive. By all accounts, no contact from owners or other off-world entities has occurred since that day.

Thus, the remaining slaves knew by the end of the second week of the invasion that their owner had either changed her plan or had lost her company. The invader with inside information about the owner believes she was convicted of using a risky invention, the new cloth for the suits, that led to slave deaths. The penalty would be death for her and enslavement for her offspring, which would cause a bidding war among other owners for her assets, including her slaves. Whatever the reason, it was clear to most invaders that they had been abandoned.

Plight of the "leftovers"

After being abandoned, invaders whose suits were still intact became obsessed with keeping them that way, while those whose suits had been damaged sometimes killed fellow invaders to obtain functioning suits. Some invaders left their posts and dispersed, singly or in small groups, to avoid capture in case an owner, old or new, arrived. Some stayed at their posts for years in the hope that they would be able to return home to their families and friends. Electrical grids were kept running for as long as possible so suits could be recharged. With a charged suit, an invader could gather food and other supplies from abandoned buildings with little or no resistance from humans. A damaged suit was almost as good during the first few years after I-Day because it took a long time for most humans to determine the way in which the suits were used to kill and to recognize factors that might inactivate the killing function.

Levels of confusion, grief, despair, and anger were high among the "leftovers," as humans nicknamed the slaves who were abandoned. When the invasion began, most slaves went about the task of killing humans rather dispassionately: it was, simply, a job. After the abandonment, many slaves were filled with rage and, unable to direct it at their owner, vented it on humans. Invaders killed humans for sport, revenge, or for no reason at all. Many survivors say this was the most terrifying period of the invasion.

This background information is critical for those seeking to understand Tall Man and the other invaders. Tall Man was caught in a difficult situation when he met Kaylee Bearovna. As the leader of his group of invaders, and as a Tzngwaneeza, he felt he must stay at his post and keep other members of the group there for as long as possible. This caused friction between him and the other three slaves: none were Tzngwaneeza, and all wanted to leave as soon as they realized they had been abandoned. Tall Man's entire extended family had been killed in a mining disaster years before, so there was no reason, other than loyalty to his owner, for him to go home. On the other hand, his mate and unborn child had just died on this world. There was no reason for him to stay.

Tall Man: His response to "being without"

While feeling caught between two worlds must have been disturbing to Tall Man, the most heart-wrenching part of his situation was that he had no family after the death of his mate and unborn child. This is one of the worst things that can happen to a Tzngwaneeza. If he had returned home, members of his species in the local community would have held many mourning ceremonies for him over a period of two years. Their word for the condition translates simply as "being without."

Tzngwaneeza have a custom that was common among cultures on this world in the past: when a family member dies, the next of kin may adopt a captured enemy as a replacement. If a wife is lost, an enemy woman is taken for a new wife; if a child is lost, the child of an enemy is adopted. There is a kernel of truth in what Kaylee says when she wonders if Tall Man is keeping her as a pet. Tall Man knew Kaylee was in the library and, with enough time and effort, could have broken in and killed her. However, his mate had disappeared on Day Three, and his focus during the days after her disappearance was on finding her. When he realized his mate and unborn child were dead, he was overcome by grief. That, combined with the fact that his owner had abandoned him, made him unwilling to continue killing humans. Trekker Tim says his father went out of his way to keep the other invaders in his group from harming his mother, hindering their efforts to break down the door and to set off more bombs. Then, when she placed the paper wreath on his mate's body, he began to see Kaylee in a new light.

Tall Man had the option of adopting Kaylee as a wife or as a child because he had lost both. From Kaylee's account of his actions during their time in the library, and from interviews with other Tzngwaneeza, we know that Tall Man intended, at first, to adopt her as his child. A human musicologist and an elderly invader analyzed the song he sang for Kaylee, as described in her journal, and they concluded the song is one Tzngwaneeza sing to children.

The Tzngwaneeza adoption period is long, with many steps to complete before an enemy makes the voluntary decision to (1) become a member of the family; (2) stay with the family in a relationship similar to that of a close friend; or (3) leave the family completely. One indication that Tall Man's intentions toward Kaylee changed early in the process took place after he sabotaged the local electrical system, which he did before they left the library together. Sabotaging the system was a sign that he was cutting off ties with his past and was no longer in league with other invaders, whose power to kill with a touch he had effectively destroyed. Presenting the hand coverings of the other invaders to Kaylee was his way of completing an early step in the adoption process, one that required him to prove he was willing and able to take on the role of her protector and provider. While this step is occasionally part of the adoption process for a child, it is always completed when taking a wife.

A casual act, one that could have been misinterpreted by Tall Man quite easily due to cultural differences between the species, probably influenced the change in his intentions. When Kaylee's hair became too tangled to comb, she chose to cut it short and to do that quickly, giving her remaining hair a ragged look. Among the Tzngwaneeza, a woman would do that only in response to the loss of a mate. We know that Kaylee looked very young, which might explain why Tall Man at first intended to adopt her as a child. However, when he saw her roughly-cropped hair, it was natural for him to assume she was old enough to have had, and lost, a mate, and that she was experiencing the same painful condition of "being without" that he was experiencing.

It is possible that Tall Man was conflicted about his relationship with Kaylee and was trying to cover all the bases, so to speak, while waiting to see how the relationship developed. It is also possible Tall Man had every intention of adopting Kaylee as his child, but she had other intentions. As we see from her journal, Kaylee began her time in the library as a child in some ways, but she left as a strong, determined, and capable adult. What we know for a fact is that Tall Man and Kaylee did become husband and wife. Blood samples prove Trekker Tim is their child, and he says it was obvious to him and to anyone who spent time with his parents that they were deeply in love.

Mating between species

Many tragedies have occurred because of misconceptions about interspecies mating. Human females have been forced to have abortions because they carry the child of an invader or descendant of an invader. Female Tzngwaneeza have been killed for mating with humans. Pregnant females of both species have been disemboweled while still alive because there is a myth that mixed-species fetuses have special powers that can be transferred to those who consume the beating hearts of the babies. Newborns of mixed parentage are killed by humans as soon as they emerge from the birth canal because it is believed that their hands have the ability to kill from the moment the child takes its first breath. Female invaders or the descendants of invaders (from the three species that have distinct sexes) who are used as sex slaves, a horrifying practice that continues to this day, have had their uteruses cut out by their human owners so the owners can proudly certify to customers that no "pollution" of the human species will occur at their establishment.

How is it possible that unions between humans and invaders can produce live offspring? This is a fundamental question that perplexed researchers for years. On this world, only closely related species can reproduce. A horse and donkey can mate and produce a mule; but a horse and an elephant, even if they could mate, are not able to produce offspring because their species are too dissimilar. Before the invasion, some scientists manipulated DNA to create chimera, new types of animals from parents that could not reproduce naturally. That was not an option after I-Day, when most labs were destroyed and researchers killed, although some people still believe there is a secret lab somewhere in the world churning out mixed-species "monsters."

While research on human-invader mating and offspring has been limited, I summarize it here. Again, it is important to remember there are four species, and six variations, of invaders.

The Ilquanoochin reproduce asexually, have no external reproductive organs, and, thus, cannot mate with humans. This hairless species, which has reddish-orange skin that feels like coarse sandpaper, was the first to be affected by the invader die-off and was hardest hit by it. We know little about them, and there has been only one reported sighting of them in over thirty years. As mentioned earlier, I have serious doubts about the veracity of that sighting.

The Glaz, the invader species with tusks and with leathery skin that peels off in large flakes, have three distinct sexes (male, female, and "hermaphrodite," for lack of a better term) in addition to their three hierarchical social levels. Their mating taboos are strict: for example, mating between Glaz from different castes is an offense punishable by death. Due to the strict taboos, none of the Glaz mates willingly with humans. However, hundreds of cases of hermaphrodites or females of the tusked species being used by humans as sex slaves, or being taken by force by a male human, have been reported. There have been no verified accounts of offspring being produced from any of those interactions.

This species was frequently targeted by human mobs because it looks like the "monster" that invaders were thought to be. Those few Glaz who managed to survive the die-off and the mobs live in relative seclusion now, for obvious reasons. Due to the small population, the many restrictions about which members of the species can mate with each other, and the presumed lack of ability to produce offspring with humans, it is expected the Glaz will die out within a few generations.

The third species, called the Frakyllo, has two distinct sexes and is similar to humans in many ways, although they have almost colorless skin, flattened foreheads, and white fur on many parts of their bodies. They are short, timid, and quite persistent (the two invaders Kaylee called The Twins are of this species), and they actively seek opportunities to mate with any species. There are hundreds of reported cases of humans mating with them but no verified cases of offspring from those interactions. Few of the Frakyllo survived the invader die-off; this species is expected to disappear within a decade or two.

This brings us to Tall Man's group, the Tzngwaneeza. Researchers were startled to discover that unions between this species and humans often produce offspring. The recent birth of twins to Trekker Tim and his wife is one of many cases indicating that the children of such unions are fertile. This species dealt with the die-off better than other invader species did. Due to the ability of this species to form unions with humans that lead to fertile offspring, and the ability of Tzngwaneeza to blend into human society due to similarities in physique and personality, they are expected to form a permanent and growing part of the population on this world and to add vigor to the gene pool.

Tall Man: Coming home

The results of blood sample analyses conducted in the past few years suggest the Tzngwaneeza can produce fertile offspring with humans because they were not so much invading this world when they arrived here as they were coming home.

Perhaps some readers will recall that the remains of a new human ancestor, called Denisovans, were discovered in Siberia before the invasion. Testing of the remains indicated that both Neanderthals and another species, which was a mystery at that time, contributed to the genetic code of Denisovans, who passed along segments of their code to some modern humans. The DNA of Tall Man and other Tzngwaneeza includes a significant amount of genetic code from that same mysterious human ancestor, indicating that humans and Tzngwaneeza are related. The Tzngwaneeza have origin myths about becoming slaves when they were captured on a distant planet. It is possible that this planet, this world, was their original home.

I ask readers to keep this in mind when they react with repugnance or violence, as many do, to children of unions between humans and Tzngwaneeza. We are judged by how we treat the most vulnerable among us, and those very vulnerable children have been treated very badly. For decades, humans could blame their actions on ignorance. No more. It is my hope that the blaming and shaming those children suffer, and the violence they endure or die from, will end as more humans come to understand that when we harm mixed-species children we are harming members of our own extended family.

Summary: Seeing the big picture

When I shared the story about six blind people trying to describe an elephant, I left out the last part. As they fight about whose description is correct, their voices grow so loud that the elephant tries to get away from the noise. It runs this way and then that way in an effort to escape. In the process, the six blind people, who refused to believe that each held a piece of the big picture and refused to work together, are trampled to death.

There is an elephant in the room, one that humans, invaders, invader descendants, and those of mixed-species heritage have been trying not to think about: another invasion.

An invader who had access to his owner and who studied business practices on his home planet believes it is possible an owner (old or new), or one of the owner's competitors, will come here in the future with another invasion force. He believes that in the confusion of a bidding war over the old owner's assets, or during the transfer of assets from one owner to another, there was a slip-up. The invader wasn't able to describe how information is recorded and stored on that planet because the method is not similar to any that humans have ever used, so he likened the process to the information recording we do with paper. Perhaps something like a map, something with the location of this planet, was filed in the wrong place: because this world and the occupying force left here are tiny parts of the owner's assets, a misfiled map might not be noticed. Or perhaps information about us was corrupted somehow, rendered unreadable, as if an ink stroke had smeared during the recording process, obliterating our line in the ledger. Or perhaps information about this world simply disappeared during the transfer process, as if a page was ripped out of a ledger. According to the invader, it is possible humans survived annihilation, and invaders escaped slavery, due to a clerical error.

The elephant story is not only about the disastrous results of humans not being able to distinguish between invader species because of their brown suits. It is also a cautionary tale about what could happen if the people of this world don't listen to each other, respect each other, and understand that each of us holds a piece of the truth. It is a story about what could happen if we don't work together to address the big picture.

Appendix Five: My Final Interview

by Klaratee of Arcadia

I was trained in qualitative field research by an anthropology professor who survived I-Day and the decade after by living in the Hoh Rain Forest. He was on a solo backpacking trip through the forest when the invasion began, and he didn't realize anything unusual had happened until a week later when he left the Hoh to return home. At the first sight of an invader touching a human, he spun his Subaru around and headed back to the forest, expecting to be overtaken at any moment by the strange things in brown suits. He was not. Because the suits tended to malfunction when wet, invaders had no desire to follow him into a perpetually rainy place.

My professor saw no humans or invaders during his decade in the Hoh. After the invader die-off, when he returned to the fragments of civilization, people asked him if it was hard to be alone for all those years. He never answered their questions, but he told me that, aside from missing his daughter, his years in the forest had been the best of his life.

As Kaylee Bearovna notes in her journal during the early weeks of the invasion, the natural world seemed to be doing fine even though humans were not. My professor said finding food in the wild was a challenge at first, but it became easier over time as the rain forest recovered from being over-loved by humans. The recovery of nature is a trend that expeditionary units have found throughout the northwest region of this continent, and the limited information I've heard from other areas of the world suggests the same process is happening there, too. Natural areas near population centers were stripped of anything that could be used for food, fuel, or other necessities soon after I-Day, but because humans and invaders tended to either starve to death or to move on after harvesting the resources, even those areas tend to be much healthier now than before the invasion.

Also, some recent research in the arctic region suggests that the sudden and drastic decrease in the use of fossil fuels due to the invasion might have had a stabilizing effect on the process of climate change. Sea level rise is less than was predicted and weather patterns seem more consistent with the historical record.

My professor said it is important to see both the pros and cons of any event. Although this is not a popular position to take, I must acknowledge, when I look at the topic objectively, that the invasion had benefits. This is true for the natural world. This is true, also, for me: I would not have been born if invaders had not come to this world.

My father used to say I was an expert at making lemonade out of lemons. I have never seen a lemon or tasted lemonade, and it is unlikely I ever will, so it took quite a while for my father to explain what he meant by that when I was a child. When he was done with his explanation, he said, "Do you understand now?" I nodded, but I didn't really understand. Lemons didn't sound like something that needed to be fixed in any way. They sounded magical, a fruit with real power.

I think that was a generational difference between my father and me. He remembered the pre-invasion world and longed for it until he died. As the child of a survivor father and an invader mother, I have never known any world but the one we live in now. The world seems lush and full of wonder to me. Everything edible tastes good the way it is. Being alive is enough to make any day a good day. I realize the world can be dangerous, but there is a spirit of excitement about it, too, something in the air that smells fresh, and clean, and hopeful.

I am not blaming my father for holding on to what little of his past he could remember. He was one of the few humans to survive d-bit (death by invader touch), perhaps because the invader who touched him had a malfunctioning suit. My father said the pain of the touch was the worst he had ever felt, and he had been shot twice while serving in the military, so he knew pain. He must have seemed dead to the invader, who left him on the side of the road where he fell. When my father came to, he escaped by picking his way north through the dense coastal forest until he found a settlement of decent survivors.

It wasn't until one of the survivors asked him his name that my father realized he could not remember it. He could remember being scared his first day of kindergarten, going to Sea World, eating ice cream for breakfast during summer vacations from school when his mother was at work, having a job at a place called McDonald's that sold hamburger sandwiches that were not made out of pig meat, and dancing wildly for hours at clubs. He could remember places and experiences, but he could not remember his name or the names of his family and friends. He said it was probably because all of them, and the old him, were dead. The name of the settlement that took him in is Arcadia, so my father called himself McDonald of Arcadia.

I was always a collector of stories. I listened, wide-eyed, around the settlement fire each night as my father and the other survivors and invaders who lived there told stories about their lives. The next day, while I picked salmonberries or gathered clams, I would tell myself the stories I'd heard the night before. I would piece the tales together word by word, saying them over and over until they were as clear, polished, and indestructible as the carnelian agates I found on the beach. After I learned all the stories people could tell about themselves, I begged them to tell stories about other people they had known. Then I polished those stories, too, and added them to my collection.

My father's favorite story was about the day my mother came to the settlement. It was during the die-off, and she was very sick. Although the humans were decent and kind, they were cautious about taking in invaders, even those like my mother who didn't wear a brown suit, because they knew invaders could pass along an illness that caused blindness. When my father told the story, he said he recalled thinking that one look at the beautiful Tzngwaneeza who would become my mother was worth living without sight for the rest of his life. His hut was at the edge of the settlement, and he vowed to the community that he would keep the woman away from them, and stay away himself, until she was fully healed if they would allow him to take her in.

Other humans, invaders, invader descendants, and people of mixed heritage came to the settlement over the years, and I was thrilled about this because each brought new stories. Then the professor who survived the invasion by living in the rain forest passed through. He was really too old to be traveling alone, but he had heard from Ishi Kenai, of the NWET, that his daughter was alive and well and still living in the family home in Malibu. His desire to see her again, to find someone he knew, was so intense that he had set off alone on a journey of many hundreds of miles with nothing but a walking stick for protection.

He told great stories around the fire the night he stayed with us. I was enthralled. There were no opportunities for a real education in our area, so my father suggested I help the professor during his trip south to Malibu in exchange for the professor teaching me something, anything. The professor liked the idea. I didn't want to leave my father and my small piece of the world, but I wanted to learn. I helped the professor reach his daughter, then I stayed with them for two years to study.

His daughter had kept his office exactly as he had left it the last time he was home, so I had access not only to his books, teaching materials, and conference papers but also to pens, paper, and a beautiful and still functioning antique typewriter (Sun Standard #2, circa 1904). My final paper, pecked out slowly on that typewriter, was a collection of stories I had gathered over the years: "Tales of Arcadia Settlement." Once the professor approved my work, I pecked out another copy to give to my father.

The professor put me in touch with Ishi Kenai, and we met on one of his survey trips. Ishi was looking for someone to collect stories from people who had served in units during the early years of the expeditionary teams. The project sounded great. I would travel with units to various posts and accompany them on survey missions. I would see other parts of this region.

We stopped in Arcadia on the way north so I could see my father one last time. I told him about my education and my new job. He loved the copy of my Arcadia stories, which he shared with everyone in the settlement. He was excited for me. He was not feeling well, but he said people in Arcadia would care for him. We both knew I needed to move on.

For several years, I worked on the stories Ishi had asked me to collect. Then Ishi came back from his final deployment. He was injured and in great pain, but he was excited about the journal he had found. He wanted to return to the JSU area to search for Kaylee Bearovna and for any information about her. He would have taken off at once if he had been able to walk.

I traveled with him on the sailboat that ferried people back and forth between the mainland and Vancouver Island, then stayed on the island to help out during his long hospitalization. When he returned home, I spent several days a week helping him with his physical therapy. I thought he might give up the quest when he was well again, but he did not. So, as he finished recovering, we laid the groundwork for the search for Kaylee, and we began soliciting food and other donations for the effort.

Ishi describes in his essay, found elsewhere in these appendices, events leading up to the first year of our search and to the discovery of the safe place, where Benji Edelstein (Kaylee's friend) and Trekker Tim (Kaylee and Tall Man's son) lived. This was the easy part of the quest. After conducting interviews with them, our search for Kaylee, or for information about her, became much more difficult.

The safe place had taken us months to find even though we knew it was within a two-day walk south of the library and, thus, in a fairly well defined and relatively small search area. When Kaylee had headed north to continue her search for Matilda, she carried a map drawn by a man who thought the child might be living with people who had a cabin fifty miles away. Benji had seen the map, but he could not recreate it due to his blindness. Trekker Tim had not seen the map, but he recalled his mother saying she would cross the mountains through a high pass and then follow a river for many miles. This gave us only a vague idea of where the cabin might be located within a vast search area of many hundreds of square miles.

As we waved goodbye to Trekker Tim and Benji after our interviews with them, I thought our search for Kaylee was about to be called off. In addition to the fact that the search area was huge and poorly defined, Kaylee had been so ill when she left that Benji was certain she could not have gone far. Ishi Kenai did not speak as we walked down the dirt road that leads from the safe place to the lake. When we reached the water, he skipped stones across the surface and watched the ripples. He turned to me and said, "Let's go home, Klaratee" (as I had expected). Then he added, "We'll come back when the mountain pass is clear of snow next spring."

We continued our search for Kaylee and the cabin the next spring. And the next. And the next. And the next. We began the search season each of those four years with a visit to Benji and Trekker Tim to bring them supplies, give them updates about our search, and see if they had more information about Kaylee. They were grateful for the items and news, but they had no news about Kaylee to offer us in return. However, they did give us Benji's picture of Kaylee so we could show it to people to see if they recognized her. Both Benji and Trekker Tim were crying when they handed the picture to me, but they insisted that I take it. They said giving up the picture would be a small price to pay if it helped us find Kaylee.

Ishi had urged friends to read Kaylee's journal, which he kept at his home on the northern coast. Many people who read the journal wanted to help us find her. By the fifth year of Ishi's quest, our contingent had grown to nineteen searchers, plus pack animal handlers and other support crew. There were so many of us that we split into five groups, one focused on the area where the Yakima River flowed out of the mountains, the others focused on four of the river's tributaries.

We had lost members of our team before. A cook drowned while trying to cross a river during the first year of our search for the cabin. A member of the support crew was captured and killed by cannibals during the second. Two searchers went missing near the beginning of the third year. We looked for them for weeks, but neither their bodies nor any sign of them was found. The fourth year of our search for the cabin was the most deadly. By May, three crew members and two searchers had died, all killed by humans. The area Kaylee had entered when she left Benji and Trekker Tim and struck out for the cabin was dangerous, and most of the danger was due to her own species.

Everyone who volunteers for our team knows they will be in danger. There are few guarantees of safety in the post-invasion world. After the five team members were lost, Ishi held a meeting to see if the remaining members of the team wanted to continue the search for the cabin or go home. It was unanimous: everyone voted to continue. I think Kaylee would be amazed if she could see how her words have inspired and moved people, so much so that they are willing to die in response to her plea to be found.

Perhaps we were willing to do this because all of us have lost so much. Survivors of I-Day feel this intensely. Like my father, many lost everyone they knew in one day. Even when family members or friends survived I-Day, most would die during the decade when invaders used their killing power, or the threat of it, to keep humans from obtaining the food and supplies they needed to survive. People gone; places gone; the world they knew gone. And with so much danger, illness, and starvation threatening us today, even younger people, like me, know too much about loss. To find something we thought was gone forever (Kaylee, her books, her library, her child) allows us to believe the world is a place where miracles can still happen. To find something important for Kaylee might be the closest we will ever come to finding something important for ourselves.

I was dealing with a health issue during that fourth season of our search for the cabin. I had told no one about it because I wanted so badly to be part of the team. I was the only one with formal training in qualitative field research. I was the only one who knew Ishi's physical limitations and could convince him to relax when necessary, let someone younger climb the highest peaks to scout areas, and take the pain pills his friend had made for him. I needed to be part of the search effort no matter what.

Then I was shot.

I don't know how it feels to be touched by an invader, as my father was, but it's hard for me to imagine anything more painful than being shot by a high-powered rifle at fairly close range. I lost a lot of blood. Despite our best efforts, the wound became infected. Although Ishi wanted me to ride home on one of our pack mules, I knew the team wouldn't be able to carry enough food and supplies to make it back if I did that. I walked most of the way on a leg that screamed at me with every step. I still walk with a limp.

But here's the strange thing: being shot was one of the best things that has ever happened to me. Honestly.

If my father were alive today, I know he would say I have taken the "making lemonade out of lemons" thing too far this time. However, if he could read my interview with Heather Jo Wilson, I think he would understand.

I like to imagine my father and mother sitting side by side wherever they went when they died, sipping tall glasses of icy lemonade and reading the story about how I was shot and about all the good things that have happened because of my injury. I like to think they are laughing and telling each other this is a good story.

Appendix Six: The Lost Child

Heather Jo Wilson

Interviewer's Note (Klaratee of Arcadia)

Ishi Kenai and our research team spent four years trying to find the cabin that Kaylee Bearovna was headed to when she left the safe place for the last time. We had few solid leads during those years. Most of the clues we found and the information we received led us nowhere. For example, the discovery, early in the third year, of a bright yellow Humvee rolled over an embankment caused us to focus all of our efforts that season on the area surrounding the vehicle. We knew the vehicle was the one we had been looking for, but we didn't know it had been stolen from its owners and ditched twenty miles away from their cabin.

During our fourth season of searching for the cabin, we found an old woman living in a dug-out cave halfway up the bluff above a river. Cannibals had camped on top of the bluff over her dug-out one night without realizing she was there. She heard them talking about two families living a few miles farther north. The cannibals had killed one family the winter before, and they planned to go back for the other that winter. It was a gruesome tale, and not much information to go on, but we headed in that direction. Two months later, we found a cabin.

I followed standard procedures for making contact: I stood at a distance from the cabin, explained in detail who we were and why we were there, and told whoever was in the cabin that we had food and supplies to trade for information. A woman shouted at us to go away. I described the food and supplies we had, and she seemed interested. We thought we heard her say it would be okay for one person to advance. I was chosen. When I was about half the way between our group and the cabin, she shot me.

Ishi ran to help, but the woman threatened to shoot him, too. I waved him away. Then I stood, swayed, and fell, hitting the ground with a thud. I didn't know at the time why my fall changed the woman's mind about us, but it did. She opened the cabin door, still holding the rifle, checked out the situation, then helped me into the cabin so she could clean and dress my wound. She told the others they could camp in the yard.

I conducted the first of six interviews with Heather Jo Wilson while she dressed my wound, which, miraculously, did not include much damage to muscle or bone. She was upset about shooting me. I believe this explains her openness to be interviewed, her speech patterns, and her unguarded responses.

She would not tell me her age, but she seemed to be close to seventy at that time. Her eyesight was excellent, often an indication of a human who has had few encounters with invaders. Her general health seemed poor. She had trouble moving about the cabin because of severe pain in her joints. Also, the disrepair of the cabin and outbuildings indicated she had no help with upkeep. In short, Heather Jo was an elderly woman in pain and with few resources and no support, who was living not only alone but also in constant terror.

Heather Jo Wilson

I don't want to live here anymore. I don't want to live anymore. I know I shouldn't say that. It's against God's law. But look what I did to you. I could have killed you. I almost killed you. It's just not right.

I'm so scared all the time. It was different when my husband was here. He did all the shooting. He's the one who liked guns. I hate them. He brought so many guns here. Every kind you can think of. And he used them. He killed invaders. He killed people. He killed anything that moved. He would come in the house with blood all over his hands. It made me sick to my stomach. I felt so terrible about that. I feel so terrible now. I feel terrible all the time. I'm so scared.

I make myself sick to my stomach now using guns. I do that to myself. Blood is on my hands. Your blood. More than I want to think about. I hate me. I do. Shooting you like that. Do you need anything? A drink of water? Some berries? Another pillow under your foot?

The day the invasion began, what you call I-Day, I thought that was the worst day of my life. Then when we were hiding in our safe room and I heard the awful sounds outside, I thought that was the worst. Then invaders burned the town, and that was even worse. The trip here was awful. So much death. So much sorrow. So many people killed by us so we could escape. As if we deserved to live. It was an awful trip. We almost died so many times. It got to the point where I didn't know who the good people were and who the bad people were. It got to the point where I forgot which type of people we were.

Then we got here, and I thought the killing was over. It wasn't. Seemed like my husband was killing somebody every other day for a while. All kinds of people. Even kids. You can't trust them, my husband said. People would come here looking for food or help, but he said it was a trap. They're trying to fool us, he said. We can't let our guard down. They want what we have. They'll take what's ours. He was a good person in many ways, but he didn't trust anybody.

This cabin belonged to his parents. It was a vacation home, but they didn't come here much. He turned it into a prepper place. That's what his friends were, preppers. Preparing for the worst. Although they had no clue what the worst was.

Before the invasion, my husband and his friends would get together, drink beer, watch survivalist shows, and talk about the end of the world. His friends had the gear, the cool stuff. He had a few things, but mostly guns. They talked about what they would do and how they would survive. It was a bunch of baloney. Nobody knew what the invasion would be like, or how bad things would be afterwards. My husband and his friends thought they'd have to hold out for a few years until things got better again. A few years. Can you believe that? Seems silly now.

Most of the guys bought cabins within about twenty-five miles of here. They figured that way they could stick together to fight off bad guys if they needed to.

My husband came home after drinking with the guys one night, and he was going on and on about how he and a friend had decided our kids would marry each other when the end came. We didn't even have kids. Turns out, we couldn't have any. Maybe we could have before the invasion, but then my husband got hurt down in his private parts and that changed things. We never had a kid. I cried about it for a while, but, when I think about it now, it was probably a good thing.

Having his friends nearby didn't work out like they planned. We would have been much better off if nobody knew we were here. As soon as one of his friends ran out of food or something, they came looking for it at our place. Maybe they went to some of the other places, too, but they always seemed to end up here. At first my husband gave them things. After a while, we didn't have much to give. That's when some of his so-called friends got angry.

A couple of them showed up one time looking for tools or something. Whatever it was, my husband had it but was using it and wouldn't give it to them. They tried to take it. Everybody pulled out guns. My husband got shot. A couple people died. It was like an all-out war from then on.

Maybe my husband being shot was why we couldn't have kids. I don't know.

Henry, the husband of the couple who took Matilda with them, he was part of my husband's group of friends. Another prepper with a place up here. Henry and his wife, Ginger, lived down the street from us back in town. But Henry wasn't like those others in many ways. He was a good person. He was the kind that wouldn't hurt anybody. He only hung out with the group because he felt he should be prepared for things. I guess it was like a boy scout thing for him.

Their house was across the street from the Gulicks' house. Henry and Ginger saw what went on over at that place. Whenever the wife or Professor Gulick was out of town, the other one had friends come to visit. Special friends, if you know what I mean. The year Professor Gulick was in Australia, Ginger said it was like there was a revolving door on their house. The wife had a different guy almost every night. When the wife was out of town, it wouldn't be just one person spending the night with Professor Gulick, Henry said. They were real sick people over there.

They weren't fooling anybody about Matilda, either. Henry said all the neighbors knew when Kaylee started babysitting

Matilda that she was the mom. Everybody knew she went to Australia with Professor Gulick, so it was easy to do the math.

Henry said Kaylee was good to Matilda. Not like that witch of a wife. Henry saw the wife hit Matilda. Hard, too, not just a swat on the seat of the pants. He wanted to say something, but you didn't do that to a Gulick. Broke Henry's heart to see how they treated that little girl. Whenever Kaylee had to leave, Matilda cried and cried. He heard her crying during the night all the time, and the wife and Professor Gulick didn't do anything about it. Social Services would've taken that little girl away from them if they had been anybody else.

They left Matilda behind in the house, you know. When they escaped. The Gulicks left her in the house and drove off. How do you do that? How do you leave a little kid all alone?

Henry didn't know at first that Matilda was there in the house by herself. He heard her crying when the invasion began, but then it was quiet. He thought her so-called parents took her with them. I mean, as awful as they were, he didn't expect them to leave her alone. He and Ginger were hiding in their safe room, so maybe Matilda made a peep during the days before the big fire, but they couldn't hear her.

Anyway, on the third day, when invaders started burning down the town and people like us who'd been hiding had to get out quick, Henry thought he heard crying. Houses burning, invaders coming, but he and Ginger still went over to see what was going on. And there was little Matilda in her bedroom, all alone, with the door locked. Locked from the outside, if you can believe that. I mean, think about that for a second. Locked from the outside. What kind of animals were they?

Matilda had no food. No water. There was a pile of poop and a puddle of pee in one corner of the room, and she kept saying she was sorry she made a mess. "Please don't hit me," she said.

"Please don't hit me." I just never knew people could be so cruel. Ginger grabbed Matilda and they drove off.

We had the Humvee back then. My husband's pride and joy. That was before one of my husband's ex-friends snuck over here to the cabin one night and drove it off. You say you found it crashed? I say it serves those guys right. I would call them something else, but I'm a Christian.

My brother had a room at our place so he could study at the university. We would have "bugged out" when the invasion began but we were waiting for him, hoping he'd make it home. We were "sheltering in place," as my husband said. But when the town started burning, we had to leave. We tried to get up to JSU to find my brother, but the street was packed with people. No way we could get through. We headed up the canyon road instead, the one that goes over the mountain pass.

That's when we saw Henry. His car had broken down. He was carrying Matilda and holding Ginger's hand, and they were running up the canyon. Cars were swerving all over the place. We saw one almost hit them.

You would think little Matilda would be crying. Little tiny kid like that. I know I was crying, for sure. Just about everybody else was crying, too. But she wasn't. She was quiet as a fawn. Eyes big, you know, watching everything. It was like she didn't have any tears left.

My husband was a good man, at least back then, but he wasn't going to pick them up. He said we probably wouldn't make it ourselves and it was crazy to take anybody else. I never argued with him about anything. My pastor said a good wife shouldn't do that, and I didn't. But I argued that day. Yes, lots of people were running. Yes, lots of kids were getting left behind or run over. But these were people we knew. I don't know why my husband stopped, but he did. They jammed into the Humvee, and we took off.

Like I said, it was a horrible trip. My husband was in kill-or-be-killed mode, and it scared me just to be sitting next to him when he was like that. We tried to keep Matilda from seeing the worst of it, but she saw plenty. She was…. Well, there's nothing more I want to say about that trip.

Henry and Ginger had a cabin two miles west of ours, but they stayed with us for a while at first so we could get this place secure. They were good people. Henry helped my husband a lot. Then we went over to their cabin to get it ready. Things were getting weird in this area, but the guys my husband knew hadn't started causing trouble yet.

I was sad when we came back to our own cabin after getting Henry and Ginger's place all spiffed up. Seemed so empty here without them. I liked having Matilda around. And Ginger, too. She was real sweet, and I knew she'd be a good mother for Matilda. I didn't know what had happened to Matilda's real mom. That child was just a little lost lamb. She once was lost but now was found, I should say. Like from that old hymn we sang in church.

We didn't get to see Henry, Ginger, and Matilda as much as I wanted. Things started getting weird. Some guys my husband knew got desperate; then they got mean. Everybody had guns, of course. They thought they were the Good Guys. They weren't. Maybe at first, but not then for sure.

I try to be a good person, but look what I did to you. I almost killed you. I could've killed you, and you were just trying to do something nice for Kaylee. For Matilda. I'm as bad now as my husband and his friends were. My husband used to say if it moves, shoot it. I always hated when he said that. Now that's how I live.

I don't want to live here anymore. I don't want to live like this anymore. There must be a better place. There must be a better way to live. I can't….

We did see Henry, Ginger, and Matilda sometimes. When there was some big project to do at their place or here, my husband and Henry got together to work on it, and then we women could visit. But, believe me, just going the little ways from our cabin to theirs was a big deal. Very dangerous. You never knew who was out there, hiding by the trail. Humans, invaders, creatures that might have been humans in the past but that you couldn't really call human anymore. Sick people, dying people, rabid animals.

We did spend a few Christmases together. That was nice.

Ginger got pregnant six times after the invasion, but she lost the baby every time. Having Matilda was a real blessing for them. They loved her. She loved them. I felt like she finally had the family she deserved. It was a good feeling. It was one good thing I could hold on to that came out of the invasion.

They were over here for Christmas one year when there was a big snowstorm, and they had to stay a couple extra days because of it. This was when Matilda was about eight. Cute little thing. Beautiful voice. I knew her grandmother, Kaylee's mom, from church, back when she was well enough to sing with the choir. Mary O'Halloran. I didn't know her well, but I knew who she was once Henry mentioned Kaylee. When Matilda sang, it was easy to tell who she got her voice from. My husband had Ms. O'Halloran as his teacher in fourth grade. Jefferson City was so small that everybody knew just about everybody in one way or another.

We had fun that Christmas. We sang, made popcorn, told stories. My husband shot a deer that fall, so we had a real feast. Then they had to go home, even though the trail still had over a foot of snow on it. I packed them a lunch to eat along the way.

You'll probably think I'm crazy, but I have these things I call "feelings." Not like the feelings everybody has. It's hard to explain. It's like I know things about people or situations that other folks don't know. Sometimes I have a feeling about what's going to happen before it happens. Strange things like that. Like a sixth sense, I guess.

I tried to tell my pastor about it once. I had a feeling something bad was going to happen to him and his family. They were planning a trip to Yellowstone, and I said they shouldn't go because of this feeling I had. He said those things come from the Devil and I should pray for the dark spirit inside me to leave. He was talking like I was possessed or something. It's a weird thing, I admit. I never thought of it as bad, though. They went on their trip, got in a car accident going through Yellowstone, and they all got banged up pretty bad. I guess if the Devil was trying to warn them not to go, that means God wanted them to get hurt. I don't know. That kind of thing is way over my head.

Those feelings might sound weird, but they really helped us out a lot over the years. I'd be doing dishes on a normal day, then have a feeling something bad was about to happen. My husband used to poo-poo my feelings when we first met, but he came to see there was something to them. I'd run and find him, tell him something bad was on the way, and we'd get ready. Sure enough, within half an hour, sometimes a lot less, an invader would come sniffing around the cabin in its brown suit, or one of my husband's ex-friends would take pot shots at the place. If I hadn't had a feeling, we could've been outside when they came, and we'd be dead.

I didn't have one of my feelings that day our friends left to go back to their cabin. Maybe I was too busy. Maybe I'd offended whoever sends the feelings. I don't know.

It was a nice day, fairly warm for that time of year. They stopped to have their picnic, and Mattie Lu—sorry, Matilda— went off the trail a little way into the woods to make a snowman. And suddenly, just like that, they were attacked. Whatever they were, Matilda saw them coming. She dug a hole in the snow, crawled in, covered herself up, and hid there during the attack. Can you imagine that? Can you imagine a kid her age thinking fast enough to do that? I would have been standing there with my mouth open, dumbfounded.

Later, much later, she said she was pretty sure they were humans, but she couldn't tell from their voices exactly who they were. Could've been guys from the prepper group, but there's no way to know for sure. She thought they were cannibals from some of the things they said. That kind of thing goes on too often up here, especially in the winter.

I don't know how long she was in that snow hole. Later, when she could finally talk about it, she said she waited until there wasn't a sound, then she waited a couple hours more.

We had a little coyote back then. Called him Yoyo because he ran back and forth so much. Cute little guy. Made a great watchdog. Barked at everything except us and Matilda. He loved that little girl. We heard something moving around outside that night, but Yoyo wasn't barking. My husband thought whoever was out there had killed Yoyo. He got a gun and was ready to shoot. Then we heard Matilda's voice. She was singing. My husband came that close to killing her. That close. His finger was on the trigger. Then we heard her singing.

She was half frozen. I thought she was going to lose a couple toes, but she didn't. For months after that she couldn't say a word. But she could sing. Strangest thing I ever saw. It was a long time before she could talk again. And a long, long time before she told us what happened that day.

Then Matilda was our little girl. She was wonderful. Such a joy to have here. That child could do anything. Show her how to do something once, and she had it. Even complicated things, like machinery. Anything needed to be done, she wanted to do it. So smart. And sweet. And sad, of course. Not a surprise after all she'd been through.

She talked about her mom a lot. Her real mom, Kaylee. Yes, she remembered Kaylee. Even though her so-called family didn't let Matilda see her momma very much, she remembered her. She drew pictures of her. I've got some of them around here someplace. I'll try to find them for you. And she didn't remember her momma just because other people talked about Kaylee. Henry and Ginger told Matilda what a good mom Kaylee was, but that's about all they knew. But the pictures she drew told me she remembered her momma very well. I'll give you Matilda's drawings if I can find them.

I don't know what year it was when Kaylee showed up. My husband almost shot her, too. That's just the way he was. But Kaylee had been around. She knew what the world was like. To make it all this way, past cannibals, invaders, wild animals, the works. Your friend there [Ishi Kenai] says you've lost people in the area between here and the mountains to the south. I believe it. It's dangerous. I thought every place was like this. If I had known there were places out there where people actually live together and don't kill each other and don't eat each other, I would have left here years ago. My husband always said it would be worse anyplace else, so I stayed.

Anyway, Kaylee knew how to do it right. She didn't come barging into the yard, like most people would. She stopped a long way from the house, far enough so we could get a good look at her and hear her but not be scared by her. Smart.

As soon as Kaylee started talking, Matilda's face lit up. Great big smile. Almost too big for her face. She looked at me and my husband and said, "Please don't shoot her. Please don't. That's my sweet momma." She knew. Matilda knew her mother's voice after all that time. Praise God, from whom all blessings flow, for that child.

Kaylee was sick. Real sick. I don't know how she made it all this way. It would have been hard for somebody in good health. As soon as Kaylee saw Matilda, she fell down to her knees and hugged her little girl and wouldn't let go. Look at me. I mean, look at me. I've got tears in my eyes right this very minute thinking about what happened that day. It was so sweet.

You want to know what love is? Pure love, I mean? That was it right there. That was it. Makes me feel better about humans when I remember that moment.

Kaylee could barely lift a spoon when she got here, she was so weak. Matilda fed her. Nice rich venison broth. Wild berries. Fresh water from the spring. They slept together. Every time I went in to check on them, they were hugging each other tight. I don't know how they got dressed or used the outhouse since they never seemed to let go of each other.

And talk? All day, and it sounded like they talked all night a few times, too. Like they were making up for all the years gone by and trying to make up for all the years to come when they wouldn't be together.

Kaylee knew she was dying. I know she did. I think Matilda knew, too. She could figure things out. I gave those two whatever they wanted and then stayed out of their way. I figured we'd have Matilda for a long time, but Kaylee would only have her for a few weeks. At most.

I don't know what was wrong with Kaylee. She said she wasn't in much pain, which was good because we didn't have medicine to give her. Not real medicine. She was slipping away, but at least it would be a quiet passing. Matilda woke up one morning with her arms around Kaylee, thought her momma might be cold, and got another blanket for her. Kaylee kissed Matilda, and then she passed over.

She's buried in the back yard. By the wild rose bush. You'll see a couple shiny stones, some sticks, a few knickknacks. Little things Matilda put on the grave over the years. Your friend says you might dig up that poor woman for some reason. Go ahead if you want to. But I'm telling you, it was Kaylee. Matilda knew. She knew in her heart.

Then Matilda was our girl again. My husband died. He had a cold, but it wasn't bad. And then he died. You know how it is. People die of things that used to be no big deal. Hard to imagine we used to go to the store, pay a couple bucks for medicine, take it, and be better. Now these things kill us.

Oh, Matilda. After her mom died, she decided she didn't want to be called Matilda anymore. She wanted to be called Mattie Lu. That's what Kaylee called her sometimes. Like a nickname, I guess. Her little Mattie Lu. Matilda didn't want a last name anymore. I guess she'd had so many last names over the years that they were kind of a nuisance to her. All she wanted was the name Kaylee called her.

Are you sure you don't know where Matilda is? I figured you folks would know for sure. Your friend said he served with an expeditionary team, and that's who she went off with. Maybe when you get home you can check for me. Somebody must know where she is.

She didn't want to leave. And it wasn't like I wanted her to go. I would've liked to keep her here forever, but that would be selfish. You see how I live. You see how dangerous this place is. I didn't want that for her. The expeditionary people were nice. A woman in the group promised she'd watch over Matilda. Mattie Lu was old enough to volunteer, so I let her go. I would have gone, too, but they couldn't take me. Against regulations, I guess.

I'll bet she's done real well with her unit. Seems like the kind of person a group like that would need. Seen the worst of things and still keeps her chin up. Still keeps a good attitude. Still thinks people and the world can be good.

Without Matilda here, this place is dead. Dead to me, for sure.

Don't even think about going over to Henry's old cabin. Promise me you won't go over there. It got snapped up fast after he and Ginger were murdered. That's what my husband said. He snuck over there a couple weeks after the attack and saw an ex-friend living in the place. Like that guy had been itching for a chance to move in. Maybe he was part of the attack. No way to know. My husband saw things going on over there that I can't talk about. Things I try not to think about. Things with kids. We always kept a close eye on Matilda, of course, but we watched her like a hawk after that. Please don't go there. Like everything else here, it's all about death.

I don't want to be here anymore. Living with the dead. I'll be dead soon if I stay. I know that for a fact. I had one of my feelings about it. I can't protect myself, and I don't want Matilda to come back and put herself in danger trying to protect me.

I don't know where I'd go if I left. Someplace I'd be safe, even for a little while. Doesn't have to be for long. Just someplace where I can sleep a whole night without worrying. I'd be grateful if you could find a place like that for me. Maybe someplace where expeditionary units pass through now and then so I could see or hear from Mattie Lu again. That would be nice.

I know it's a lot to ask, especially coming from somebody who shot you. I'm never going to forgive myself for that. God might forgive me, but I won't. I am so sorry.

But it would be nice to feel safe again, even if it's just for a day or two. I know it's a lot to ask, but do you think you could do that for me?

Heather Jo Wilson

Interviewer's Follow-up Note (Klaratee of Arcadia)

When our team left the cabin to head home, Heather Jo
Wilson came with us. In addition, we brought the remains
of Kaylee Bearovna. When Ishi was serving with the U-22s,
that would have been forbidden. But, because he was a private
citizen, it was not. The only problems were finding a safe place
for Heather Jo to live and finding a place to reinter Kaylee's
remains.

Trekker Tim and I had fallen in love during my yearly visits
to the safe place, and we were planning to marry at the end of
the search season. We were told we most likely could not have
children because we were both of mixed heritage. However,
during our most recent visit to the safe place, I had become
pregnant. I didn't tell Trekker Tim or Ishi because they would
want me to leave the search team for my safety and for the
safety of our child. For some reason, I had a strong feeling it
was important for me to see this season through to the end.

It's a good thing I was with the team. When I fell after being
shot, Heather Jo said she could tell I was pregnant. She had
one of her feelings, and there was something strange about the
way I fell, and then she knew. That is the only reason she let us
stay. That is the only reason she agreed to be interviewed. That
is the only reason we now know what happened to Kaylee
Bearovna and her daughter, Matilda.

Without the information Heather Jo gave us, our search
could have continued for years with no success. Or we could
have moved on to the cabin near Heather Jo's, the one she
said we should not visit, and walked into a deadly situation.
Although I do not believe in God in the same way Heather
Jo does, I believe the series of events that led to us finding
Kaylee Bearovna is more than coincidence. Some might call it

the action of a higher power. Some might call it luck. Either way, I am glad I was able to play a small part in the successful conclusion of our search.

Ishi has requested that the next NWET unit that passes through the area investigate the situation at the cabin that belonged to Henry and Ginger. Also, he has asked that they do a more thorough, and forceful, survey of the area north of the mountains, where we were searching. Something is going on there that makes the area much more dangerous than others in this region.

Ishi believes people will want to visit the JSU library once Kaylee's journal is published. Some will come because they view it as a shrine to human history and the pre-invasion world. Some will come to conduct research. There might be only one person a year for a while, due to the dangers and difficulties of travel. But, as he says, it takes only one person to break a lock or a window and make the library and its contents vulnerable to incursions. Even if the person who breaks in has good intentions, others who gain access to the library might not. He does not want the books to be harmed, not after Kaylee worked so hard to protect them.

Ishi suggested that Trekker Tim and I become caretakers for the library and the grounds around it. We agreed.

After leaving Heather Jo's cabin, our team returned to JSU and turned several classrooms in the building next to the library into a home for our family (I gave birth to our twins later that year, at Christmas time). Several other classrooms were made into apartments for Heather Jo, Benji, and people who visit the library. We plowed the Quad and planted a garden. In the center, we reinterred Kaylee's remains. The bloodstained library doorstep sits on top of her grave now, making the spot an invasion memorial. Trekker Tim and I take our twins, Rose and Jefferson, there often to honor their grandmother.

One final note: Heather Jo refused to provide us with a blood sample due to her religious beliefs. After I gave her a tour of the library, I showed her the bloodstained doorstep where the young man with hazel eyes had died (this was before we moved the stone to the Quad). I did not tell her the gender of the person who died there, I did not describe the person in any way, and she had not read Kaylee's journal yet. When she saw the stone, she gasped, knelt, put her hand on it, and closed her eyes. When she opened them, she said it was her brother who had died there. I asked her to describe her brother. The description matched the one in Kaylee's journal, including the clothes he was wearing on the day of the invasion, when he left Heather Jo's house and headed to campus to study for his final exams.

I realize many young men with hazel eyes were on campus at the time of the invasion. I realize several of them could have been wearing the same clothes as the man Kaylee describes. Heather Jo's refusal to provide a blood sample means the rest of us will never know for sure if it was her brother who died there.

Our doubts mean nothing to Heather Jo. She knows it was her brother. Finding out what happened to him, even though the knowledge came almost fifty years after the event, has given her a great sense of peace.

Appendix Seven: A Witch, Two Mothers, and One Sweet Momma

Mattie Lu

Interviewer's Note (Ishi Kenai)

The final part of my quest to find Kaylee Bearovna and those with whom she was connected took about two years and focused on discovering what had happened to her daughter, Matilda. Mattie Lu, as Matilda liked to be called, had left Heather Jo Wilson's cabin years before with a unit of the NWET. Heather Jo did not know which unit it was or where they called home. After helping my research team create housing for those who wanted to live by, or visit, the JSU library, I returned home to follow up on this lead.

I have friends and colleagues from my days in the NWET, but contacting them (or anyone outside one's own settlement) takes persistence, patience, and a portion of good luck. Between some of the largest settlements, those with as many as one hundred inhabitants, a few indirect communication methods have been established: groups that function like a cross between couriers and the old postal service; rudimentary telegraph systems; occasionally short-range radio set-ups. However, most people who want to contact someone outside their locale must either travel to the person's door themselves or give a letter to an ET unit being deployed to that area and hope the unit finds the person in question.

I used a combination of methods in my search. I visited NWET friends and colleagues within walking distance to ask for any information they might have about someone named Matilda Lucille Bearovna Gulick Mendez (Henry and Ginger's last name) Wilson, Mattie Lu, or a combination of those names. I sent letters to ET units elsewhere. I asked a sailor, one who I knew was engaged strictly in legitimate trade, to check for information about Mattie Lu the next time he stopped by the Rogue River settlement on his way down the coast—a woman who lives there has been collecting and compiling all of the census data gathered by NWET units for years. Most of my work involved sending letters and waiting for replies, but I made several short trips to follow up on leads.

After about eighteen months of searching, I had learned that Matilda served with Unit 4 of the NWET for fifteen years under the name of Mattie Lu. She was injured in an attack on the unit during her third deployment, and the injuries were serious enough to make it impossible for her to participate in expeditions after that. She continued to volunteer with Unit 4, serving as the lead strategist and administrator. According to people who served with her, Mattie Lu was a wizard at obtaining food and supplies, moving them and her unit from place to place, and making sure any families of unit members were well cared for in their absence.

Her most remarkable skill was keeping vehicles and other equipment in working order. Every person who served with her had a story about coming into the shop at any hour of the day or night and finding Mattie Lu, covered with grease and grime, adding one of her homemade solar panels to a water tank or retrofitting an old vehicle with one of her famous (or, before she had all the bugs worked out, infamous) biomass gasification units.

None of those who served with Mattie Lu knew where she had gone when she resigned from the NWET.

On my search, I ran into ET friends. Two had been young adults on I-Day and had lost their sight due to the illness invaders inadvertently passed to humans. One was living with a friend, but the other was on her own and struggling to survive. She had heard of a place on Vancouver Island that takes in those who are elderly and blind. I promised to check out the place, called Haven, the next time I was in that area.

My visit to the area came sooner than expected because my old injury flared up suddenly one day, leaving me unable to walk. A friend found me trying to crawl to the house from my garden, where I had fallen. He carried me to his sailboat and ferried me over to Vancouver Island for more surgery and several months of recovery at the NWET hospital. When the surgeon heard I was planning to go on a trek as soon as I left the hospital, she refused to sign my release papers. I volunteered at the facility for another month while waiting for her okay. Finally, I met a man with a booth at the street market who knew the location of Haven and was planning to make his first supply run to a place near there the following week. He offered me a ride in his donkey cart, and the surgeon, very reluctantly, let me go.

Every mile seems twice as long when one is sitting on top of boxes in the back of a donkey cart. By the time I reached my turn-off, after days of travel, I could barely walk. The man promised to pick me up in a few hours on his way back, and I began my painful hobble up the long road to Haven.

I was impressed by how carefully the place was laid out in terms of security, always my first concern. The road passed through a meadow that appeared to surround the knoll on which Haven was situated. Anyone approaching the knoll would be clearly visible. The entrance gate was sturdy and guarded. Several sighted people roamed the grounds, inconspicuously but attentively, to make sure all was okay. A dense and very tall hedge of blackberry bushes surrounded the entire place. Later,

I discovered there was a metal fence inside the tangle of berry bushes. It was so well hidden by the brambles that not even my discerning eyes could spot it.

I passed large produce and herb gardens on my walk along the road from the gate to the main building. The road was shaded by fruit and nut trees. Wide paths, lined with potato plants, led from the road to a barn, outbuildings, cabins, and a new half-finished structure. After I knocked on the front door of the main building and was waiting for a reply, I noticed that the window boxes held strawberry plants. My friend would be safe here and would have more than enough to eat.

The owner of Haven was down at the docks when I arrived, trading produce for fish and seafood, but an assistant gave me a tour and introduced me to blind and sighted residents. While we discussed the timing of my friend joining the community (the building under construction was a cabin that would be hers), the assistant packed a basket of food and water for my journey back to the hospital. As I was leaving, she happened to mention that the owner, Mattie Lu, would be sorry she had missed me.

I cried at the beginning of my journey, when I read Kaylee Bearovna's journal. I cried that day, at my journey's end.

When I brought my friend to Haven, I began a series of interviews with Mattie Lu. It took a while for me to become comfortable with her habit of using rhetorical questions, but I developed a simple system for dealing with her special speech patterns: if she asked a question once, I didn't answer it; if she asked the same question again, I didn't answer it; if she asked it a third time, I knew she wanted an answer.

The interviews never lasted for more than a few minutes because Mattie Lu was in constant motion. She was in her late forties at that time, and she has a paralyzed arm, a severely twisted back, and no sight in one eye (results of injuries she sustained while deployed with her NWET unit years ago), but neither time nor injuries have slowed her down. Mattie Lu is the heart of Haven, and she likes to be involved in everything. No one minds this because she is consistently entertaining and upbeat. As one resident told me, being around Mattie Lu makes jobs go faster because they seem like play instead of work.

I stayed at Haven for over eight weeks on that second visit. I had brought along Kaylee's journal, the piece Klaratee wrote, some of Mattie Lu's drawings from her early years (Thank you, Heather Jo, for sharing them), and summaries of interviews we conducted with Benji Edelstein, Trekker Tim, and Heather Jo Wilson. Every time I mentioned leaving, Mattie Lu said she hadn't finished reading those items yet and needed "just a couple more days."

I stayed and helped out while waiting for her to finish. I put the roof on my friend's cabin. I made blackberry jam and elderberry cordial, and I put up more jars of applesauce than I had ever seen before. I participated in the nut harvest festival. I sang baritone during the thrice-weekly community gatherings, which always wrapped up with a sing-along. Although I suspected Mattie Lu had read her mother's journal and the other materials many times, I didn't mention that to her, in part because reading them was her only way to be close to her family and in part, I admit with a little guilt, because I realized I didn't want to leave.

However, I had promised the doctor who did DNA testing for me that I would gather blood samples in an area where some of his relatives might be living. I needed to be on my way. Before I left, Mattie Lu handed me her mother's journal, then surprised me by asking when I would be back. I surprised myself by saying, "Soon."

Mattie Lu

I enjoy complexity. The more details and intricacies there are in machines, travel plans, strategies, logistics, garden layouts, recipes, or just about anything, the more I delight in them. I like to discover how one thing is connected to another, and then to another, and how all of those things work together to create the finished product, the desired outcome. That's what makes life interesting for me. Nothing is simple if you keep your senses and curiosity alive and focused on the world. Nothing. And why would I want it to be?

On one of my deployments with Unit 4 of the NWET (the U-4ias), I met an elderly man who had been a clinical psychologist before the invasion. He was working with children of invaders; I believe "descendants" is the correct term today. Those children have many excellent qualities, but they tend to be easily agitated, to sleep so lightly they suffer from constant sleep deprivation, and to feel as if they can't let down their guard.

Does this surprise anyone? They were born here but are treated like outsiders. I've seen them hunted by humans for sport. Also, their ancestors were slaves for hundreds of generations. Their cultures developed over thousands of years around the need to be prepared at any moment for their lives to be disrupted, often in major ways, by the whim of an owner.

The psychologist said I reminded him of the descendants. He said I should really try harder to "not sweat the details." He said I should do something relaxing, maybe take up meditation. Or maybe do some deep breathing exercises. He said those types of relaxation methods would work best if I sat by a stream, in a meadow, in a forest, or in some other "simple place."

First of all, I don't sweat the details. I revel in them.

Second, there is nothing simple about a stream, meadow, forest, or other type of landscape. Do you know how many creatures live in streams? How many single-celled organisms swim around in them that we can't see? How many types of plants grow in a meadow? How many wiggly, creepy, crawly things live in those plants? How many tiny creatures live in the soil under plants? How many insects fly around the meadow and land on plants? And forests are not simple. Oh, no, my friend. Forests are some of my favorite places because there is so much going on in them, so much complexity.

I know he was trying to help, but I wasn't built that way.

Maybe that's why I have been able to deal fairly well with complexities in my life. Having one family, then another, then another, and then another. Would I have preferred to be with my biological mother, Kaylee Bearovna, every moment of my life? Of course. I remember her as kind, funny, sweet, comforting, warm, and every other good thing you can say about a mother. But my life became complicated, and that's the only type of life I know.

Those times when the Gulicks wouldn't let me see my mother? I remember that, too. How could I not? My sweet Momma came for an hour or two sometimes, but they always made her leave. I cried whenever she left. They hit me, but I cried. I couldn't stop crying. I think that's when they started locking me in my room.

Which was not a bad place. Not at all. Professor Gulick's wife, who shall be referred to from here on out simply as The Witch, loved to shop, and she bought things for me and for my room. She didn't do it to make me happy, of course. She did it so she could show off when her friends came to visit or to spend the night.

Most of the things she gave me were garbage. Plastic things that are probably cowpie-looking disks of ugly melted goo now and will still be making this world ugly for as long as it exists. I saw toys like that when I was with the U-4ias: half a doll's head stuck to a hard black puddle that used to be the rest of her plastic body. From when invaders burned towns and cities. But The Witch hit the mark once in a while and gave me something I liked. Why not? Even a blind pig can dig up an acorn now and then.

My favorite thing was something she didn't buy. Promise not to laugh? The rug in my room. I think it had belonged to the Gulick family for a long time. They called it an Oriental rug. It had amazing colors and intricate designs. Flowers, birds, wild creatures, trees, little brown people, symbols that didn't mean anything to me but must have to the person who wove the rug. All the designs wound around each other and were connected by vines and little squiggly things in the borders. I loved it.

The Witch didn't like me to mess up my crib, which she kept crammed full of pillows, stuffed toys, and other things I wasn't allowed to touch. Everything in the crib was for show. We wouldn't want a baby to spit up on anything that cost that much, would we? We wouldn't want the blanket to be rumpled, or the pillows to be askew, would we?

She put me on the floor. That's one of my first memories: lying face down on the floor. When Momma Kaylee came to babysit, she held me in her lap when I took my naps. But when she wasn't there, I slept on the floor. In fact, I practically lived on the floor. I had a blanket and a pillow, and I had my amazing rug.

I spent so many hours tracing the designs in that rug. Sometimes I would try to follow a single vine all the way around the edge of it. Sometimes I told myself stories about the strange little people who lived in the rug. Sounds odd, doesn't it? That's just the way I was.

The only bad things about the room were the lack of food, water, and a toilet. Most of the time I didn't mind being locked in because that meant I didn't have to deal with the other people in the house. Some of the visitors were pretty strange. Some were scary. But when The Witch or her consort locked me in, and there was nothing to eat or drink, and there was no way I could go to the bathroom, I didn't like that part.

I had a…. Stop me if this gets too disgusting, okay? I had a set of plastic tile things that hooked together. They came in a tub with a top that snapped on tight. When I was locked in my room and couldn't hold it anymore, I would dump out the tiles and use the tub for my toilet. That's what I had, so that's what I used. I could put the top back on the tub and hide it in the closet. It didn't smell if I put the top on tight. But I had to remember to dump it in the toilet when my door was unlocked, and I couldn't let The Witch see me do that. I don't like to talk about what The Witch did to me when she saw that.

That's why I was crying the day Papa Henry and Mother Ginger found me. It wasn't because The Witch and her consort were gone: I was happy about that. It wasn't because of the invaders: I had been watching them through my window for two days as they went up and down the street touching people. They even came into the house once (they didn't get me because my door was locked), but I wasn't afraid of them because they looked like the little brown people in my rug. Except some had six fingers instead of five. I saw them take off their gloves when they thought all the people were dead. I wasn't even crying because I was hungry and thirsty, although I was. I was crying because the tub was so full it spilled on the floor, and I didn't want to be hit.

I could tell many stories about my life. The day the fires started and we left town, our trip to the cabins, my happy times with Papa Henry and Mother Ginger, their death, living with the Wilsons (Heather Jo was a great mother, too, by the way), my years with the U-4ias. Everybody has stories like those. Why would anybody want to read about those things?

All I really want to talk about is my sweet Momma, Kaylee Bearovna. It's very important to me that people who read her journal understand who she was so they don't get the wrong idea about her.

Shall we begin?

First, my mother was neither an adulterer nor a murderer. If anyone finishes reading this and still thinks she was, I have failed in my task. I understand why she felt that way about herself while she was under siege in the library. She was experiencing intense and negative emotional stress. Who wouldn't view the world and themselves darkly in a situation like that?

However, I have read my mother's journal; I have read the "smoking gun" letter that Professor Gulick sent to her, the letter she always carried and later entrusted to me; and I discussed these issues with her during the short time we had together at the Wilsons' cabin before she died. The terms "adulterer" and "murderer" do not apply to my mother. Period.

Let's deal with the issue of murder first. On the third day of the invasion, my mother heard the screams of children outside the library. The children were my friends from pre-school, who had been hiding with Teacher June somewhere on campus since the invasion began. I wasn't with them because Professor Gulick had not dropped me off at pre-school two days before, on the morning of I-Day.

He and The Witch were having a very big and very loud fight on I-Day morning, a fight that had been going on all night. When I tiptoed down the hall to use the bathroom, after it was light out, I saw them hitting each other. They saw me, locked me in my room, kept fighting, and, as far as I can tell, forgot about me. Completely. They were screaming because of the fight, then the house was quiet, then they were screaming because of the invaders, then the house was very quiet for two days, and then the fires started.

Momma told me she realized at once that I was not with the pre-school group, even before she looked out the window, because she didn't hear my voice. Did she hesitate to help the other children? No. Did she pause to consider her own safety before rushing out of the library? No. Was there anything else she could have done to save them? No. I believe she worked as hard to save the children as she would have worked to save me.

Her response to children in danger was gut-level, but her response to the young man with hazel eyes was carefully considered. She chose to communicate with him, a sign she was willing to trust and take in a stranger. She developed a plan to help him. She was thinking about how to feed him once he arrived. She figured out the timing of his dash to the RAW perfectly. She did not unlock the door before signaling for him to start running because that could have endangered both of them.

Tripping after she slid down the ladder was a mishap. It was not manslaughter. It certainly was not murder.

The children, the young man with hazel eyes, and all the people my mother tried to save over the years died because of the invasion, not because of things she did or didn't do. She realized this when she told me those stories at the Wilsons' cabin, although she still tended to regard herself as a failure in many ways and still felt guilty.

That's not hard to understand, is it? As strange as it seems to us now, before the invasion most people never faced a situation where their actions meant the difference between life and death, to themselves or to anyone else. Now, everyone has been in situations like that. We regret our actions, but we move on. That's the only way to survive, right? There have been far too many murderers since the invasion began. My mother was not one of them.

Now, about adultery. There was none. Never. And this is where my mother's story and my own get more complicated. Remember the "smoking gun" letter she mentions in her journal? It's about to come into play.

The truth is that The Witch and her consort expected Kaylee's Australia trip to result in her becoming pregnant. They figured she would fall in love with Professor Gulick.... Let's just call him The Warlock, shall we? They expected that The Warlock would charm my mother into having an affair with him (or he would drug her, take her, and then convince her she had slept with him willingly), she would become pregnant, and they would manipulate things to end up with the baby.

Once Kaylee and The Warlock were in Australia and he realized she was not going to succumb to his charms, he had to come up with another plan. The clock was ticking. She had to become pregnant fairly soon so the birth could occur before they both returned to JSU. He admits in the letter that he drugged Kaylee the night of the party. He admits that he joined her in bed. That's why she remembers smelling his aftershave lotion. He admits that, much to his dismay, he was so drunk he couldn't, well, follow through with his plan.

What did The Warlock do when he was incapable of impregnating Kaylee? He tricked someone else into doing it for him. There was a student at the party who had a huge crush on my mother, unbeknownst to her. The Warlock convinced the young man that my mother liked him but was too shy to tell him. He told the young man she was waiting for him in the bedroom so they could be intimate. However, because she was shy, she would pretend to be asleep.

Are you thinking what I did when I heard this? Of course you are. This is one of the oldest tricks in the literature books. I haven't read as many as I would like, but I've read enough to know The Warlock did not come up with that idea on his own.

What happens when a brilliant but unconscious young woman and a brilliant but almost unbelievably gullible young man get together? Me.

My mother told me she considered the encounter rape, but she did not think of the young man as the rapist. He was something they called a nerd. Or a geek. I'm not sure which of those words she used. Maybe both. She said that meant he had little experience with other people, especially women. He was easily manipulated by The Warlock, who held a high position, had many powerful friends and colleagues, and seemed to have no reason to do something evil. She said my father was, in her opinion, harmed just as much as she was that night. She placed all of the blame for that harm on The Warlock.

When my mother told me about this at the Wilsons' cabin, she apologized for discussing difficult subjects with someone so young (I was almost thirteen at the time), but she said she knew I would understand because I was an "old soul" and "wise beyond my years." She said she knew that about me from the day I was born. I don't think I have any special wisdom, but by that age I had seen many of the ugly things people do to each other, and I understood the subject that she seemed so desperate to discuss with me before she died.

There was one question I didn't have time to ask my mother. Why would The Warlock admit to these things in writing? Was he full of remorse for what he had done to my mother?

Was he ready to take the punishment he deserved? Had his wife, The Witch, cast a powerful spell on him so he suddenly turned into a decent human being? As my mother would say, no, no, and absolutely not.

After Momma died, I read the letter. The Warlock says his wife suspected he was having an affair with the male student they had hired to watch me. The Witch threatened to tell everyone her husband was gay unless he gave her most of his inheritance. The Warlock wanted Kaylee to tell people she had had an affair with him, thus muddying the waters on the issue of his sexual preferences and, hopefully, discouraging his wife from going ahead with her plan.

After everything he had done to Kaylee, all the agony he had put her through, he wanted her to lie for him to save his fortune. Can you believe the nerve of that guy?

Maybe those kinds of things still happen, but I don't think they happen very often. People have too many other things to worry about, like trying to stay alive. You don't like somebody in your household? Leave them. And if you really hate them, take all the food with you. You have an issue with your mate? Wait until a freezing cold night and, when they go outside to use the outhouse, bolt the door so they can't get back inside. Problem solved.

Do I approve of those methods? No. I'm just saying I've heard stories about people using those simple, straightforward methods to deal with difficult relationships.

Remember in that earlier interview when I talked about enjoying complexity? You might recall I said I like it in just about everything. If I were writing notes about this interview, I would underline those last three words. One exception? Close personal relationships. Those things drive me batty. They are much too complicated.

There were times before I was injured when guys wanted to be more than friends with me. I tried twice, but those relationships didn't work. Even after I was injured and ended up looking like the branch of a corkscrew willow, a few guys expressed interest, but I said no. I knew there was no hope of a positive personal relationship for me.

Friends are good, though. Friends I can deal with. Did you think I didn't like any kind of relationship? Not true. I do like relationships, but they have to be simple.

And children? I get along great with them. I've had a chance to be around only a few over the years, because there aren't that many children to be around, but we always became best buddies in record time. Children tend to be straightforward in their wants and needs. I like that.

The folks who live here? I have no problem getting along with them. I've found that elderly people tend to wake up happy most mornings just because they're alive. They know they can't make it on their own, so any care you give them during the day is appreciated. And they give back more than they get. They have so much to offer.

Being blind changes how people relate to each other, too. Blindness is a constant reminder that we need each other, and that goes a long way toward making relationships positive. The people here, blind and sighted, know I need them. I can do many things, but I can't do everything. I need them, they need me, and everything works out fine.

I set up this place for elderly blind people for two reasons. First, I did it because I wanted to help the world. Doesn't it seem like most ex-NWET folks end up doing this kind of thing? Like you [Ishi] going to all the trouble to find people you don't even know. I knew one U-4ia who took in orphans, another who ran a small school in his shack, and another who went fishing every day and donated everything he caught to the local community.

I guess you spend years trying to help people with the ET unit and it gets to be a habit. A good habit. Do you know any ex-ETs who decided to cheat people out of food or supplies after they retired? Or set up a brothel? Or train dogs for those awful blood fights? I sure don't.

The second reason why I set up this place? For Momma. Kaylee would be the same age as some of these folks if she had lived. And here's something no one knows but me: Kaylee was going blind when she found me at the Wilsons' cabin. She didn't tell her son or Benji because they wouldn't want her to go off to find me if they knew. By the time she reached the cabin, she could make out shapes, but that was about it. She said the whole world was blurry to her except for me.

It's not hard to understand why she went blind: her husband was Tzngwaneeza, the invaders who gave the disease to humans that caused them to lose their sight. I'm sure Tall Man came down with something that seemed like a cold, then he recovered in a few days, and my mother began the long, slow process of going blind.

From what I saw while in Unit 4, the disease caused blindness in humans who were teens or adults at the time of the invasion, but it doesn't seem to affect those of us who were children on I-Day or were born after the invasion. If that's true, my mother's generation will be the last to go blind from that disease.

My mother's generation suffered the most from the invasion. They went through the worst type of agony: losing just about everything they knew and just about everyone they loved. They are the reason those of us who were children on I-Day were able to survive. When I think of what my mother went through to find me, I cry. When I think of what she went through to protect her son, I cry. Caring for people here is caring for her.

There was a time when I wanted to find my father. I ran into a man once who had a boat and was planning to sail to Australia. I don't know why he wanted to go, but he was taking other people along, too. I wanted to go. I wanted to search for my father. But I had a one-year commitment to the NWET, and I needed to honor that, so I didn't go.

I hope to contact my father some day. I know his name, but not much more than that about him. However, I just happen to have made a new friend named Ishi, a guy who is a genius at finding people. Who knows? It could happen.

My brother, his family, Benji, and Heather Jo? I would like to see them someday, too. But this corkscrew back of mine doesn't allow me to travel far, and I don't expect they will be able to travel for many years. Too dangerous for the children. If you see them again, tell them I understand. Tell them it makes me happy knowing they are alive and well and out there doing good things for the world. It makes me happy knowing they are taking care of the library Momma loved.

I love my life now. I wake up every morning early, anxious for the day to begin. I can't wait to see the people here. I can't wait to start working. I can't wait to see what our community accomplishes during the day. There is complexity in our relationships here, but that's because each of us is an important component in a complex entity.

I am in a safe place now, a true haven. I know that would make Momma happy.

Books that Sacrificed Printed Pages for My Journal:
An Oddly Annotated Bibliography

Day Eight: *Flowers of the Farm*, by Arthur O. Cooke. Accidentally ripped out last page of text. Used it to begin a journal. Really feel bad about ripping out that page.

Day Nine: *Gossip in a Library*, by Edmund Gosse. He says, "Voltaire never made a more unfortunate observation than when he said that rare books were worth nothing, since, if they were worth anything, they would not be rare." Dowager Gulick gushes over Gosse, so his are the 1st printed pages I've ripped out on purpose.

Day Ten: *The Book of War*, by Sun Tzu. In war, "At first, be as discreet as a maiden." I've got that part down.

Day Eleven: *Travels in Alaska*, by John Muir. When I am reading Muir's books, I no longer feel trapped....

Day Twelve: *Chronicle of the Conquest of Grenada*, by Washington Irving. Poor guy writes a book based on a monk's journals, then finds out the monk never existed. Or did he? No matter—W. I. still gets a 2nd edition.

Day Thirteen: *The Khaki Kook Book*, by Mary K. Core. Bottom line: She believes Indian cooks are great & not as dirty as you might imagine. Yes, she said that.

Day Fourteen: *The Professor*, by Charlotte Bronte. Full disclosure: I hate him. Then I think about Matilda.... It's complicated.

Day Fifteen: *Notes from the Underground*, by Fyodor Dostoyevsky. My father's favorite author. "From one prison to another. I haven't died yet; I am already dead."

Age 3

Day Sixteen: *The Divine Comedy*, by Dante. Not funny.

Day Seventeen: *On Nothing & Kindred Subjects*, by Hilaire Belloc. Kith & kin—gone. If there is anything out there except nothingness, please, I don't want to know.

Day Eighteen: *Medicina Flagellata; Or, The Doctor Scarifyd*, by Anonymous. Worst preface ever. There's a good reason why this person chose to remain anonymous.

Day Nineteen: *Eureka*, by Edgar Allen Poe. Poe's work has bright spots. To M: "And thus thy memory is to me like some enchanted far-off isle in some tumultuous sea...."

Day Twenty: *White House Cook Book*, by F. L. Gillette and Hugo Ziemann (White House Steward, 1887). "Cooking, Toilet and Household Recipes, Menus, Dinner-Giving, Table Etiquette, Care of the Sick, Health Suggestions, Facts Worth Knowing, Etc., Etc., The Whole Comprising a Comprehensive Cyclopedia of Information for the Home." Is the White House still there? If so, who is inside?

Day Twenty-One: *Tales from Shakespeare*, by Charles and Mary Lamb. I was going to dub this book "Cliff Notes for Kiddies," but it's not bad. They wrote it mostly for girls because boys, at that time, had access to their father's library (yes, they said "father's" not "family's") but girls, most often, were not allowed access. Nice idea.

Day Twenty-Two: *Chaucer's Translation of Boethius's The Consolation of Philosophy*, by Geoffrey Chaucer. So much literature written in prisons over the centuries, & I am drawn to it like a moth to flame. I cannot resist it. There is no danger in this obsession, only comfort, hope, & light.

Day Twenty-Three: *Marvels of Modern Science*, by Paul Severing. Sure, sure, they're all amazing & marvelous—until they stop working.

Day Twenty-Four: *Forty Centuries of Ink*, by D. N. Cavalho. I love ink: the smell of it in new books; the way it flows—slightly viscous & glistening—from a fountain pen; that moment before it soaks into a piece of paper, when a word that has just been written w/ ink enters the world, hesitates, shines. But there are some places, delicate places, where ink does not belong.

Day Twenty-Five (A): *Old Christmas*, by Washington Irving. Illustrations by R. Caldecott and James D. Cooper. Stories like those my grandmother told. She grew up in a world I couldn't imagine. Now I live in a world none of us could have imagined. BTW, great pictures, Mr. Caldecott.

Day Twenty-Five (B): *Two Tragedies of Seneca — Medea and The Daughters of Troy*, translated by Ella Isabel Harris. Many similarities between their lives & mine.

Day Twenty-Six: *Mathilda*, by Mary W. Shelley. I think of you every day. I wish we could be together, especially at Christmas. You are gone, I expect, so all I can give you is the gift of remembrance & a record of your existence. You were here, Matilda; you are always here w/ me.

Day Twenty-Seven: *The World Set Free*, by H. G. Wells. He warned us, but did we listen? Perhaps the world is being set free now. Maybe destruction will set us on the path.

Day Twenty-Eight: *Wild Flowers*, by Neltje Blanchan. She says, "[A flower] is a sentient being, impelled to act intelligently through the same strong desires that animate us, and endowed with certain powers differing [from ours] only in degree…." Maybe this is true for a pac, too?

Day Twenty-Nine: *Life in a Thousand Worlds*, by W. S. Harris. He has seen them all on his journey of the soul.

Age 5

Day Thirty: *Round-About Rambles*, by F. R. Stockton. Sweet, funny, touching. Just what I needed today.

Day Thirty-One: *In Defense of Women*, by H. L. Mencken. Nothing makes an invasion pass more quickly than a laugh, especially at the expense of women, right?

Day Thirty-Two (A): *The Foolish Dictionary*, by Gideon Wurdz. Get it? Giddy on words? These entries make me laugh out loud. Wish that reaction hadn't been reduced to a cliché. Irrepressible positive emotions feel great.

Day Thirty-Two (B): Prologue to Malory's *King Arthur*, by William Caxton. This is like reading the "begat" parts of the Bible. Another prologue/preface monstrosity that makes me want to scream "Get on w/ it, already!"

Day Thirty-Three: *Introduction to the Propyläen,* by Goethe. 1st issue of art mag published in the 1700s. More words in intro than in a year's worth of art mags today. Seriously, I just wanted to see some pretty pictures.

Day Thirty-Four: *Journal of an African Cruiser*, by H. Bridge; edited by Nathaniel Hawthorne. Reading about southern climes makes me feel warm. Much on Liberia's re-colonization: Seemed like a good idea at the time, but….

Day Thirty-Five: *Heidi*, by Johanna Spyri. 1st book I owned, a gift from my mother when I was 5. Really missing her & Matilda today.

Day Thirty-Six: *A Narrative of the Expedition to Botany-Bay*, by Watkin Tench. A country ships prisoners to a distant continent & forces them do hard labor in horrible conditions to build a colony for the country that discarded them. What could go wrong?

Age 6

Day Thirty-Seven: *What's the Matter with Ireland?*, by Ruth Russell. Driven wild by deprivation; trying to survive w/ an overpowering alien nation next door; a speck of life clinging to the world's far edge. Ask me about it.

Day Thirty-Eight (A): *The Irish Fairy Book*, by Alfred Perceval Graves. I've used prefaces/intros from this book & the two that follow to honor the 12 pre-school children & their teacher who died on Day Three of the Great Invasion. May they spend eternity in a place w/ an endless supply of books.

Day Thirty-Eight (B): *Little Women*, by Louisa May Alcott. A gift from my mother, who called me her little Jo.

Day Thirty-Eight (C): *LuLu's Library*, by Louisa May Alcott. I used to read this book to the children when I volunteered at the campus pre-school.

Day Thirty-Nine: *How to Live on 24 Hours a Day*, by A. Bennett. Early 1900s upper class life "hacks." Ask the maid to prepare a tray each night with items you will need to make a light breakfast—including a spirit-lamp to boil water—so you can get to work early in the a.m. w/o bothering the help. Why didn't I think of that?

Day Forty: *The Colloquies of Erasmus*, by Desiderious Erasmus. Quote for Dowager Gulick: "Do not be guilty of possessing a library of learned books while lacking learning yourself." One for me: "In the country of the blind the one-eyed man is king." I'm flawed, but I'm alive, which, oddly enough, makes me humanity's best hope in this tiny bit of the world. But, hey, no pressure.

Day Forty-One: *The Mantle, and Other Stories*, by Nicholas Gogol. He caused quite a stir back in merry olde Russia.

Day Forty-Two: *The Works of Christopher Marlowe, Volume Three*, by Christopher Marlowe. "Come live with me and be my love...." My favorite part? Where to buy his "Hero and Leander" script in the 1600s: "[To] be sold in Paules Church-yard, at the signe of the blacke Beare."

Day Forty-Three: *The Kitchen Encyclopedia*, by Anonymous/Swift & Company. They made margarine back when it was a modern miracle. A book-long ad.

Day Forty-Four: *The Writings of Henry David Thoreau*, by H. D. Thoreau. If I had been alive when Thoreau was at Walden pond, he would not have lived there alone.

Days Forty-Five and Forty-Six: *In the Arctic Seas ~ A Narrative of the Discovery of the Fate of Sir John Franklin and His Companions*, by Captain M'Clintock. Impossible to read w/o putting on a sweater. I kept the heat lamp close by while I devoured this.

Day Forty-Seven: *History of the Expedition under the Command of Captains Lewis and Clark*, by Meriwether Lewis and William Clark, edited by Paul Allen. I am trying hard to overcome my fear of what awaits me outside the RAW. Unlike me, these men seemed to wake up every morning & say, "Let's see what's out there."

Day Forty-Eight: *The Universe a Vast Electric Organism*, by George W. Warder. Reminds me of another George W. Both of these guys were absolutely sure they were right, although facts indicated otherwise; both believed people would someday recognize the brilliance of their ideas. Still waiting.... This G. W. believed the sun is not hot, is inhabited, & is "the intellectual and spiritual center of our system of worlds." Seriously, what more can I say?

Day Forty-Nine: *Pathfinders of the West*, by A. C. Laut. She liked Lewis & Clark, so we agree on that.

Age 7

Day Fifty: *Astounding Stories of Super-Science*, edited by Harry Bates. Super-cool scifi mag that began publication in 1930. Some titles from 1ˢᵗ issue: "The Beetle Horde," "The Stolen Mind," & "Phantoms of Reality." What more could I ask for?

Day Fifty-One: *The Mushroom, Edible and Otherwise*, by Miron Elisha Hard. I have never liked mushrooms. In fact, most of them make me gag. Something about the texture. But I'm about to enter a world where most of the available food will be whatever grows wild. Apparently, there are mushrooms aplenty around here, so I might as well figure out which ones won't kill me.

Identification Note: *The Psychology of Singing*, by David C. Taylor. The language isn't exactly melodious, but there are many gems in here about the connections between singing & positive emotional health. I believe that humming can be just as good for lifting the spirits.

Bibliography: *Leaves of Grass*, by Walt Whitman. A very dear & very old friend of mine. I am tempted to take this book w/ me, but I won't. Doesn't make sense to do that. Thank goodness I have so many of his poems memorized. When it comes to the old question of "how shall we live," Walt said it best: "...read these leaves in the open air every season of every year of your life, re-examine all you have been told at school or church or in any book, dismiss whatever insults your own soul; and your very flesh shall be a great poem...."

Kaylee Bearovna

Illustrations by Walter Crane
from the following books

Pages 135, 155: *Agatha's Husband: A Novel*, by Dinah Maria Mulock Craik. Illustrated by Walter Crane. London: Macmillan and Co. 1875.

Page 83: *"Carrots:" Just a Little Boy*, by Mrs. Molesworth. Illustrated by Walter Crane. London: Macmillan & Co. 1876.

Page 300: The Children of the Castle, by Mrs. Molesworth. Illustrated by Walter Crane. London: Macmillan and Co. 1915.

Pages 16, 55, 216: *A Christmas Child: A Sketch of a Boy-Life*, by Mrs. Molesworth. Illustrated by Walter Crane. London: Macmillan and Co. 1880.

Pages 165: *A Christmas Posy*, by Mrs. Molesworth. Illustrated by Walter Crane. London: Macmillan and Co. 1888.

Pages 72, 111, 166, 283: *Christmas-Tree Land,* by Mrs. Molesworth. Illustrated by Walter Crane. London: Macmillan and Co. 1884.

Pages 38, 265: *The Cuckoo Clock*, by Mrs. Molesworth. Illustrated by Walter Crane. London: Macmillan and Co. 1895.

Page 246: *Grandmother Dear: A Book for Boys and Girls*, by Mrs. Molesworth. Illustrated by Walter Crane. London: Macmillan and Co. 1878.

Pages 44, 68: *Household Stories by the Brothers Grimm*, by Jacob Grimm and Wilhelm Grimm. Illustrated by Walter Crane. London: Macmillan and Co. 1899.

Pages 7, 96: *Line and Form*, by Walter Crane. London: G. Bell & Sons, Ltd. 1900.

Pages 121, 177, 236: *The Necklace of Princess Fiorimonde and Other Stories,* by Mary De Morgan. Illustrated by Walter Crane. London: Macmillan & Co. 1886.

Page 143: The *Tapestry Room: A Child's Romance*, by Mrs. Molesworth. Illustrated by Walter Crane. New York: The Macmillan Company. 1899.

Page 28: *Two Little Waifs*, by Mrs. Molesworth. Illustrated by Walter Crane. London: Macmillan and Co. 1883.

Additional Illustrations by Lucy T. Furuheim

Pages 286-298.

Pearl (as a child), courtesy Darcy Hogan.

About Pearl Larken

Pearl, who was nine years old when the Great Invasion began, lives in a village on the Pacific coast so small and remote that invaders didn't reach it until a week after I-Day. The invaders killed most of the population, including Pearl's father and sister, before they were driven away by a fierce storm. They didn't burn the buildings before they left, and the village has rebounded over the years as survivors are drawn to it by the promise of shelter.

As a child and teen, Pearl helped her mother care for orphans and the sick and wounded. Later, she served for decades as the only literacy teacher in the area. Now she is the village herbalist, mushroom provider (for food and mood), and button maker. Pearl is a founding member of the "We Survive" book group.

About Kate Boyes

Kate grew up on the banks of Crocker Creek, her dearest friend. When she wasn't puddling around in the water, she was tramping through the woods that extended for miles on each side. Every tree, stone, and being—seen or unseen, sentient or not—had a personality and a story. Those early experiences influenced her master's thesis on bears, her doctoral work in environmental sociology, and her creative writing.

Kate's creative nonfiction is published in a number of anthologies, including two volumes of the American Nature Writing series. As a travel writer for Fodor's, she contributed to their *Historic America Guide to the Old West, Gold Guide to the Rockies, Skiing USA*, and the guidebook created for the 2002 Winter Olympics. Writing a biography of Paul McCartney for Lucent Books gave her an excuse to belt out Beatles tunes whenever she wanted, a practice she continues to this day. Kate's latest play, which deals with the issue of homelessness, was produced by the Red Octopus Theatre Company in 2018.